SEXUAL
INTEGRITY

SEXUAL INTEGRITY

A NOVEL

J.A. DENNAM

CLEiS
PRESS

Published in the United States by Cleis Press, an imprint of Start Midnight, LLC, 101 Hudson Street, Thirty-Seventh Floor, Suite 3705, Jersey City, NJ 07302.

Printed in the United States.
Cover design: Scott Idleman/Blink
Cover photograph: iStock
Text design: Frank Wiedemann

First Edition.
10 9 8 7 6 5 4 3 2 1

Trade paper ISBN: 978-1-62778-204-3
E-book ISBN: 978-1-62778-205-0

Library of Congress Cataloging-in-Publication Data is available on file.

A FAT RAINDROP HIT THE WINDSHIELD WITH THE force of a gunshot. Her world grinding in slow motion, Brooke Monroe looked past it and watched as the seafood restaurant's front entrance dimmed in the approaching storm. Just fifteen yards to the door...

Could she make it?

With narrowed eyes, Brooke grabbed her purse from the passenger seat of her Audi, curled her fingers around the handle, and yanked it open. Battling gale-force winds, the sole of her left shoe hit the pavement with the first lightning flash. Her door slammed shut in time with a thunderclap. Clutching her purse with the fierce determination of a soldier on the front lines, she plowed through resisting forces and weaved through a line of parked vehicles. The raindrops doubled and then tripled. Then, with just five yards to go, the encroaching wall of rain arrived with gusto, tackling her to the ground in a hail of luke-warm bullets.

With a cry of defeat, Brooke got back on her feet and dove for the door handle. Once she was safely inside, the torrent was muted to a low hum as she stood there dripping on the entryway mat.

Her skirt and blouse clung to her like a transparent skin. The leather purse she'd purchased in Galveston was now a heavy, wet blob at her side. Her auburn hair was plastered across her face in dark, stringy hanks. Two women who waited on a padded bench shot to their feet and came toward her with wide-eyed concern.

Amy and Miranda, of course, had showed up on time, managing to outrun a typical Naples, Florida storm.

"Oh no, look at you!" Amy fussed as she tried to make sense of Brooke's hair. As usual, every petite and perky feature was cover-girl ready from her styled blonde bob to her platform pumps.

"Wear this. It'll hide your bra." Miranda shrugged out of her suit jacket and wrapped it around Brooke's shoulders. Of course, now everyone would be ogling the Latina's voluptuous curves, but perhaps it would work in their favor during this unscheduled meeting. For the first time, Brooke secretly hoped her new boss was a letch as well as a heartless bastard.

Okay, it wasn't really a meeting, but more of an ambush—a desperate attempt to reclaim the jobs of nearly thirty employees who'd been let go during the surprise takeover of her father's graphic-design business by Ken Stevens of Master Ink Innovations. Amy and Miranda were there to symbolize the casualties: living, breathing examples of professional people who deserved to work under the Master Ink banner.

And then there was Brooke: a sopping-wet windblown wreck who couldn't appreciate the opportunity she'd been given to do that very thing. How unfair was that? As the two unemployed women fussed over her appearance, Brooke blinked at them through wet eyelashes. "Some representative I am, huh?"

Amy's pout came with a sympathetic laugh. "Oh, sweetie, look on the bright side, at least you weren't wearing mascara."

When they finally entered the restaurant, a blast of air conditioning accompanied the smell of steamed shellfish. Her arms covered in goose bumps, Brooke made one last attempt to finger-comb her hair.

"Here, wipe off your glasses."

A cloth napkin appeared over her shoulder. Brooke accepted the offering that Miranda had just pilfered from a stash by the hostess stand.

"Hello," greeted the hostess behind the stand. "Will it be just the three of you today?"

"We're meeting Ken Stevens," Brooke informed her. "He has a three o'clock reservation."

"Oh. He didn't say anything about a party of five....I'll go ask."

Amy and Miranda pushed her forward after the hostess, cutting through a nearly empty dining room. Brooke stumbled as the adrenaline-based percussion of "Wipeout" pulsed from the speakers overhead. While her sensible shoes made a path of wet footsteps in her wake, Brooke couldn't help but think that the song's maniacal laugh had been recorded just for her.

Go ahead. Mock me. I'll leave here with your balls in my clutches too.

When they passed the lighted bar, she held her wire-rimmed glasses upward for inspection. Now sufficiently dry, she put them back on her face just before she collided with a thirty-something man waiting for his drink. His amused glance darted over her sodden appearance. Brook instantly bristled against the judgment she saw in it.

"Ladies." His voice was suave and smooth, just like the half smile that accompanied it. He had deep-set eyes, an aristocratic nose, and a strong jaw. His thick hair was light brown with gold highlights and just long enough to graze the collar of his casual sports jacket. Yes, definitely the GQ type who took pride in his appearance.

She could practically feel Amy marking her territory.

"Local or tourist?" Amy asked him with a megawatt smile.

The man's gaze, still smug with ridicule, flashed briefly in Brooke's direction. "Depends on who's asking."

It was an obvious brush-off that left Brooke out of the running— as if she were even interested! Rolling her eyes, she tugged at Amy's wrist. "We aren't here to pick up strays, remember?"

Her haughty dismissal only made him laugh. "Ouch!"

"Definitely tourist," Miranda guessed as they continued their journey through the restaurant. "That sunburn is fresh."

As they approached the booths, the storm clouds outside moved on. Light sliced through the picture windows, showing the modest restaurant's marine-themed décor and leaving the streets beyond the windows to steam-dry in the sun. Still soggy, Brooke seemed to be the only reminder of what had just come and gone in typical southwest Florida fashion.

The hostess finally noticed she'd been followed. "Oh!…here they are. Should I get menus?"

The man in the booth didn't exactly look like a shark. His round face had a jovial appearance that went with the mustache and balding head, but Brooke didn't let it fool her. There was a heart of stone beneath that extra-extra-large T-shirt. And probably a hairy back too.

"We won't be eating, thank you," Brooke said with a tight smile, hoping to project her unwillingness to share a meal with the man who'd just purchased her hard-earned future like a six-pack of beer.

The hostess hesitated for a moment and then slowly retreated to her station as Ken Stevens watched them. He seemed to know exactly who she was and didn't bother to ask before shoving a forkful of salad into his mouth.

Brooke adjusted her glasses and introduced herself. "Mr. Stevens, my name is Brooke Monroe. We haven't met because I was on vacation when my father sold his business to you. While I can assume that the unfortunate timing was not an accident, I refuse to believe he was aware of your intention to fire his entire staff."

Stevens shoved in another bite and spoke through the mouthful. "I take it you're here to change my mind."

"I am."

"While I admire your loyalty, Ms. Monroe, no one in my position would keep an overpaid staff."

Noting his blatant lack of compassion, she glared at the top of his shiny head, glad that she'd practiced her speech in the car. "These women are very good at what they do. Miranda offers amazing technical support, and Amy is a phenomenal account specialist. They represent everyone you just left jobless. All I ask is that you consider their performance and compare it to any of your employees' work. In other words, why fix what isn't broken?"

"I wouldn't have been able to acquire your father's business if it wasn't broken," he answered.

This was something Brooke still could not understand. She knew Monroe Graphics had been struggling, but she never got that it was hovering on the verge of bankruptcy. She had grown up with the thriving graphic design business and vowed to run it as well as her parents did when it became time for them to retire—which was apparently now. How could Stanley Monroe sell her birthright without so much as a heads-up to his only child?

The pain of that particular betrayal was still very raw, but being forced to work for a heartless man like Ken Stevens was even worse.

"If you don't consider rehiring at least half of our employees, I refuse to work for you," Brooke threatened.

Now the middle-aged man put down his fork and pushed the salad aside. His T-shirt bore a Stanford University alumni logo, along with a few pieces of lettuce that rested atop his protruding belly. He leaned back and regarded her with a hint of amusement behind hazel eyes that, she was positive, hid many secrets. "You are aware of the employee agreement you signed?"

"I am." *Now*, she added silently. It would be much too embarrassing to admit that she'd signed something without reading it, or that her father had taken advantage of her trust in order to trap her into such an agreement. Then again, it wasn't the first time he'd resorted to such tactics, acting as a "protective parent looking out for his only child." Chewing on that bitter truth, Brooke's composure slipped a notch.

"You're also aware of the non-compete clause in that agreement?" Ken asked next. "If you quit or are terminated with cause, you cannot use your connections or expertise against my company for a year."

Her shoulders stiffened at the reminder. "I don't believe you'll give me the opportunities you and my father agreed upon."

"Excuse me." A waiter cut through and deposited loaded dishes of crab legs, garlic toast, and rice pilaf onto the table.

A look of delight crossed Stevens' features as he scoped out each plate. "Regardless, it's your only shot at ever managing Monroe Graphics the way you planned." He picked up the crab fork. "Now, since this meeting was supposed to take place tomorrow morning, you can either sit down and join me for a meal or leave me to mine. Ladies, have a good day."

Even though Brooke never ate at three in the afternoon, she took a seat and stubbornly crossed her arms, daring him to try and scare her off. "Mr. Stevens..."

The waiter reappeared with another tray of food and unloaded it before her. Stevens broke a crab leg in half, spritzing crab juice in her direction. Once again, Brooke was seeing through spotted lenses.

"I was already managing Monroe Graphics," she continued tightly. "It's the vice president position you're taking away from me. Once my father retired, I was supposed to step into that role, and I am more qualified for it than anyone else."

"Takeovers are never pretty," he explained while dipping strips of crabmeat into melted butter. "When I go back to Sioux Falls, this new branch of mine will be thriving and in the very capable hands of someone I trust. Ethan was my first choice to run things here and, by continuing as senior manager, you will assist him with the transition." Ken put a napkin to his greasy lips and gave her a sarcastic smile. "Who knows, with your loyalty and cooperation, maybe one day you'll make VP too."

Amy and Miranda fidgeted on the sidelines. Caught up in her own dismay, Brooke had nearly forgotten they were there. "Mr. Stevens, I've been chasing that dangling carrot far too long. I see now I've only been amusing my father, and I'll be damned if I'll perform for your amusement too. Don't expect to see me in the conference room tomorrow morning."

On the verge of tears, Brooke slid out from the booth, having effectively given up her career. Quitting meant that she'd have to honor the non-compete clause and stay out of the graphic design business altogether.

"Ethan will be sad to hear that, Ms. Monroe," Ken said with tactful reserve. "He was even prepared to let you keep your corner office despite the fact that it should go to him. Then again, he does love the view from there."

Momentary shock halted her footsteps. Stevens must have known just how much she coveted her eighth-story view of the bay marina and its bustling activity. "I thought you would be taking my office," she said. "It's the biggest one."

"I'm too busy for scenery. I'll be taking the one adjoining the conference room."

That was why her father had chosen that office as well. Eyes narrowing with impudent fury, Brooke set her teeth. "Who exactly is this Ethan person? Besides my replacement—"

"That would be me," said a familiar voice behind her. Brooke whirled around to find her worst nightmare in the form of Mr. GQ himself, standing there with two drinks and a cocky smile. He set the tumblers down and extended a hand. "Ethan Wolf."

When she refused to shake it, he simply shrugged and sat down in front of his food. While she watched, he dove into his own plate of crab legs, clearly unaffected by her looming presence.

Amy finally found her voice. "Come on Miranda, let's get our own table."

Brooke barely noticed her friends walking away. Sure, she was disappointed that they hadn't fought for their jobs more, but the thought of this arrogant playboy, Ethan Wolf, taking her corner office view brought her fight up to a whole other level. She clutched the strap of her damp purse in a deathlike grip.

Look at them: sharing a meal on a Sunday afternoon, two men who obviously "bond" outside the office.

It begged the question of what qualifications Mr. Wolf actually had: Love of the same alcoholic beverage? A past with the boss that included a few laughs? Ethan was dressed in expensive clothes and looked like the kind of guy who enjoyed flirting with women, then rudely shunning the ones who didn't appeal to him. His manner alone suggested someone who was overly confident and used to getting what he wanted. He probably drove a sports car and carried his little black book in a fancy European shoulder bag.

Her experience with men like Ethan was short but sad. She had almost married one until her father had interfered in that relationship too. When faced with the right kind of ultimatum, Brandon had up and moved to the Midwest to exchange vows with the first curvaceous tart who spread her legs.

Brooke took a deep breath, closed her eyes, and let it out slowly. Brandon said he had left because she was too career-focused and uninterested in having children right away. But she was only twenty-nine, for Christ's sake, and she'd worked too hard to get where she was.

And if there was any motivation for keeping her office, it was to keep this weasel-faced player out of it. She squared her shoulders in preparation for an even bigger battle than she had first imagined. "Mr. Stevens, I'd like to make a proposition." Both men looked up at her as if they were surprised that she was still there. "Assuming you know my past track record with client relations, you can see that I would be quite an asset to your company."

"Of course," Stevens added easily enough. "That's why it would be a shame to lose you."

"I was wondering how much experience Mr. Wolf has had in the trenches."

Ethan's fork hovered pre-bite. "What does that have to do with anything?"

"Character," she stated with articulate care. "While I'm sure you have a nice degree on your wall, I have first-hand experience in every facet of the business, something you couldn't possibly gain in the classroom."

"I've done my time as an account specialist."

Stevens interrupted their verbal battle with the wave of a hand. "You mentioned something about a proposition, Ms. Monroe?"

"Yes." She took a steadying breath. "Since you so blatantly pointed out that I should prove myself first, I'd like a legitimate opportunity to do so."

"He already has a VP." Ethan cracked a crab leg and managed to spritz her eyeglasses as well.

Nostrils flared, Brooke removed her glasses and cleaned them with a napkin. "I have connections that go much further than your empty handshake ever could, Mr. Wolf. You say you have experience? I'd really like to see it."

A brow cocked upward as amusement deepened the lines around his intense blue-gray eyes. They silently mocked her choice of words, promising a whole world of "experience" if she wanted to see it that badly.

"I do believe she's challenging you, Ethan," Stevens said, voicing her thoughts outright. "Something tells me that the next few months will be quite interesting for both of us."

When Brooke placed her glasses back on her nose, it was with a determination to grind Ethan Wolf's confidence into a fine dust that could be blown out of town by the next gale. "You seem like a shrewd businessman, Mr. Stevens. Certainly, you'd want the best person for the job."

"I won't give you Ethan's job."

"I'm not asking you to give it to me." She jerked her chin in Ethan's direction. "I want to earn it, as he should."

The light in Ethan's eyes changed from amusement to anger. "I don't have to prove myself to Ken," he stated. "I earned my title a long time ago."

"So did I," she hissed back through clenched teeth.

"I guess the difference lies in the employer, then. Yours sold out. Get over it."

A low gasp came from two booths away as Amy and Miranda

eavesdropped. *Get over it?* This pretentious jerk couldn't know what those three words had just earned him.

Brooke ripped off her mental boxing gloves, ready to go at it bare-knuckle style if necessary. "I believe your vice president feels threatened, Mr. Stevens."

Stevens was already watching his dinner companion over a loaded forkful of rice pilaf. "You think so?"

"I'm inclined to ask what grade he's in, but I'm in no mood to dodge spitballs next."

Ethan snickered into his plate.

"Do you feel threatened, Mr. Wolf?" Stevens asked.

"I decline to answer without a straw at my disposal," Ethan retorted.

It was a good thing there weren't any straws around or Brooke would have poked them into his eyeballs. "And this is the man you want to give a corner office to?" she pointed out with disdain.

To her surprise, Stevens laughed. Ethan Wolf also smiled, but it held a promise of something dangerous if she tried to take him on. Though he didn't have the dark, smoldering looks of a movie star, he was certainly handsome enough. Add a little false charm and there was his advantage. But it seemed that Stevens was as dedicated to his employee as it was the other way around. Brooke—a mousy workaholic who couldn't charm a seagull with a handful of breadcrumbs—didn't stand a chance.

Why even waste her time when it was obvious she was dealing with children? With her chin up, she pivoted to storm out, with or without her friends.

"Ms. Monroe."

Her wet hair fanned out around the lapels of Miranda's too-big jacket as she turned with attitude.

With his fork, Stevens pushed the remaining kernels of seasoned rice toward the center of his plate. The clatter heightened her nerves until she realized he was deep in thought. "If Ethan agrees, I'll let you compete for the position."

As she processed this, Ethan's gaze shot up in surprise. "Why would I do that?"

Stevens met it from across the table. "Because you love competition. This is perfect for you, especially right now."

Covert signals flew between the two men with quiet intensity. Brooke's lips spread into a slow smile as the sense of victory surrounded her.

Sure enough, Ethan let out a breath, sat back, and grabbed a napkin. "Alright, but as *acting* vice president, I get to add a stipulation to this so-called competition."

Stevens nodded once. "Let's hear it."

"When Ms. Monroe loses to me, I want her to spend the remainder of her twelve-month employee agreement as my personal secretary."

"You already have a—"

"I believe you mean *administrative professional*," Brooke interrupted with a bright smile, earning Ethan's extended gaze. "And I'll agree to those terms as long as the corner office stays empty until it's been won. We can each take a cubicle in the main work area."

Brooke knew she'd struck a cord when a riotous anger replaced Ethan's carefree mood. The thought of him enjoying her leather reclining chair with its six-point massage made her boil. Watching him do it through the window of his private reception desk was worthy of a dramatic dive from the roof of their eight-story building.

"Sounds fair," Stevens said. "Since this isn't exactly a conventional way of doing things, I assume a handshake will suffice in sealing the deal."

Brooke barely heard the man since she was returning Ethan's death-ray glare. Did Stevens really expect her to believe that the man was willing to let her keep her office? He'd probably already spent time in her leather chair; studied the fishing boats as they unloaded their catches directly into the back doors of bayside seafood joints; watched the seagulls fly overhead while the pelicans bobbed on the waves below in competition for the same snack.

Though she hadn't accomplished everything she'd set out to do that afternoon, Brooke reveled in the glow of achievement. Once she was VP, she would have the power to get Amy and Miranda's jobs back, as well as the other terminated employees she felt were worthy. To her, it was already a done deal.

She cocked an eyebrow, meeting Ethan Wolf's glare with equal fervor. Yes, this time she would welcome the storm that brewed ahead.

DRIVING AT NIGHT WAS THE PITS IN SOUTHERN
Florida. Ethan turned on his windshield wipers and cleared the
condensation that impeded his view. The humidity was stifling for a
northerner born and raised in South Dakota. How in the world did
people breathe down here?

He squinted and tried to look past the thick, twisting Banyan trees
rising from just about every manicured lawn he passed. The average-
sized home in this neck of the woods must have five thousand square
feet of living space at the least. And though Ethan enjoyed the view of
lit up beachfront mansions, the sound of Brooke Monroe's snotty little
voice continued to plague him.

The fucking nerve of some people. When he'd agreed to upend his
whole life and move to southwest Florida to help run Ken's new division, it wasn't supposed to come with risk. Not that he feared losing to
Brooke…the woman was a train wreck who dressed as if she'd raided
her mother's closet, not to mention a native who'd allowed herself to
get caught in the only ninety-second downpour of the day…wow.

His body jerked with a laugh. Even her pretty friends appeared embarrassed to claim her as their only representative. He remembered her stringy hair and dripping skirt, and those gigantic green eyes that never lost their primness behind her wire frames. She had fucking fangs for Christ's sake, venom-tipped, pointy little canines gnashing at him while he struggled to enjoy his first taste of fresh seafood in ages.

Well, she could take her judgment and shove it up her watertight ass. He'd worked hard all his life, earned every right to run this new office. He also understood how the world worked—never rode mommy and daddy's coattails to the point of complete, sheltered ignorance. Hell, would she even be able to function without them?

Why she bothered him so badly was what bothered him most. It wasn't because she'd seemed to judge him at first sight. If she wasn't interested in him, fine. But to dismiss his not-so-subtle hint for her company with a comment about strays was downright bitchy. She was the one who was all wet and disheveled. For some odd reason, that had stirred his interest in her even more than when he'd seen her picture on a shelf in her corner office.

Not anymore. What he'd dismissed as shallow had been nothing more than a raging hatred for someone she had deemed to be the enemy. Considering her position, it was something he could sympathize with...if she hadn't pushed every sensitive button he had to push.

And that was why she bothered him so much. He'd lost his cool, said some things he shouldn't have, demonstrated the same lack of tact she had. Not one single pair of beguiling green eyes was worth that, no matter how long he'd gone without sex.

Not that he should have nurtured any sort of attraction for a fellow coworker, something that was largely frowned on by his boss.

When Ethan awoke from his reverie, he found himself in a completely different part of town—east of the city where flat, barren stretches of road disappeared into the night, and intersections and streetlamps were few and far between. When visiting Naples before, he'd found himself in these parts once or twice and had taken advantage of their reputation as a problem area for law enforcement.

The threat of a hefty fine and a suspended driver's license was much greater in Florida than where he'd come from, but the need to drive beckoned more.

Just one more time.

He rolled up to the last stoplight for miles. Since nothing and no one was around, he stopped at the green and waited. Seconds later, someone pulled up to the crossing in a purple, modified Supra with tinted windows.

A little rev here, a bigger rev there. Ethan crawled through the lit intersection and waited. Sure enough, the Supra turned and followed. When it caught up, Ethan rolled down the window.

"You can't be serious, man," the other driver shouted as the sultry air pushed around them.

Ethan grinned. "Is that thing even legal?"

"Does it matter?"

Asking questions wasn't smart, especially with a stranger, but no one would believe he was a cop anyway. Not in his ride. "It may."

The guy jerked his chin. "That's a Miata, dickhead. There's a reason we don't see many of those on the scene."

Ethan shot forward a few yards to make a point. *Shut up and try me.* The Supra caught up and its driver laughed through the darkened window. "It's your funeral, friend. On three?"

They both stopped and squared up—one vehicle high in street cred, the other with a much different reputation in cool. But Ethan knew that his Miata had a bit more than just sex appeal. He and his brother-in-law had spent countless dollars and hours rebuilding his 2008 MX5 into the lone Super20 concept car that Mazda had reintroduced at SEMA in 2011. All it took was a few simple modifications, from the Cosworth engine, the widened wheelbase, racing beat header and exhaust, down to the custom yellow paint scheme. Her black fender flares and side skirts made her an edgier MX5 with a street-tough style. Ethan didn't care that she was slower than most on the straights. Since he had no business behind the wheel of a legit racer, his souped-up Mazda was more of a consolation prize than anything else.

He might lose tonight, but he'd win by tapping into his inner bat-out-of-hell, a release he hadn't enjoyed for more than a year. They'd stopped beyond the amber glow of the last streetlamp. With nothing but their dashboard lights to see each other by, they waited in the dark, keeping a constant eye out for anything that looked like law enforcement. Engines revved. While he counted, Supra gave him a look of surprised approval.

On three, tires squealed. Ethan shot forward from second gear and made it to fourth at 60 mph. The car beside him screamed along with air whooshing through the open window, floating forward and back in a bid to outrun. Ethan's blood raced too as the centerline blinked faster and faster in his headlights. When they broke 100 mph, the roadside blurred. His eardrums whirred with a good kind of pain. The next stoplight grew larger in the distance, a small sign of life in the middle of a desolate place.

They hit 110 miles per hour and Ethan edged forward. Either the Supra wasn't so super, or the guy behind the wheel knew something Ethan didn't. In a street race, cops usually pursued the car in front.

"Shit." He eased off the accelerator, letting the Supra shoot forward. Just then, red and blue lights lit up the night.

It was a sight no driver wanted to see, but for someone like him, it could be a devastating blot on an otherwise-clean record. He made an executive decision and held his breath. While the Supra blasted through the intersection, Ethan yanked on the parking brake and cut a hard right. The Mazda drifted through the turn as if it had wings. When the world straightened again, he watched in his rearview mirror as the cop tag-along chose which one of them to pursue.

The police car's siren pulsed loudly behind him and then faded as it went after the Supra. Ethan sat back and gripped the wheel with a resounding whoop of victory.

When he pulled onto his street a half-hour later, he realized he'd just spent a good forty-five minutes without Brooke Monroe even entering his head. For most of the drive home, he wondered if he should push his luck somewhere else, or if the Supra's driver managed to outrun his tail.

Ethan wheeled into the driveway of his lavish condominium, vowing to keep his latest escapade a secret. His neurosurgeon would fly down from South Dakota and make him write *"I will die next time I break my skull"* one hundred times with a piece of chalk on the pavement of whatever road he was caught on.

With his heart rate back to normal, he parked in the underground garage and rode the elevator up to the fourth floor. When the doors parted, his phone rang. He answered with a smile as he sifted through the keys on his key ring. "I was just thinking about you."

His twin sister's voice immediately took on an apprehensive tone. "Dare I ask what you were thinking about?"

"How much I'm going to miss my part-time job."

"What part-time—oh, you mean your excuse to torture yourself."

Though Ethan helped run the motorsport track that belonged to his sister and brother-in-law, it was more out of an innate need to feed his addiction rather than to earn a paycheck, even if it would only be as a spectator from now on.

"Ethan, I've watched you contemplate the risks far too long. You are physically impaired, and sneaking onto the track at night when no one is looking will only lead to disaster one day."

"I only dipped my toe. I didn't even make it into fifth gear."

"No excuses. This move is the best thing for everyone, especially for me. I nearly lost you. You can't put me through that again."

"I won't," he grumbled. Besides, the only thing around was that public drag strip in Immokalee, and until he settled into his new life, scheduled races weren't in the cards. Spontaneity was all he could fit in for now. And tonight's race would have begun and ended a whole different way if he'd been behind the wheel of his M3 turbo, may it rest in peace, or pieces rather.

At least he'd managed to survive the wreck that had taken his beloved BMW and left him nearly blind in one eye and with a slight vertigo problem. After months of healing, both physically and mentally, Ethan had decided to take his doctor's orders to heart. Find another addiction, whatever it was.

"Just promise me you won't do anything stupid on the streets," Harper pleaded. "You know how Florida is."

The sound of sirens rushing through an intersection still reverberated through his head. "Yes, and you also know my car won't give these guys so much as a woody."

"That's not a promise."

What he'd already done that night was definitely stupid, especially allowing the Supra to take the left lane where he couldn't see him as well. If he planned to become a full-timer in this city, he'd need to keep it down. Focus on settling in, bury himself in work, and hope it was enough to keep his restless spirit in check.

"Are you settled in?" Harper asked.

"Almost." Once inside the spacious condo, Ethan plunked the keys down on the granite-topped bar on his way into the living room. "I took the guest room. Adrianna's is a little too pink for me."

Harper chortled a laugh. "And she was so looking forward to sharing her princess boudoir with her favorite uncle."

"I'm her *only* uncle."

"Oh right." As if she were surprised by the well-known fact. "And what a sport you are for filling in as her only aunt too."

The razzing he took for allowing his four-year-old niece to make spriggy ponytails all over his head had not died down apparently. In fact, his scalp still tingled with the painful memory since he'd lost nearly half his hair one root at a time pulling out the entangled rubber bands. Ethan ran a hand through it as he crossed over to the sliding glass doors. The terrace called to him even at night. "When are you coming down?"

"Adrianna and I will be there in a few days for a visit. But if you mean for the winter, Grant is planning to shut down the track in late October."

"That's at least five weeks. I should have my own place by then."

As Ethan leaned against the railing, warm salt air enveloped him. For some reason, it wasn't stifling up there. He supposed the privacy had a lot to do with that.

Twinkling lights reflected off the Venetian Bay to his right. Small waves lapped over the white sugary beach to his left. The luxurious peace of this city was reserved only for the rich since no middle-class resident could afford it. Savoring the lap of luxury, Ethan breathed deeply, took it all in, and let himself relax. Hurricane Brooke with her path of destruction was no longer on the forefront, replaced by the memory of screaming engines and the sound of his sister's voice.

STOMACH LURCHING WITH NERVES, BROOKE leaned against the back of the elevator as it began its climb to the eighth floor. She closed her eyes, clutched the handle of her briefcase, and effectively bolstered her courage against the enormous changes taking place in her life. It was Monday, her first day under a new employer.

God almighty, what had her father done? Brooke ran down the list of what must have occurred since the day she left for vacation.

No...*before* she left for vacation. The man who had sired her—whom she would now refer to as Stanley—had been busy making plans without her. Then he had guilted her into a seven-day hiatus she never wanted, all so that he could execute his scheme in secret to avoid the inevitable confrontation. Since when had her father become a coward? Since when had he become a liar?

"Your grandmother wants you in Dallas by Saturday afternoon," he had said. *"This may be your last chance to see her alive."*

Bullshit. As soon as she'd entered Thorncliff Retirement Center's lobby with a bouquet in her hand and tears in her eyes, the seventy-eight-year-old spud dragged her all the way down to Galveston for a full week of art galleries, theater, nude swimming, and enough dirty martinis to pickle a whale, all while Brooke watched from under a wide-brimmed hat and five layers of sunscreen.

It turned out that Nana Louise had a bucket list. Who better to chauffer her around than a granddaughter with "no fella to take the starch out of her britches?" That was code for *how could you have let a fiancé slip out of your fingers?*

Unfortunately, when they returned to Thorncliff, her parents were waiting with bright smiles that reeked of something wrong.

That was the day her world fell apart—the day her parents broke the news that Monroe Graphics was no longer theirs to run.

The elevator dinged out the sixth floor. Brooke snapped to attention and checked her hair for fly-aways. All was good. It was at least dry this time, pulled back in a low ponytail, perfect and professional. So were her clothes: a beige pencil skirt that reached below the knee and a white buttoned blouse that was closed up to her throat. This time she wore heels so that if or when she ran into Ethan Wolf, he wouldn't have the chance to look down at her again.

Shoulders back. Chin up. Bend a knee before you pass out. Which she did just before the doors finally slid open on the eighth floor.

To her enormous relief, the Monroe Graphics insignia still graced the wall behind the reception desk, which was placed right in the middle of the building. It was dramatic and modern, curved with a strip of backlit chrome running its length. To the left were the administrative offices. To the right was the creative team's domain.

A stranger sat behind the desk, but Brooke was prepared for that. She approached with a smile, fully intending to bank left and head toward the administrative side. Her smile faltered as soon as a man in blue coveralls popped up out of nowhere. He was holding a sign that he must have been in the process of hanging. It was the smaller print that hammered home the gravity of her arrangement.

A division of Master Ink Innovations.

"May I help you?"

Brooke blinked down at the receptionist. The woman's black bangs, smoky eyes and cocoa skin glowed against the computer screen as she looked at Brooke with expectation. Unable to recover a smile, Brooke managed to introduce herself. "Brooke Monroe. I work here."

"Um…hold on."

The woman's voice halted her progress down the sunlit hallway. Brooke watched her in dumb shock as she picked up the phone and dialed an extension.

"Yes, sir, I have a Brooke Monroe here. She says she…oh…." She turned around and glanced at the sign above her. "Yes, okay. Sorry." Once she put the phone down, she looked at Brooke with apology. "You can go back."

Permission? She needed permission to enter an office she knew better than her own townhouse? An office that bore her surname for God's sake? Brooke swallowed back a sudden wave of fury and took in two recuperative breaths. "Thank you."

It came out as a constrained attempt at civility, but the new receptionist had already moved on, hunkered over her keyboard like a dutiful employee, leaving Brooke to stew alone.

Again, she felt as if she'd been dismissed, but in her own office this time. Far from deterred, she walked along the row of windows letting in the eastern sunshine, which brightened the russet colored walls and filled the place with a creative kind of energy. The hall opened into a main pool of cubicles, half of them already occupied by new faces. At least the art was still up—mural-sized pieces showcasing Monroe's highest achievements on the lofty walls overhead. Half of those achievements were hers, not that anyone here would know that. Brooke supposed that Stevens simply hadn't gotten around to taking them down yet.

Even though the general appearance was the same, the soul of the place was notably gone. A jolt of loss went through her at the absence of Amy's blonde head, always with a phone to her ear, and her father scoping out the latest projects with a bagel in hand. This was the *new* administrative department, a dozen or so strangers who'd already made themselves at home.

It was the first time Brooke wondered whether Stevens had had enough time to hire locally. So removed from this sudden takeover, Brooke naturally assumed that he'd brought his own staff from South

Dakota. But that would be absurd. The cost of living here was more than double that of most places. Unless he owned a hotel in which he housed his travelling circus, there was no way all these people could have settled in so quickly.

"Brooke."

She whirled around, nearly dropping her briefcase. Ken Stevens stood there with his hands in his pockets, looking considerably more professional than the last time she'd seen him. He was shorter than she had imagined, his nose nearly level with hers. Of course, her only sight of him had been in a booth with lettuce all over his shirt. She wanted to ask him how long he had planned this expansion, but couldn't for fear that she'd look even more stupid in the eyes of someone so gauche.

"Mr. Stevens," she murmured, soaking it all in. "Before our meeting, I'd like to get some things from my office." His eyes twinkled at the correction she made first. "I mean...the office that will soon be mine again."

He chuckled and indicated that she follow him with the wave of a hand. "I already had the files removed from it, but you're welcome to retrieve your personal items. In the meantime, this will be your desk." He stopped in front of one of the cubicles. It was plain with an L-shaped desk wiped clean except for a computer, a stack of empty trays, and a stapler. Swallowing her disappointment, she dropped her purse and briefcase into the partitioned box before her—one that used to belong to a young man who'd only been employed there for three weeks.

"I'll be in the conference room when you're ready," Ken said, his shadow moving across the taupe-colored partitions. The windows behind him offered a view from the west side of the building and would brighten later in the afternoon sun. Her father had ensured that the private offices and conference room would share their generous bounty of light with the rest of the floor through inner glass walls. The corner office was the only one that was remotely private with just a thin strip of glass to see through from the main work area. She headed that way.

The door was slightly ajar. She pushed it open and was relieved to see that her office was empty. It still looked the same. Her few belongings were still on the modern, black mahogany desk and the matching bookshelves behind it. Her potted Ficus tree thrived in the corner, adding a splash of green to the wood-and-leather decor.

And, of course, there was the view offered from a whole corner of shaded glass. *Her* view. She approached the windows, looked down and watched a pair of fishing boats glide through the canal toward the open gulf. Morning sun cast a golden shimmer over the V-shaped wakes they left behind. High masts filled the marina to the right, bobbing on the stirred-up surface of the water. Beside the marina was a rustic marketplace waiting for the ten o'clock opening rush. Until then, its boardwalks and tropical signs remained quiet with anticipation.

And so did she. Her creative mind took in the sights thoughtfully. How could she ever give this up, especially to that pretentious blowhard Ethan....

"Are you lost?"

Spoken by the very man of her thoughts, his words came with a slight accent as if he fancied himself a smooth-talking southerner. To Brooke, Ethan Wolf's voice was the symbol of her own doom, which reinforced her resolve to keep this particular office out of his grasp. "Not anymore," she answered with her nose to the glass.

Behind her, he moved across the plush carpet until he appeared in her peripheral vision. "Nice," he said. "I do like to look at pretty things."

When she finally stole a sideways glance, it was to see that he wore a tailored gray suit with a black shirt and tie—dressed for success and oozing with casual confidence. Unfortunately, she still looked up at him despite the heels. "Then I hope you brought a nice poster and some thumb tacks, because it will be the only view you'll get."

Her clipped remark was met with a smooth chuckle. He leaned one hand against the double-paned glass and shoved the other in a pocket. She noticed that he wore no cologne and no jewelry, a sort of lackluster representation of the label she'd pinned on him. Amy would

probably say that he emanated enough raw sex appeal on his own...
something Ethan probably thought as well.

When he spoke, Brooke jerked her gaze away, horrified by the
possibility that she'd been staring.

"Something tells me the next two weeks are going to end in my
favor." He let out an exaggerated sigh. "But you can still admire the
view when you bring me my morning coffee."

Brooke clenched her jaw against an urge to tear into him, knowing
it was exactly what he wanted. Instead, she walked to the desk and,
with her back to him, said, "It's a shame you can't move in today as
you'd planned." Grateful for the distance between them, she began
collecting the few framed pictures and personal items that marked the
coveted space as her own.

"I'm a patient man, Brooke," he said behind her. "The outcome
will be worth it."

Then he left. With nerves abuzz, she packed up and took her
armload of meager items to the doorway. She then turned and gave
the room one last look. A piece of hair fell from her smart ponytail
onto her nose. She blew it away and maneuvered the door shut with
her foot.

Moments later, she entered the conference room. This was supposed
to be a simple overview of what was expected of her in order to win
the position that she'd already earned. Both Ken and Ethan leaned
back in their chairs simultaneously.

Great, twins. Seeing as how they were such buddies, she knew that
Stevens would favor Ethan.

She took a seat on Ken's other side at the long conference table,
its polished veneer surface reflecting the cloud-studded sky from the
vast window beside it. A hint of lemon oil stirred in the air along
with Ethan's cool amusement. Ken got down to business. First, he
covered the basics from commissions to benefits, which were in line
with what her father had provided for his employees. After that ten-
minute spiel, Ken handed them both a two-page list of rules and
expectations.

"Ms. Monroe, I think we're all aware of your feelings regarding this buyout, so I'll skip to the disclaimers."

She placed her hands in her lap and listened in stony silence.

"There will be no bias in this competition, by me or by any of my employees. Most of the people here are new to both of us and have no stake in the outcome. This will be based solely on new business since that is where you and Ethan have equal footing. The receptionist has been instructed to divvy out sales calls equally between you. Whoever lands the biggest client within a two-week period will win the corner office, as well as the VP position. Should you lose, you'll finish out your twelve months here as stated in the employee agreement." He leaned forward and laced his fingers on the table. "As for Mr. Wolf's provision...my conscience requires me to ask if you're still agreeable."

His question blindsided her for a moment. Did he really care if she'd be miserable as Ethan's personal secretary? "And if I'm not?"

He nodded once. "Well, now is your chance to change your mind."

A part of Brooke's heart thawed a bit toward her new boss. Though it was tempting to back out, it would be the same as admitting defeat. "Yes, I'm still agreeable," she mumbled.

Ken filled his lungs and shook his head. "Okay, then. In the meantime, you'll still be required to assist Mr. Wolf with the transition. I can't afford to halt everything while you two have a thumb war."

She accepted the folder he shoved in her direction. It was two inches thick, sectioned with colorful tabs, and titled "Transition Procedures." She turned a few pages, fighting back a look of distaste. "I understand."

"This may translate into overtime, depending on how full your day becomes due to said thumb war."

The thought of wasting a moment of her time training someone else for her job didn't sit very well, but she nodded anyway. A commitment of twenty minutes a day to the two-inch file should be sufficient enough.

"And even though we're continuing to use the Monroe name," Ken continued, "you won't conduct any business without including the Master Ink affiliation. Shannon Webber is handling the marketing materials. You'll need to see her regarding your new business cards as soon as we're done here."

"Which one is Shannon Webber?"

"She's in the office next to mine." He pointed directly ahead. "Besides Ethan and my lead illustrator, she's the only other employee I brought with me from headquarters. She's in charge of bidding projects."

Brooke thought about that as she watched Ethan struggle to suppress a smile. "Excuse me, but in order to land big clients, we need to put out competitive bids. How do I know this Shannon won't tip the scales in Ethan's favor?"

Ken shrugged. "You're familiar with the economics here, Ms. Monroe. If you question a bid, you're welcome to bring it to my attention."

"But—"

"Unless you suspect me of tipping the scales as well." His look dared her to accuse him. The truth was, however, that this contest between her and Ethan could only benefit him during the takeover of a floundering business.

"Of course not," she said with sincerity. "And I appreciate the opportunity you're giving me, I truly do. I just have one question."

"Shoot."

"When I win VP, what position will Mr. Wolf have here?"

Across from her, Ethan continued to stare, only now with a touch of annoyance.

"That'll be between me and Mr. Wolf," Ken said in the utmost professional manner. "Now, after you get things squared away with Shannon, I'll expect you to be present for orientation which will take place in the main work area."

BROOKE READ THE WHITE TAPE ON THE DOOR
that bore Shannon Webber's name in red marker. She'd caught sight
of a wild mane of wheat-blonde hair through the glass and the shape
of a man who was directly on the other side of the door. Out of habit,
she simply walked in without knocking...and encountered a blessedly
familiar face.

Her eyes widened in shock. "Roger!"

Roger Kerrigan, her long-time coworker and friend, grinned and
then laughed when she threw her arms around him. "Please tell me
you still work here," she breathed.

"I got the same deal as you." He held her out at arms' length where
she could take in his simple, blessed familiarity. Goofy in many ways,
youthfully handsome, and always the loud one at any party, Roger was
either loved or hated. "They're keeping me around to hold the new
system administrator's hand for a while," he added.

At that moment, Brooke loved him more than anything, no longer
feeling awkward and alone. She still had Roger—the twinkly-eyed

cad with an oversized grin that some would call lecherous. Despite the empty passes he'd made at her through the years—which left her unaffected yet very flattered—she'd always valued his company.

"Ahem."

Brooke glanced past his shoulder and got her first good look at Shannon Webber. The new bid specialist was a picture of thick blonde hair and high-shine lip gloss—an all-American shampoo commercial with a neon smile. No wonder Roger was camping in here.

"Oh, I'm sorry." Brooke matched the woman's smile, hers every bit as counterfeit. "I'm Brooke Monroe." She grabbed Roger's wrist in a clandestine death grip and said through her teeth, "Let's do lunch, shall we?"

Roger gave a nod and backed out of Shannon's office with notable tension. "Ladies...."

Before the door shut behind him, Shannon was standing, extending her hand over the desk. "You must be the Monroe on the wall," the woman said, her fluffy, shoulder-length waves bouncing with the force of their handshake. Then Brooke was handed a piece of paper. "Fill this out so I won't get any information wrong on your new business cards and marketing materials."

That was it. No "sorry for the takeover," or "we'll take good care of your business," or "don't worry, I won't seduce Roger to the dark side." Having worked hard to earn the respect she was accustomed to, Brooke was left feeling just as insignificant as she had during her first encounter with Ethan. Shannon Webber was just another invader who'd raided, plundered, and occupied her world within mere days... or so it seemed.

But when Brooke won VP, Monroe Graphics would be hers again. And that would fix *everything*.

A wave of content swept through her. She sat a little taller as she filled out her form; this time her smile was genuine when she handed it back.

WITH KEN'S PRIVATELY SPOKEN WORDS STILL soaking in, Ethan left the conference room just as Shannon's door opened. Brooke walked out, looking much too sure of herself, with a tilt in her proud chin. Hands in his pockets, Ethan gestured toward the two cubicles beside them: "Looks like we're neighbors."

She visibly stiffened. "Unfortunately."

He studied her for a moment. Despite the red hair, her skin was surprisingly milky white and free of flaws. Her face was delicately shaped, with a small nose that complemented the cupid's-bow shape of her mouth. Once again, he was talking himself out of an attraction to her, something he'd been doing since first spotting her in the corner office that morning.

Yes, any physical appeal that Brooke possessed was dampened by the look of censure blasting from her stark green eyes.

Then again, that was kind of cute too…and Ethan loved a good challenge. "Will it hurt too much when you hear my voice as I secure the biggest client?" he goaded, finding a new appreciation for that look of censure.

In her prim little outfit, Brooke replied, "I'll be too busy in the conference room satisfying *my* biggest clients." He cocked his brow at that, which caused an adorable hint of color to seep into her cheeks. "I meant…going over projects," she added.

Ethan decided that his competitor was easily thrown off balance, a weakness that should work in his favor.

Starbucks coffee in hand, Shannon came out and joined them. His long-time coworker reached up and straightened his tie for him, giving away the status of their friendship—a friendship that had been sorely tested since his accident. It was no secret that she'd had feelings for him, but Ethan lost a lot the day he crashed, including his sense of immortality. Life had suddenly gotten serious, which meant no room for starry-eyed, sympathy-driven fools. His resulting mean streak had lasted too long, and Shannon had developed one in return, leaving their friendship in a state of awkward limbo.

He'd often wondered if he should take her to bed just to get it out of the way and move on. She had a great rack, and the rest was all slender curves that fitted the blue pantsuit she wore like a department store mannequin...curves he'd always wanted to see without clothes on. But that would mean going against Ken's strictly enforced code of ethics.

"Are we ready for the big event?" Shannon asked, flaring her big brown eyes.

Now at her desk, Brooke spared the woman a look as she emptied her briefcase. "What big event?"

"Orientation. Everyone's going to gather in here for an official introduction to Master Ink Innovations." Shannon blinked and laughed a little. "You didn't know?"

Ethan had to admit that Shannon could come off as a bit supercilious to anyone who didn't know her. This was Brooke's first taste of that, and he braced himself for the inevitable clash. Sure enough, the woman didn't disappoint, throwing a glare over her shoulder that would have melted glass. "You mean did I know that it was time for orientation, or that it was a *big event?*"

Ethan whistled a response before turning away. *Attitude, attitude.* Shannon followed him to his desk just one partition over. "What's her problem?"

"Too much sour in her kraut," he replied through the corner of his mouth.

Brooke's red head popped up over the partition. "What was that?"

He powered up his computer. "I said you must have doubts, about winning VP."

"Nope, no doubts."

A dark-haired man approached carrying a coffee mug that said *Keep Calm and Press Ctrl-Alt-Delete.* He stuck out a hand in Ethan's direction. "Roger Kerrigan. I'll be assisting the new systems administrator."

Ethan returned the handshake and introduced himself. "I take it you're the other Monroe employee who was allowed to stay on."

Allowed. He inwardly cringed at his own use of the word, but smiled blandly at Brooke's killing glare.

Roger nodded in answer, though a chill had entered his eyes. "Brooke and I have been working together for over six years." He moved over to her desk and sat down on the corner as she organized it. "You're lucky to have her. She has connections all over town." Brooke nudged him in the arm. He shrugged. "What?"

"I'm sure we'll work very well together," Ethan said through a tight smile. *As long as she knows how many sugars I take in my coffee.*

Roger leaned in close to Brooke for a private conversation as the noise around them began to escalate. Ethan could sense Shannon's super senses kicking in, for the woman had an uncanny knack for picking up on anything that wasn't meant for her. He, however, tuned out entirely as the creative staff started filing in from the other side of the building. He recognized Bill Knight, the lead illustrator whose legendary temper tantrums had been known to bring an entire office to its knees. If the man weren't so damned brilliant, another firm would be dealing with their unfortunate but creative secret weapon.

Ethan jerked out a nod of greeting. Bill returned it, claiming a place against the wall with the other artists. "What's so special about the darkroom?" he heard Shannon ask above the gaggle of voices.

"Uh...nothing...is special about it," said Brooke, effectively recapturing Ethan's attention. She appeared flustered, more embarrassed over Shannon's eavesdropping than pissed. Roger simply buried his face in his coffee mug.

Ignoring those clear signals to mind her own business, Shannon persisted. "Then why did Roger call it special?"

The man sputtered and puckered his face as if it were a ridiculous notion. "It's not even really a darkroom anymore," he added, "more like storage for old film-developing equipment and stuff."

"Yes, and there's a slight infestation problem in there." Brooke bumped Roger off her desk and practically yanked him away by the ear. "It's full of spiders and bugs," she threw over her shoulder.

Shannon's eyes narrowed as she watched them walk away. "Aren't they cute...."

"Cute?" More like suspicious, Ethan thought, following the

couple's progression as they made their way to the copy machine.

"Roger obviously has a thing for Brooke."

No shit. "Why would anyone have a thing for her?" His voice reeked of a foul mood.

Shannon giggled and nudged him with her elbow. "Shame on you. She's okay looking. Nice enough figure. *Love* her coloring."

Not that Ethan needed the reminder. "She's been a shrew since we met."

Shannon laughed again, propping herself against the edge of his desk. "Why, Ethan Wolf, is your pride hurt that she isn't fawning over you?"

He gave her a quelling look on the way to his own chair. "No way do I want those fangs of hers anywhere near me."

"Fangs?" She reached back and took a few of the candy corn from the dish he always kept nearby.

"Yeah, didn't you notice?"

She shrugged while she ate. "Guess not. Then again, I wasn't staring at her mouth."

He covered the dish as she attempted to take another. "If you can't play nice, go away."

Ken appeared from his office, took a place in the front of the crowd, and held up both hands in a bid for silence. The din subsided and the entire staff settled down for orientation. Forty-five minutes later, half of them filed out and headed back toward the creative side. On her way by, the receptionist leaned over Ethan's desk and graced him with the smell of lilac perfume and a view of her creamy milk-chocolate cleavage. As a result, he found himself wondering why all the full-timers never seemed to have tan lines. "Can I help you?" he drawled when she swiped a piece of candy from his dish.

"I can help you." The woman placed the candy on her tongue and took it in with suggestive slowness. "Take care of that sweet tooth, I mean."

Ethan had to admit that she was a gorgeous example of a Florida native with curves in all the right places, large sexy eyes, and the soft features of a makeup model. But a proposition of that nature was no more than a dangling carrot that he could never have.

"You're very kind," he said carefully since he didn't want to piss off the woman who fielded the calls. "But I get plenty of sugar outside the office."

She bit her satiny bottom lip between her teeth and stared at his mouth. "You're adorable. I'm Letreece, by the way. Let me know if you need *anything* at all." Her fingertip brushed a trail down his arm as she straightened up and walked away.

For an instant, the backlight from the windows offered a revealing look at her silhouette through a black skirt. If Ethan didn't know better, he'd swear she wasn't wearing underwear.

"I see we're already off to a great start."

He spun around and realized he'd just been caught ogling the receptionist's ass by none other than Brooke Monroe who'd returned to her desk with perfect timing. Great. "Before you even say it, I let her down softly."

She blew out a disgusted laugh as she sat down. "You can camp under her desk for all I care, as long as we get the same number of calls." Her chair rolled and she peered around the partition. "And I will be paying *very* close attention, Mr. Wolf."

AT LUNCH, BROOKE AND ROGER MANAGED TO
secure a place in line at the nearby Chipotle; it usually moved fast
enough to accommodate their hour-long lunches with plenty of time
to spare. She'd already explained her competition with Ethan in the
car. Now she needed to know whether Roger had her back.

The line moved forward as hungry customers walked by with their
trays. Brooke inhaled the scents of braised pork and fresh cilantro, her
stomach grumbling in protest. "I'm not asking you to spy, Roger," she
clarified. "Just keep your ears open. You know, make sure everything
stays on the up and up."

Roger sucked air through his teeth. "I don't know, Wolf doesn't
strike me as the type who'd cheat."

He was right. Ethan had as much to prove as she did since he'd
come fresh from a management position as well. They truly stood on
equal ground. "But Shannon is another story," she thought out loud.
"That woman has everything to gain by having Ethan on top. I mean,
did you see the way she draped herself all over him?"

"I don't think they're sleeping together, if that's what you mean."

She rolled her eyes and took another step toward the counter. "It wasn't a sexual reference, Roger, though I'm sure they've slept together. There probably isn't a female in South Dakota who can't pick his dick out of a lineup."

Roger gave her his toothy grin. "You sound jealous."

"Don't be an ass." She paused to place her order and moved along the counter picking out what she wanted in her burrito. When Roger caught up to her, she was near the register fishing for her wallet. "And I can't believe she eavesdropped on our conversation, *especially* when you brought up that awful darkroom."

He loosened the knot in his tie. "It's not awful. It's an important piece of Monroe history."

She paid and made her way through the restaurant with her tray. Once she filled her drink, she chose a place by the window and sat down on the high stool. Roger followed close behind. Through a mouthful of pork and rice, Brooke picked up where she'd left off. "I'd rather that darkroom be long forgotten. It's a *stain* on Monroe's history."

Roger handled the gigantic burrito with expertise. "I never got your aversion to it," he answered and then took a big bite. "Ith a well-known fack people work bether afther athieving orgathm."

Brooke watched the food roll around in his mouth while he spoke. "That's disgusting, Roger."

He swallowed. "It's the truth! And you know those creative types. They expect special privileges to keep their imaginations well oiled. No pun intended."

"I'm a creative type," Brooke reminded him. "And I don't require special oiling."

"Not many people are as pristine as you."

Yes, it was no secret that Brooke stayed far away from the dark-room and its lurid reputation. Though the revolving door to it was located on the creative side of the floor, it was next to the conference room and the walls were paper-thin. Roger explained that the danger of being overheard was half the fun. There was probably something to that, but respect meant a lot to Brooke and she'd worked hard to earn it. Respected women weren't caught with their panties down in secret rooms that reeked of sex.

"Does the new boss know about your other skills?" he asked, dropping the subject of the darkroom all together.

Brooke shook her head and wiped her hands on a napkin. "No. Stanley thought it was best that I focus on one thing."

"You're calling him Stanley now?"

She waved away Roger's look of disapproval. "I'll call him my father again when he quits ruining my life."

"You still blame him for running Brandon off," he accused her through another mouthful. "I keep telling you, the guy was cheating on you, Brooke."

"I realize that now, but this has nothing to do with Brandon and everything to do with Monroe Graphics." After seventeen months, two weeks, and five days, Brooke was certainly over the humiliation of her fiancé's betrayal. She took a breath and checked her tone. "And if anything good comes from this takeover, it's that I get to start fresh. No more double duty."

"But you like double duty, and you could really make it big as a designer." Roger had always been her biggest advocate when it came to her art. "You certainly seem more comfortable wearing your artist hat than your management hat, or even your IT hat. Hell, what department *haven't* you cycled through?"

Sometimes she wondered if he was right. "You know how easily I get bored. The administrative end of it has more staying power with me."

He regarded her in silence for a moment. "Or you could use this opportunity to do what you really love. Have you thought of pitching your web design ideas to Mr. Stevens?"

Her shoulders slumped. The possibility of ever seeing her new project come to fruition was now gone forever. Knowing this, she refused to let herself go there. "I'm more focused on getting VP. I'm entitled to it, Roger. Not only that, but I can start hiring some of our old staff back."

Roger's dark eyes turned all soft. He leaned over, gave her a peck on the forehead. "You're hopeless. Do you hear me?"

Brooke felt a tug of melancholy as his good mood surrounded her. "I'm so glad you're still with me. Have I told you that?"

"Mm-hmm."

She watched him eat, again noting that nothing ever seemed to get him down. "Why are you so happy about this takeover?" she asked.

"Money," he answered matter-of-factly. "I got a raise despite my bump down in status."

She laughed and shook her head in mock disgust as she wrapped up the other half of her burrito to take home. "You have no integrity."

His eyes twinkled. "Not a single shred." And he shoved the last humongous bite into his mouth.

Toward the end of her first day, Brooke had managed to schedule two meetings with old clients and draw in one new for a total of one magazine ad, a gift card design, and a whole line of new branding. Normally she'd chalk it up as a good day, but Ethan had scored bigger with his one hook: a textbook layout with the potential of winning a whole series of five.

It had been torture listening to that call through the partitions. Just thirty minutes to go in the day and he would have fallen behind with his own sad accumulation of niche jobs. The man had gotten lucky.

Or was it luck after all? With a sigh, Brooke resigned herself to two weeks of deep suspicion. Could she really trust anyone here except Roger?

The answer was no, never. It was hard enough explaining to a particular Monroe client that she was back to pimping jobs and the reasons behind it.

"But I'm partial to Zhon's work," the client had said in her ear. "You wouldn't happen to know where he is now, would you?"

Since it had been literally two days since she'd returned home from her vacation, Brooke didn't know where any of Monroe's former artists had gone yet. "We have a gifted new team of designers, Mr. Barlow." At least she *hoped* they were gifted. "I'm sure we can have some suitable ideas for you when we meet on Wednesday."

"What if I don't like them? How do I know I'll get the same customer service? Have your rates changed at all?"

Since he'd been a client for two years, Brooke knew his particular tastes. All it would take was a little liaison work. "The bid should be compatible with past jobs. As always, we'll offer you up to six design concepts. If none of them suit you, I'll be happy to recommend another firm."

"Sounds fair. I don't mean to be a pain in the ass, but I don't like change."

You and me both, she felt like saying, but managed to bite her tongue.

She'd felt a little better after speaking with the artist whom Ken Stevens—the acting project manager since they didn't have one yet—had assigned to the job. Her name was Penny, a pixie of a woman who worked with her knees beneath her chin most of the time. Brooke instantly liked her. When they had come up with a rough draft, Brooke was able to convey that the client preferred dark with exploding light graphics to the more subdued textures Penny had first suggested. This was what Ken needed her for: knowledge and understanding of their existing customer base. But old business wouldn't win her VP.

Ethan emerged from Shannon's office, lost in a cell phone call. "We're in the process of bidding that project right now, Mrs. Stanhope. I'll have a figure for you by morning." He barely spared her a glance before sinking behind the partition. His chair creaked. The keyboard tapped out a string of noise. As Brooke eavesdropped, she rolled her eyes in disgust. What a conman. His voice was dripping with sex appeal, and Brooke made a mental note to pay attention to that from now on. If the majority of his calls were from women, she'd know that their receptionist had failed to remain impartial.

God, what a pig. At least Brooke was smarter than that and would never fall for his charms. Sure, he had a certain amount of sex appeal.

He looked good in a suit, he knew how to smile, and he walked with a natural swagger that projected high levels of testosterone. But she had too much pride to notice those things, let alone waste time thinking about them....

When Ethan hung up, he summoned her, which she promptly ignored. "Monroe," he repeated. "I know you can hear me. It's quarter to five and I want to get out of here on time."

"So get off your ass and come to me if you're in such a hurry," she sniped, pulling the two-inch file from her drawer.

There was a long, drawn-out sigh. "I see you're determined to make this as painful as possible."

Brooke slapped the folder on her desk and voiced those three little words that had set this whole competition in motion. "As you so kindly said to me: Deal with it."

"What—?" His chair creaked again and he appeared around the corner. "Is that why you're acting this way? Because of some remark I made at that restaurant?"

She flipped the folder open with attitude. "Maybe I just don't like you, Ethan. Is that so hard to believe?"

"Kind of, yeah."

Oh, the arrogance! She turned toward him, compelled to count out his many flaws. "You are selfish, egotistical, deathly afraid of losing to a woman, and you have horrible taste in candy."

Amusement softened his expression. "I'll make a deal with you," he said with his arms crossed. "If you manage to outsell me tomorrow *and* manage to remain civil all day, I'll wash your car."

He'd probably make fun of her practical four-door sedan, no matter that it carried the highest safety standard in its class. "Just washed it."

"Fine, then I'll gas it up for you."

Gas, huh? Brooke hid her interest in the contents of the folder. "And if I lose, I assume you'll want the same in return?"

"Oh, I'll definitely want that carwash. Too many love bugs down here."

Yes, those black and red insects, always connected in flight, were thick enough to keep a windshield thoroughly coated in guts. But the man knew how to drive a hard bargain, especially when gas prices were through the roof. With a sigh, she relented. "Alright, it's a deal."

He made a sound of triumph. "In the parking lot, after work, on a day of my choosing." When she rolled her eyes upward, he explained, "As much as you like to play in the rain, I don't. And I plan to be watching from my lawn chair."

Play in the rain…his subtle reminder of her sorry state when they met was a low blow. She rewarded him with a bland smile. "Oh, you shouldn't concern yourself with getting wet, Ethan. Most filling stations come with a really big canopy overhead."

He shrugged. "I'm good with that. If you can manage to hold your tongue for nine hours straight, I win either way."

"You know what I think?" Ken asked from his office doorway. "That you two need to spend more quality time together."

As panic set in, Brooke leaned around the partition to find her new boss massaging his temples. "That's not necessary, sir."

"I want at least an hour on that transition file starting now," he snapped. "And no bickering!"

"But it'll be almost six o'clock before—"

"And if it keeps up, you'll give me another hour tomorrow." Before either of them could argue, he retreated back into his office, leaving the door open a crack.

Ethan blew out a frustrated breath. "Yes, sir."

By the end of Tuesday, Brooke was glumly searching the forecast for days with no rain. Why she ever agreed to Ethan's challenge was a mystery. She could have just left things the way they were, but she'd know better from now on. How could she possibly outsell him when all he seemed to get were female clients? They melted like butter at the sound of his voice—instantly succumbed to his crafty words and whisky-coated chuckles.

It was painfully clear that she'd have to adjust her strategy, turn on some charm of her own. Gaining new clients had been a struggle for

Monroe Graphics in the last year or so, but Brooke had been distanced from that department for a long time while deeply engrossed in other facets of the business.

No, the only explanation for Monroe Graphics' failure was Stanley Monroe. Her father had fought retirement until it was too late, and he had simply grown lax. She had detected the fatigue, but had failed to sense the impact of his neglect. It just wasn't like him. Then to sell out and move to their second home in Dallas before the ink had even dried....

Did that man even know how shell-shocked, grief-stricken, and painfully alone he'd left his daughter? Why hadn't he warned her? Why hadn't he tried harder to leave her something or at least allowed her the opportunity to try to save the business?

"Looks like you're in luck for the rest of the week," Ethan said from the other side of the wall. "There's rain in the forecast every day until Monday."

Having worked up a good anger, Brooke sniped, "Oh joy," and instantly thanked the heavens that Ken had already left for the day.

"Come on, it's not so bad. Want to play double or nothing? Tomorrow may be your lucky day."

"Fuck off."

As soon as the words escaped her mouth, an exaggerated gasp came over the partition. She put her face in her hands.

"Why, Miss Monroe," Ethan gushed. "Such language. Is this what I can expect from my personal secretary?"

Brooke slammed her palms against the desk, pushed off, and stalked around to his side. He was munching on a candy corn, deeply engrossed in his computer screen, clearly not intimidated by the fact she hovered like a lethal cloud. Her eyes darted to the glass bowl of candy. She grabbed it, picked out one of the brightly colored triangles and held it up. While Ethan watched, she gave it a good long lick and then buried the contaminated piece deep in the bowl. When she slammed it down with a thunk, he appeared to be in shock, which filled her with childish satisfaction.

"That...," he said as she stomped back to her desk, "...was grossly immature."

Tucking her skirt beneath her, she calmly reclaimed her seat. "Want to tell me again how you like your coffee?"

"I can't believe you just did that."

"Neither can I, but I feel much, *much* better now."

"Guess I should have known that losing to me would turn you into even more of a bitch."

"Good." Ken's voice came from around the corner. He appeared with briefcase and keys in hand, startling them both. "I see we're all geared up to spend another hour on that file."

Brooke opened her mouth to argue.

"And," he added before she could, "I think it's only fitting you do it in the corner office. Don't you?" He looked between them as if expecting a comment. When only tense silence followed, he nodded. "That's what I thought."

TEN MINUTES INTO THEIR PUNISHMENT, BROOKE
sat with her face on the desk and her high-heeled shoes in the corner.
Ethan stood at the window, hands in his pockets watching the rush-
hour traffic go by. They hadn't spoken a word since the door closed.
Not a lick of productivity had been accomplished, but it was highly
suspected that their boss could care less about the two-inch file.

Ethan was the first to crack. "This is torture."

With a heavy sigh, Brooke peeled her face from the desk and
propped it between her palms. "Yup."

He twisted around and fixed her with a look. The top of his shirt
was unbuttoned revealing a hint of firm, tanned skin. "Want to order
Chinese?"

Her natural inclination was to say no, but her stomach rumbled in
agreement instead. "Sure."

He took out his cell phone and hesitated. "Do I need to worry that
my food will find its way into any of your orifices?"

The absurdity of his statement accompanied by his censuring glare made it difficult for her not to smile. "Not if we eat without speaking," she managed with a straight face.

A while later, the air was thick with the aromas of chow mein, pot stickers, and orange sesame chicken. Brooke had solved their bickering problem by pulling up an episode of "Revenge" on the computer, which Ethan agreed to as long as she didn't get any ideas. They watched TV and ate in silence, relaxed, feet up and—most importantly—quiet. When their time was nearly up, the door opened. Shannon's head popped through it.

"Ooh, dinner and a movie," she crooned. "Isn't that...cozy?"

Brooke choked on a mouthful of noodles. Ethan paused the show, his profile stern with annoyance. "What are you still doing here?"

Shannon walked over and snatched one of his pot stickers. "Waiting for you." She took a dainty bite, the small dumpling clasped between two pink fingernails. "We were supposed to have a beer after work, remember?"

How cozy, Brooke thought with an internal snarl. She picked up her drink and loudly sucked out the last of its contents.

Ethan picked up his own soda. "It'll have to be tomorrow."

"That's the second time you postponed on me," Shannon argued.

"Sorry." He jerked a thumb in Brooke's direction. "Blame her."

"Excuse me?" Brooke said through her straw.

"You're the reason we keep having to stay late."

"Unbelievable." She got up and started clearing away her share of the mess.

Shannon helped him clean up his and asked, "Is there a rule that says you can't be out past six?"

"I have a date."

"With who?"

"My neighbor."

That was a friggin' surprise. Brooke went for her shoes, promising herself not to ever again give Ken a reason to punish her this way.

Shannon wrinkled her nose. "Mable Shoemaker? Isn't she like eighty years old?"

Ethan gathered up his jacket and briefcase. "Seventy-nine. I promised to escort her during a sunset walk on the beach in exchange for a loaf of banana bread."

As the three of them walked out together, Brooke felt the tug of a reluctant smile. Shannon outright laughed, shook her head. "You whore."

"You don't understand." He leaned down and whispered, "It's *really good* banana bread."

By the end of the next day, Brooke was regretting her decision not to compete for double or nothing. Her phone soliciting had paid off in a big way, leaving Ethan in a cloud of dust.

Moreover, a sign that read "Respect the corn!" had been taped to the side of his new lidded jar that was secured with a small padlock. Why he'd chosen to do that rather than simply lock the whole thing in a desk drawer was beyond her. On occasion, she'd hear him open the jar, take out a small pile of candy, and then replace the lock. It made her smile every time since such acts of paranoia—in fact, anything that made his life more difficult—put joy in her heart.

Surely, they were neck-and-neck in sales, especially now that the bids were rolling out and coming back signed. It was getting harder to secure times for the conference room, and some client meetings would have to be held in one of the empty offices. She and Ethan alone were keeping Shannon busy, never mind what the other two account specialists were bringing in.

Still, they both had yet to secure any big, new, VP-winning accounts.

Roger spent more than a little time at her desk, getting regular updates. Shannon also kept close tabs on things, clearly rooting for team Ethan. In doing so, Roger and Shannon had struck a little bet of their own as to who would win the position.

Since she and Ethan had already spent their lunch hour with the dreaded two-inch file, Brooke rejoiced in the fact that Ken had no reason to keep them after work and had gone home early himself. She knew because she watched him from the hall of windows, making sure to track his progress all the way to the first stoplight. Not that she planned to fight with Ethan, but it was nice to know their boss wasn't within earshot just in case.

What a silly man to think that forcing them together would solve their issues. Okay, maybe yesterday afternoon wasn't so bad. She was sure it was because she and Ethan didn't actually work and instead wasted an hour of their day in an idle, stress-free environment. It wasn't as if Ken checked on their progress or anything.

But today she could go straight home, climb into her flannel pajamas, make dinner, and satisfy her creative side in her own studio until bedtime. Just like every other day....

Why did that sound so damned sad all of a sudden?

Roger showed up to see how things were going. Having shed his jacket and rolled up his shirtsleeves, he appeared just as relaxed as when he'd worked for her father. At least some things remained familiar, she thought with a smile. He leaned against the partition and spoke low. "I take it you had a good day?"

For the first time, Brooke noticed how much she appreciated the crinkle of his eyes when he smiled at her. His presence had quickly become a breath of fresh air amid the hostile work environment. She removed her glasses and returned his grin while rubbing the exhaustion from her eyes. "I did, but I'm ready for a hot bath and a glass of wine."

When she opened her eyes again, his blurry form was leaning in a little closer. "You have such beautiful eyes," he observed. "Ever thought about wearing contacts?"

This time, his compliment had an effect. She felt a small warmth bloom in her chest as she put the wire-rimmed glasses back on her nose. Now she could clearly see the way his defined jawline actually made his lips look fuller, more inviting than she'd ever noticed before. "Do you think I should get contacts, Roger?" she asked softly.

"Oh, please," an annoying voice came from over the partition. "If you two don't get a room, I'll be forced to wear my noise-cancelling headphones."

The warmth turned into full-fledged heat that rose clear up to the roots of her hair. Roger stood up a little and peered over the partition with an air of amusement. "Dang, Wolf, you sure know how to piss on a moment."

"I don't know what kind of frolicking went on here before, but Ken doesn't allow 'moments' between coworkers."

Roger stifled a cough with his fist. Brooke widened her eyes, begging him not to bring up the darkroom, knowing exactly where his mind had just gone.

Ethan must have noticed because he too stood up and peered over the wall. "I'm right, aren't I? You two are a couple."

"We are not nor have we ever been a couple," Brooke emphasized in a panic, fearing that Ethan may try to get one of them fired. "A man and woman can be good friends without more entering into it."

His brow creased with a frown of doubt. "Sorry, Brooke, but guys have one-track minds. Whether you know it or not, your friend Roger has envisioned going to bed with you many times, just like he has done with all his other platonic female friends."

"*Daaaaaang!*" It almost came out like a whine as Roger pierced him with a look that screamed *shut up!*

Ethan met it with a shrug. "It comes with the Y chromosome. Everyone seems to know it but her."

Brooke watched with horrified fascination from her chair below. The two men were so close in size and height, she wouldn't know the difference from behind if not for the hair. And the feet. Roger had enormous feet. Did he really want to sleep with her?

As the thought rolled through Brooke's mind, Roger began to back away. "Dude, things just got awkward. I'm out of here." He mimed a silent apology to Brooke and, with a casual walk, abandoned the administrative side of Monroe Graphics.

Brooke turned her rage on Ethan, who winked at her in return. "You're welcome," he said before disappearing back into his own workspace.

"For what?" she hissed. "Putting a strain on the only friendship I have in this office?"

"No, for opening your guileless little eyes to the ways of men."

He was getting ready to leave. Most folks had already gone home, and Brooke had no desire to be the last one left in the office. She shut down her computer in a race to make a dramatic, angry exit. "Who knew you were such a sore loser," she grumbled.

"Excuse me?"

She grabbed her briefcase and purse and turned off her light.

"You're just pissed because I did better than you today."

Halfway down the darkened hall of windows, Ethan caught up to her as she sprint-walked toward reception. "Believe me, I'm used to competition, Brooke," he said behind her, his voice taking on a tone of ridicule. "At least you won't find me spewing profanity when I'm under pressure."

Deciding against the elevator, she took a hard right and entered the stairwell. The door slammed in his face. She heard *"shit!"* and felt a jolt of supreme satisfaction for proving him wrong.

But it wasn't long before he was sailing down the stairs behind her. "You know what your problem is?" he asked, his tone more harried than before.

"That you didn't take the elevator?" She clutched the strap of her purse high on her shoulder as she rounded each landing in the windowless, vertical tunnel of stairs.

"You're mad at yourself for being duped," he said.

Brooke made a face. "What the hell are you talking about?"

"Why do you think your father sold Monroe Graphics without telling you?"

"Because he wanted to protect me."

"No, because he *could*. You've ridden his coattails for so long, you never learned the basics of running a business or how to spot the warning signs when it's in trouble."

"It wasn't in that much trouble," she denied hotly.

"See? That's what I mean. You may have connections, but you're too naïve and too unobservant to do Ken any good as VP."

They reached the ground floor at the same time where she turned on him in a fury. "It wasn't my job to be observant, it was my father's."

"As *senior manager*, it wasn't your job?"

She couldn't exactly tell him her role as senior manager was a bit different than most. She'd stepped into it to replace her ailing mother, but she had largely remained a part of the creative department.

As she pondered her answer, Ethan stepped closer, his energy wreaking more havoc on her frazzled nerves. This anger between them was more charged than anything she'd experienced, and damn it, she knew it was mostly her fault. But she couldn't help it. He was stealing her future.

His voice rumbled above her. "Vice presidents don't make excuses, Brooke."

"I'm not," she ground out. "Things were run differently, that's all. If I had been in charge, this takeover would have never happened, and I'll be damned if I'll let you sink your hooks into me any further than they already are."

His eyes darkened to a stormy blue. "I think you hate me more than the takeover." He took another step, forcing her to back up. "Why is that, Brooke? What did I do to you besides say a few poorly chosen words?"

She swallowed the softball in her throat, hoping he didn't notice. "Is it so wrong to fight for what's rightfully mine?"

"Is it so wrong for me to accept a promotion from my employer?" he came back with incredulity.

"Yes, when it's *my* promotion," she hissed. "*My* office. *My* eleven years of hard work you see every time you walk in there." She poked a fingertip into his chest and hit solid muscle. "And when I get that corner office back, you may as well pack your bags because I'll be rehiring my old staff and there will be no room for *you*."

Looking down at the spot she'd touched, Ethan's mouth thinned into a dangerous line. "Wow, lady, you never quit, do you?"

Something in his demeanor told her she'd pushed the wrong button. His next words confirmed it.

"For your information," he said with deceptive calm, "I had no intention of taking that corner office from you. I actually felt a little sorry for you. But now the gloves are off, and I'm going for gold."

"Good!" Brooke fired back. "Because I don't want or need anyone's pity, *especially* yours."

She dove for the exit door's push bar, but Ethan held it shut, preventing her from leaving with the last word.

"If you think for one second that you'll have the power to run me out," he said, "you're more naïve than I thought."

With a look of supreme annoyance, she faced him beneath the glow of artificial light. "I'm not as naïve as you think. I see through you, don't I?"

His brow went up. He backed away and gave her full access to the door. "I stand corrected. Maybe I'm wrong about you after all."

With a satisfied nod, she threw her weight against the door and dashed out into a complete and utter downpour. Her body instantly revolted against the rush of water already flowing down her back and into her high-heeled shoes. Slowly, she turned around and glared at him through the roaring curtain of rain.

Ethan gave her a salute from his dry haven and yelled, *"Then again, maybe I'm not!"*

6

"THERE SHE WAS, CAUGHT IN THE RAIN *AGAIN,*
looking at me as if I had personally seduced Mother Nature into
pissing all over her dramatic exit."

Shannon's delighted laughter rose above the sounds of the few
patrons milling and drinking around them. "Oh, Ethan, I would have
loved to see that. What did she do next?"

As they leaned against the bar together, Ethan's eyes continued to
scan the beer garden's meager crowd for any pretty face that might
take him away from Shannon's. He'd found a few over the last couple
of days, but none that interested him enough to take them home. Now
his coworker's presence in his favorite place to wind down was met
with mixed emotions, especially since he couldn't sleep with her. And
that's what he needed right now. A good lay. Maybe then he'd get
Brooke Monroe out of his head.

Why she was there in the first place was beyond all comprehen-
sion. Was it because his own problems had waned under the enormity
of hers? Was it because she kept pushing him with that pointy little

finger of hers until he said stupid shit like *I felt sorry for you?*
God, he should have known better. If anyone understood the
degrading nature of those words, it was him. How many times had he
shunned the people he loved because he feared their pity?

As if on cue, Ethan's vision wavered a bit and the neon lights
behind the bar began to spin. A slight shake of his head put everything back to rights…well, mostly. He should be grateful that his long
bout of recovery had finally ended and that partial blindness was the
only permanent byproduct of his accident. Brain surgery, traction, and
months of rehab had provided a better outcome than what the doctors
had predicted, at least. He was talking normally, walking, and—most
importantly—driving. The fact he'd cheated on his vision test at the
DMV was beside the point.

With his mug to his lips, Ethan caught sight of a brunette over the
rim whose pretty brown eyes grew heavy with suggestive promise. It
was a look he'd seen countless times, one that had lost its power when
shit got real. But his physical needs were fully recovered now, awake
and kicking. They'd been ignored far too long, and it was beginning
to affect his train of thought.

A hand waved in front of his face. "I said, what did she do next?"
Shannon repeated, still overcome with the giggles.

With a pang of annoyance, Ethan brought himself back to the
conversation at hand: Brooke Monroe, the little shrew he'd come here
to forget. "She lifted that head of hers and leisurely walked to her car
as if it were raining down sunshine."

Shannon's mug lowered. "Really?"

The memory spurred a chuckle, the brunette all but forgotten.
"And get this," he said. "The moment she got behind the wheel and
shut her car door, *boom!* It stopped raining."

"No!" Shannon gushed.

"I swear to God. It's like Mother Nature actually does have a hit
out on her."

When he took another long pull of beer, Shannon said, "Or that
Mother Nature has a crush on you."

He swallowed loudly and nodded. "That's also a distinct possibility."

She laughed again, but their shared hilarity died down to an uncomfortable silence. As Shannon looked at his hands, her mood sobered. "Are you worried at all that she might win the job out from under you?"

The thought had crossed his mind now that Brooke had proven to be a worthy opponent. "Nah," he answered with false nonchalance.

"Why would Ken do that to you anyway, especially if she's not qualified for it?"

As he pondered Shannon's question, all the resentment from that day at the restaurant came back. Ken Stevens—an objective man by nature—had sat across from him and explained how Ethan needed a challenge. The man had been a valued supporter; ever patient when Ethan was at his worst, he knew how restless he'd become. But there was another possibility he was forced to consider. "I think he feels sorry for her."

Shannon's dubious look questioned that. "What if she does win?"

Ethan recalled his private exchange with Ken after Brooke had left the conference room that first morning. "He told me I'd have two choices. I could go back home and be co-vice president of the Sioux Falls division or—"

"*Co*-vice president?" Shannon screwed up her face. "You can't work beside Jackie Jackhammer. It was hard enough working *under* her."

Ethan couldn't agree more. "I know, I know. My other option is to stay on here and work under Brooke."

"Doing what?"

He shrugged. "We'd still need a senior manager."

"You can't be co-VP here?"

"Nope. Not until our new baby grows up a bit."

Her brown eyes filled with what he never wanted to see again: sympathy. "Oh, Ethan. What do you think you'd do?"

"I don't know. But I can't blame Ken for the outcome of something I agreed to."

She peered at him through her lashes. "But you aren't worried."

"I'm not worried." He took a long, liberal drink, praying for the alcohol to kick in soon. "What really chaps my ass is that I can't look for a place of my own until I know for sure."

Shannon put her heavy mug on the bar and moved closer, placing a hand on his sleeve. "Keep your eyes open. She might try to cheat."

Something told him that Brooke wasn't the type to do that. The one good quality about her naïveté was that it came with an innocence he almost...*almost* admired. Ethan looked down at Shannon's hand as it inched up his forearm. "How would she cheat?" he asked.

Her eyes also followed her touch. "I heard your potential client Romcore is looking at bids from another agency."

"So?"

"When Ken fired the old staff, they scattered to who knows where. Brooke now has friends who work for other graphic design agencies."

"You're suggesting she's underhanded enough to leak information?" When Shannon answered with a pointed look, he shook his head. "She'd have to hack into your system—or mine—in order to obtain anything valuable."

"Or have her friend Roger do it."

She was right. If Brooke had it in her to cheat, it would be easy. "Keep my bids low enough and we'll see what happens," he suggested with a cocked eyebrow.

"Can't be too low or it'll look like I'm biased."

Again, he looked down at her wandering hand. "Aren't you?"

"Absolutely." Her answer came with seductive undertones that reminded him of the sex he hadn't had in forever. "I don't want to work under her either."

As the heat built in his crotch, Ethan had to remind himself again why he swore to never get into Shannon's pants. It was more than just her friendship with Harper. As long as they worked together, their relationship needed to remain uncomplicated. She knew his feelings on the subject since they'd discussed them before.

But the way she looked at his mouth indicated the woman didn't care. He checked his watch and then downed the last third of his beer in one shot. "I gotta go."

"Ethan?"

"What?" He slapped fifteen bucks on the bar, enough to cover both their drinks and a generous tip.

"It feels really good to laugh with you again," she said.

"No, Shannon."

Her look intensified. "Ken never has to know."

"We aren't sleeping together."

"You need it. I need it." When he hesitated, she grabbed his sleeve. "It's just sex. No strings attached."

With a will of iron, he very carefully removed her hand. "This place is full of easy men. Go find one and quit trying to complicate our friendship."

"You'd rather I sleep with a total stranger?" A hint of danger entered her eyes. "Don't be an asshole, Ethan. If you keep turning me down, you're going to miss out on the best booty call you've ever sunk your teeth into. *Literally.*"

Though he tried to let that one pass, he just couldn't. Curiosity, lust, and a little bit of masochism begged the question: "What does *literally* mean?"

Her smile had a feline quality that tightened his gut. "I like it rough," she purred, "I like to be tied up. I like submissive roleplay. I like teeth marks on my ass."

Holy shit! Ethan could handle rough. Hell, rough was exactly what he needed in his current mood. As her gaze continued to bore into his, a white-hot need to drag her into the ladies room began to drown out all common sense. He swallowed it back, but not before the evidence began to show itself down below.

"Say something." Her voice had taken on a desperate tone. "Come on, after a confession like that, don't leave me hanging."

Speechless, he decided not to even try and explain why he was turning her down again. But when he simply backed away, the flash of anger in her countenance was explanation enough.

"Fuck you, Ethan," she hissed. "Some day you'll come crawling back and *I'll* treat *you* like an asshole. See how you like it!"

Friday morning rolled around, marking the end of the first half of Brooke versus Ethan. They'd managed to stay neck-and-neck throughout most of the week, and the pressure was beginning to have a strange effect on those keeping close tabs. Brooke knew most of the office was rooting for Ethan. He was good at charming the women and bonding with the men. She was good at bonding with her desk. Not that it would matter in the long run.

In the break room, surrounded by acrid warmth and a hint of burnt popcorn, Brooke was reaching for the coffee pot when someone tapped her right shoulder. When she twisted around to look, Ethan moved in from the left, claiming the coffeepot first.

"I think I still see a little wet behind the ears," he murmured at close range.

Brooke jumped back as if she'd been zapped and watched in dismay as he emptied the pot into his mug, leaving only a few drops for her.

"And you call me immature," she yelled as he strutted out of the break room.

Monroe's receptionist made it through the door before it closed. Letreece, showing off her curves in a red stretch tunic, tucked her lip between her teeth as she watched the man walk away. "Damn if that white boy doesn't know how to fill out a suit," she groaned.

Brooke rolled her eyes as she dug the coffee out of the cabinet. "He's a jerk."

"He's not a jerk." Letreece reached past her in search of a coffee mug. "I watched him ruin a perfectly good shirt to help that scary chick from creative get her car started yesterday. All the other guys walked on by without so much as offering a hand."

Ignoring the urge to ask questions, Brooke put on a mask of indifference and stifled a yawn. "Hmm. You must have watched for quite a while in order to know that."

"Hell yeah. An incredibly fine ass was hanging out from beneath the hood of a car, you know. After an eyeful of that, I was sweating more than my Mountain Dew."

A vivid picture of Ethan's butt popped into Brooke's head before she could stop it. The slight thrill that followed was dismissed as a brief moment of insanity. "Are you entirely ruled by your hormones, Letreece?" she asked with growing annoyance.

The woman pushed herself up onto the countertop and gave her a once-over beneath shiny black bangs. "Maybe if you'd listen to yours once in a while, you'd get a crack at Mr. Wolf yourself."

"No thanks. I had one like him before."

"What happened?"

"He got married on our wedding day." She gave a dry smile. "Without me."

Letreece took the empty pot Brooke handed her and filled it under the faucet on her other side. "That's harsh. No wonder you're such a prude."

The accusation made her frown. "I'm not a prude."

"Come on, girl, everyone thinks you're still a virgin."

It stunned Brooke for a moment that anyone would care enough to discuss it. "Would that be such a bad thing?"

The woman let out a lusty laugh. "Someone as uptight as you needs a man in her life."

Hearing her grandmother's words regurgitated by Letreece made her lift her chin a notch. "I'm not uptight, just...very focused."

Letreece handed the full coffeepot back. "So I'm going to guess that your man left because you didn't give him any booty." Then she laughed at Brooke's answering look of chagrin. "Every woman in my family has gone through divorce except for my Aunty June. You know what she told me?" When her question was met with silence, she answered anyway. "If you want a man to stick around, all you gotta do is feed him and fuck him. Simple as that."

Brooke made a sound of wry amusement as she carefully poured the water into the machine. "Your aunt sounds lovely."

"She's a mean bitch."

The water dribbled over the side.

"One time," Letreece continued, "she whacked my Uncle Leroy upside the head with a two-pound bag of brown sugar. Poor man saw stars for three days."

Brooke tried to hide her laugh. "With brown sugar?"

"Girl, that shit'll fuck you up if there's enough attitude behind it. It was a hell of a cleanup in aisle six that day, and I ain't lying."

"And they're still married?"

She held up her hands. "Like I said, feed him and—"

"Got it. Yeah..." Brooke tapped her nails on the countertop. "Only problem with your theory is that Brandon and I had plenty of...you-know-what."

Letreece hopped off the counter and leaned in close. "If you still call it *you-know-what*," she whispered, "it wasn't that good."

While the receptionist went about her business, Brooke frowned down at the coffee pot now filling with a stream of rich, brown liquid. Since Brandon was the only man she'd been to bed with, she had only assumed that the sex was okay. He had certainly seemed to enjoy it at least. Then again, it had always bothered him that she couldn't have an orgasm....

It had been a full ten minutes since her first attempt to fill her mug. By the time Brooke finally emerged with a full cup of java, the main work area had come alive with the beginnings of a new day. Since having her first friendly conversation with someone other than Roger, she felt a bit better about confronting all the new faces.

But it still didn't prepare her for the commotion coming from Ethan's side of the partition, which had exploded with the pitter-patter of little footsteps and pixie-like giggles.

"Come here, princess," Ethan said with an air of excitement. "Give me a squeeze."

"I couldn't find you!" came the voice of a small child.

"Didn't you notice the candy corn on my desk?"

"It's not in our magic dish."

When Brooke realized they were talking about *the* bowl of candy corn she'd defiled, her face flushed with embarrassed heat.

Ethan cleared his throat, as if speaking directly to her through the wall. "I had to hide the magic dish from an evil sorceress."

Brooke rolled her eyes.

"Why?" the child asked.

"I caught her trying to poison our corn so I put it under lock and key." He must have produced that key because the child made a sound of wonder.

"Can I do it?"

As they fiddled with the lock, a woman joined them. "Not exactly the breakfast of champions."

Though Brooke was curious, she refused to look up as Ethan greeted the woman with warm affection. Who was she, anyway? A girlfriend? An ex-wife? Probably, since Ethan had expressed a willingness to buy a drink for anyone who passed muster. Pig.

"Where've you been?" Ethan asked.

"In Shannon's office catching up," the woman answered. "What's with the cubicle?"

"Just a temporary arrangement. I was telling the princess here about the evil sorceress who's out to get me."

"She poisoned our corn!" the little girl exclaimed through a mouthful of candy.

Feeling as if she was about to face the firing squad, Brooke buried herself in her email, struggling to ignore the banter next door.

"Well, she put a spell on my office too," Ethan continued with a dramatic rumble in his voice.

The child whispered, "Do you need my magic wand so you can turn her into stone?"

He chuckled. "Nah. I'm going to defeat her the old-fashioned way, with my brains."

"I like my idea better," the child replied, clearly disappointed by his lack of imagination.

While they all laughed, Brooke sunk lower in her chair. Nothing like being stuck out in the open while the pot shots flew overhead.

"Brooke, why don't you stand up and meet my family?"

The blood drained from her face. Was the man actually going to call her out in front of a kid? Introduce her as the mentioned evil sorceress?

What...an...asshole.

AS BROOKE MENTALLY PREPARED HERSELF FOR A
direct hit, someone entered her cubicle. She turned to give a hesitant look over her shoulder. There was a gorgeous, willowy blonde
dressed in a chic shorts ensemble, regarding her with friendly curiosity.

"Hi." She stuck out a hand. "I'm Ethan's twin sister Harper."

Twin sister? Brooke caught the amused glint in Ethan's eyes as he
looked down at her from above the partition. "Uh…" She took his
sister's hand in a firm grip. "Brooke Monroe. Nice to meet you." A
little carbon copy of Harper appeared at her side and leaned against the
woman's legs. "And you must be the princess," Brooke said.

"Adrianna," Ethan said. "My niece."

"Are you the evil sorceress?" the little girl asked through a mouthful
of fingers.

Ethan shook his head with a smile. "Come on now, does she look
like an evil sorceress to you?"

The little girl thought about it with a cute tilt of her head. "No."

With the verdict out, Brooke's shoulders instantly relaxed.

"So you're the Monroe that Ethan told me about," Harper broke in and then flashed him a look of confusion. "She isn't anything like you described."

"Yeah, I thought you said she had fangs," Adrianna added with a giggle.

Again, Brooke rolled her eyes upward to the man hovering over them. Ethan shrugged. "Guess I'm the only one who can see them."

So her canines were a little pointy. Her mother had always said it was an adorable feature. Before she could defend herself, Harper gave Ethan's face a little shove. "Ethan, quit." Then she spoke to Brooke. "I grew up with the jerk, so I feel your pain. But, believe it or not, he really does have a soft side."

A sudden liking for Harper developed in Brooke's war-torn soul. In spite of their similarities in looks, the woman shared none of Ethan's nasty traits. "Does he?" she answered. "Guess I'm the only one who can't see it."

Harper laughed, garnering a scowl of disapproval from her brother. At that moment, Brooke wanted to know more about the poor girl who'd been forced to share a womb with Ethan. "Do you live here or are you just visiting?" she asked out of genuine curiosity.

Harper looked down at her child, who was actively tugging on her shorts. "My husband and I have a winter condo that we're loaning to Ethan while he looks for his own place."

"Oh? In town or on the beach?"

She dug through her purse and produced a handheld video game for Adrianna. "On the beach near Venetian Bay."

That meant a Gulf Shore Boulevard address. "The view must be spectacular," Brooke said as the environment filled with electronic sound effects. "And we all know how much Ethan appreciates a good view, especially when it doesn't belong to him." When she looked up, she saw that his eyes had narrowed to dangerous slits.

Harper chuckled from behind her palm. "I can certainly feel the love between you two." Then she leaned down and whispered, "But be gentle. His head isn't as hard as you think, which we all found out last year when he wrecked his race—"

"Okay!" Ethan clapped his hands once. "Time for a tour. The princess is getting restless and that game is disrupting the workplace."

Before they left, Harper said her goodbyes and the little girl scrunched up her face with an implied warning: Mess with Prince Ethan and she'd get the wand. Brooke waved at Adrianna, knowing Ethan had a devout fan in that one.

In the aftermath of such an interesting exchange, Brooke was left wondering about the accident Harper had hinted at. It wasn't hard to see Ethan as an adrenaline junkie, and the photo on his desk of him propped against a white BMW covered with sponsor logos now made perfect sense. There had been other people in the photo with him, but she had refused to linger over it lest someone mistake her interest.

But she had absolutely no interest in Ethan Wolf. Oh, there was no denying a certain appeal to those penetrating blue-gray eyes…when they weren't laughing at her. And they were *always* laughing at her.

An image of Ethan gallantly fixing the scary chick's car in the parking lot came to mind. And him escorting an elderly lady during a sunset walk on the beach. To think of him as a nice guy would be to admit her role in drawing out his inner asshole. With a sigh, she concluded they were like oil and water, or fire and gasoline rather. They simply did not mix without an explosive reaction. To men like Ethan—like Brandon—she was an easy target, only this time she refused to take her licks lying down.

The phone on Ethan's desk rang. Soon she heard Shannon's voice through the partition. "Yes, Mr. Troll, I'll personally hand him the message. I'll have him call you right away. My pleasure, bye now."

Brooke's first thought was how could such a sweet woman like Harper be friends with a pretentious snob like Shannon? Her second thought was why was Shannon suddenly answering Ethan's phone?

Some of her questions were answered later when Ethan's sister reappeared at her desk. Harper was alone, which meant that Ethan was somewhere showing off his niece, and probably swarmed by adoring women in the process.

"I don't mean to bother you," Harper said as she rested an arm on the partition, "but I feel the need to make some apologies for my brother."

"Believe me, that's not necessary."

"I just want you to know he isn't normally so…difficult. He's dealing with a lot of changes right now, and he doesn't like to be told he can't do something. It pisses him off. Makes him more determined to do it, which is why we worked so hard to get him away from— never mind, you probably aren't interested in the details."

But the woman was clearly itching to provide them. And, damn it, Brooke's curiosity was peaked. "Is this about the accident you mentioned?" she asked.

Harper's light blue eyes reflected gratitude for the green light. "He suffered some pretty bad injuries, some that he'll never recover from. But the driver who hit him was paralyzed from the waist down, and Ethan at least acknowledges he could have fared worse. He was a good driver, Brooke," she continued with a hint of adoration. "A *really* good driver. I mean, he was *this close* to a podium finish in last year's Majors Tour."

Brooke watched Harper's thumb and forefinger press together ever so tightly, feeling the woman's angst. "What's a Majors Tour?"

"It's like NASCAR for the best of the best in amateur racing except with a lot more turns. When he made it in, he was so focused it was scary. I remember thinking the only thing that could keep him from that checkered flag was if someone wiped him out. And that's exactly what happened."

Though Harper was doing her best to keep her regrets from showing, Brooke felt them just the same. She pursed her lips together and nodded. "I'm sorry, I didn't know."

"He could have avoided being hit, but it would have put him in the grass where there was a camera crew filming the race. Not that he remembers it, but I watched him make that decision, that sacrifice.

When his injuries forced him out of the tour for good, it broke his heart. That racetrack is like a drug for him, and it would have only been a matter of time before he did something stupid. So, you see…he needs to be here, away from all that. To discover other hobbies, other obsessions, like golfing or fishing."

Ignoring the slight pull on her heart, Brooke focused on the latter. She had quite a few hours of deep-sea fishing under her belt since she'd practically grown up on her parents' thirty-six-foot trawler. She'd always loved the peace, the downtime, and then the adrenaline rush that came with reeling in a large catch. "I don't think Ethan would be satisfied with any sport that requires patience," she deduced with certainty.

Harper shrugged a slim shoulder. "I just want him to stay long enough to give a different life a chance."

The purpose of their conversation was becoming clearer to Brooke. "And you're afraid he'll move back home if I win this competition of ours."

"Honestly…I don't think you'll win." When Brooke lost what remained of her smile, Harper held up a hand. "And that's said with the utmost respect toward you. It's just that Ethan doesn't lose."

Shannon appeared with her pink handbag and a set of keys. "I'm ready whenever you are. Where are Ethan and the munchkin?"

"Probably stuck in the creative department," Harper answered with a laugh. "Adrianna was fascinated with all the colors and the gadgets. She asked one of the artists if they were Walt Disney's elves."

While Shannon ushered her away, Harper turned and gave Brooke a quick wave. "Thanks for listening," she said. "And for the record, I think you're a very nice person."

Friday morning, Brooke found herself in Ken's office being subjected to a lecture about the conduct expected of Master Ink employees. While he droned on, she drifted in and out of flashbacks of her father there, doling out a similar routine. Then she'd wake up and wonder what the hell this stranger was doing surrounded by Stanley Monroe's stuff.

The wall-to-wall bookshelves, the reserved mahogany furniture he'd chosen from Rhodes when she was only five and hated furniture shopping.

The Appalachian Brown paint color she and her mother had spent a weekend afternoon applying to the walls.

It had been quite a project to clear all the clutter in order to *get* to the walls, yet this stranger preferred it clean and unadorned with the evidence of his long, prosperous career.

"I didn't summon you here to hold a private conversation with myself, Ms. Monroe."

Brooke tore her gaze from the empty bookshelves and refocused to find Ken's stout features brimming with impatience. "Huh?"

His mustache twitched. "Do we need to start over?"

She swallowed and fidgeted in her seat. "No, sir, I heard you." It seemed that someone had filed a complaint against her and Roger after all. The fact that Brooke had to defend herself in that light royally pissed her off. She'd worked far too hard to have her reputation sullied by the likes of Ethan. "And I *assure* you Roger and I are only friends. In fact, I wholeheartedly share your views on interoffice relationships, I always have."

Except now she was nursing a bit of a crush on Roger, especially since he hadn't exactly denied Ethan's accusation that he'd wanted to sleep with her. Did he? Was that why their recent exchanges had become laced with suggestive undertones that made her want to rip off his clothes?

Ken blew out a frustrated breath, rubbed at his temples. "So you're saying that these accusations are unfounded."

Harper had warned her that Ethan didn't lose. Did that mean he'd stop at nothing to win? Brooke held Ken's stoic gaze and said, "Absolutely. The fact Mr. Wolf would make them just proves how desperate he is to win this competition."

"I didn't say that Ethan made those accusations."

She paled at the irritation on her boss's face. "I'm sorry, I assumed—"

"You two do a lot of assuming!" Ken's voice rose as his bald spot grew even pinker. "Frankly, I'm getting tired of the drama, even though I'm partially to blame for agreeing to this damn competition in the first place. I suggest you both grow up before I give that corner office to Shannon instead."

"Shannon!"

"She's the only one not wreaking havoc on my blood pressure." His gaze jerked upward. "And what do you want?"

Brooke realized Ethan must have entered the scene because his negative energy emitted the power of a heat lamp on her back.

"I just got off the phone with Ted Troll of Romcore," he said behind her. "It turns out our competitor submitted a lower bid than ours."

Ken leaned forward and folded his hands before him. "That bid was at rock bottom. No one could have beaten it and still turned a profit."

So that was the message Shannon had taken earlier. It was good news for Brooke since Romcore was a big-enough client to have won Ethan the VP position. As she celebrated on the inside, the two men continued to banter over her head.

"They could if they beat it by a narrow-enough margin," Ethan argued, "which they did."

Ken's look darkened with suspicion. "How narrow?"

"Narrow enough to suggest a leak."

Only when a stiff silence followed did Brooke detect the accusation in Ethan's tone. A quick glance over her shoulder confirmed the worst. She sat back, dumbstruck for a moment. "You've got to be kidding. Now you're accusing me of corporate espionage?"

"Nah," Ethan drawled. "That would suggest you have some kind of vendetta against me."

Anger sent her straight out of her chair. "Just the other day you were calling me naïve!"

"I'm beginning to wonder," Ethan countered with annoying calm. "Romcore's isn't the only bid to fall short by a thin hair. There've been others, all mine, all potentially big clients."

Her hands balled into fists at her sides. "Even if I were losing to you—which I'm not—I wouldn't be so desperate as to cheat. My ethics are quite intact."

His look turned droll. "Somehow I doubt your ethics override your hatred for me."

"You *pig!*"

"STOP!" Ken's voice boomed. Brooke jumped and snapped her mouth closed. Once Ken rode out the tense silence for a moment, he spoke quietly. "I think we all need to take a breath." When Ethan opened his mouth, Ken held up a silencing finger. "If there's enough evidence to suggest a leak, I assure you it will be thoroughly investigated. In the meantime, I propose we take this competition out of the office."

From Ethan, "What does that mean?"

"It means that you two need to decompress and I need alcohol. Preferably something I can rip the cork out of with my teeth. So during your eleven o'clock lunch break, whoever can find and bring me a bottle of 2010 Duckhorn Cabernet first will get to add this week's total sales to that of your biggest client. You'll both be reimbursed for the wine, of course."

As they absorbed this odd request, Brooke met Ethan's intense gaze from his place by the door. Adding more sales—even small ones—to the pot could make a huge difference if their biggest clients were of a similar size.

Ken barked, "Are you two just going to stare at each other or get me my wine?"

His words finally broke through their stupor. Brooke spoke over Ethan as she searched for something to write with.

"What year was that?"

"Duckhorn what?"

When Ken repeated his instructions, she scribbled them down on a borrowed pad of sticky notes and then whirled around to beat Ethan out of the office.

Much to her dismay, he was already gone.

She found him at his desk audibly asking his phone to search for the nearest liquor stores. They couldn't leave for another ten minutes, which would give her time to make a few phone calls of her own, so she grabbed her cell and headed toward the hallway of windows where she wouldn't be overheard.

The second call scored big. Since she'd made a wine purchase or two in her lifetime, Brooke was somewhat knowledgeable about who was most likely to carry what. And DeBuer Cellars had not one but two bottles of 2010 Duckhorn Cabernet at ninety-five bucks a pop.

When she ended the call and turned around, she found Ethan standing right behind her. Before she could blast him for eavesdropping, he held up a hand.

"Hey, I was just headed for the restroom."

"Oh, I'll just bet you were," she raged, shadowing his footsteps all the way down the hall. "And you have the gall to accuse *me* of cheating."

"Brooke, right about now, I couldn't give a shit what you think of me." Before pushing through the men's room door, he stopped and turned suddenly. Brooke stumbled in her heels to avoid a collision. "But now that I know what you're up to, I'll do what it takes to win this."

"I didn't leak any information," she ground out.

The glint in his eyes told her it was too late. "Whether you did or not, I won't take the chance." He pressed a fingertip into her shoulder, giving back what she gave him in the stairwell. "Consider yourself warned."

As soon as the digital clock above the conference room showed eleven o'clock, they engaged in yet another race for the stairs. It was raining on the other side of the windows, but this time Brooke didn't care. Getting wet was worth the sacrifice, and she knew Ethan would be getting wet this time too.

But by the time he burst through the door, the shower was already over. Typical Florida sunshine filled the stairwell. The clean scent of ozone and wet earth met her the moment she also reached the landing. Brooke kicked off her heels and ran with them in her grasp through the cool puddles. Luckily, she'd scored a much closer parking spot than he.

Once behind the wheel, she didn't bother taking the time to roll down a window to relieve the oven-like heat or to even look and see where Ethan was. The tires of her Audi skidded on the wet pavement as she backed up and then skidded again when she threw it into drive. With a clear path to the exit in front of her, a smile of victory curved her lips.

A smoky blue sedan came out of nowhere and stopped, blocking her path. Brooke slammed on the brakes, sending rivulets of water down the windshield. "Damn it, get out of the way!" she raged, with her horn blaring.

Then she looked closer...and saw Shannon behind the wheel, the woman's smile beaming through the reflection of her own rain-dappled windshield. What the hell? Just then, a yellow-and-black sports coupe zoomed past Shannon's rear end, claiming the exit first.

Ethan's elbow jutted from the open window.

BROOKE SCREAMED OUT HER FRUSTRATION. When Ethan only smiled and saluted in passing, she rolled down the window and threatened to ram Shannon's car. With a casual whistle on her lips, the woman finally moved out of the way.

Brooke floored the gas pedal. Within seconds, she was at the first intersection with her blinker on. Only then did she turn on the wipers to clear her view. Ethan was three cars ahead in the same lane. Since she was no match for someone who'd done his share of competitive driving, she took that moment to reach for her phone and hit redial.

"DeBuer Cellars, may I help you?"

She put a pleasant smile on her face, hoping to project it through the phone. "Hello, is Sid working today?"

"Yes, he is."

"May I speak with him, please?" The arrow turned green and the line of cars began to move.

"He's in the back. Let me get him for you."

"Thank you." While Brooke was on hold, she noticed that the cars weren't moving. When she craned her neck to look, it was to find a yellow-and-black sports car blocking the way. The car behind Ethan honked. She honked too. As precious seconds ticked by, more cars in the lane began to honk. Just as it hit Brooke what he was doing, the arrow turned yellow and Ethan slowly gave his car gas. Just one more car was able to get through behind him, leaving Brooke and the rest to wait for the next green arrow. As her anger doubled, someone leaned out their window and yelled, "Asshole!"

The fact he'd pissed off others in order to slow her down was testament to how far he'd go to win this particular round. Brooke peeled her white knuckles from the steering wheel and turned on the air conditioning. As her immediate surrounding cooled, she rolled up her window and took a deep breath.

Calm, she needed to remain calm.

A man's voice came over the phone. "This is Sid."

Still boiling from the green light episode, Brooke had to force the smile back into her voice. "Hi, Sid, it's Brooke."

"Hey, I've been wondering about you."

Since she'd met him through her ex-fiancé, Brooke never thought too much about dating Sid. This time, however, she wondered how the flirtatious essence of his words could work to her advantage. "What about me?"

The arrow turned green and the car in front of her began to move.

"I thought maybe you'd be up for a drink so you can tell me all about your vacation."

She wanted to scream that it had all been a big sham to get her out of the state. Instead, she said, "I'll definitely have that drink with you, but for now I need a *huge* favor."

"Sure, what's up?"

As she drove at a reasonable pace now, calm reentered her bloodstream. "As long as I don't get stuck at anymore lights, I'll be there in about four minutes. I was wondering if you'd let me in through the back door."

"Sure. Any particular reason?"

"You have two bottles of 2010 Duckhorn Cabernet on your shelves. I'm in a big hurry and I need you to hold them for me so I can be in and out of there as quickly as possible." Before Ethan got wind of what she was up to.

"You know they're almost a hundred bucks apiece, right?"

Knowing she'd only get reimbursed for one, Brooke chalked it up to a necessary expense. "Do you take credit cards over the phone?"

"Sorry, no, but I'll keep an eye out for you."

Since she'd lost sight of Ethan long ago, she focused on reaching the back of the liquor store in one piece. The wet streets were horrible as usual, as heat and steam rose upward to distort her view ahead through the slow-moving traffic. When she finally wheeled her car into the crowded strip-mall parking lot, Brooke followed the drive that would take her to the back of the shops. Once there, Sid's mop of red hair glowed like fire in the early afternoon sun. True to his word, he had the door propped open.

When she was parked, they rushed inside together.

"So what's the hurry?" he asked as he passed her on their way to the register up front.

She kept her voice low, scanning the large rustic showroom for signs of Ethan. "I'm late for work," she said as she spotted Ethan's wavy hair bobbing down one of the wine aisles. "I'll wait here." She handed Sid her credit card.

He took it, his hand white with an abundance of red freckles. "I'll be right back."

Hiding behind stately displays of fine wines, Brooke watched in pained suspense as he reached beneath the counter and set the bottles in plain view. If Ethan spotted them before they were paid for, he could possibly finagle the employees into letting him have one. The register beeped out a sale. Ethan's hair had moved to the end of the aisles and was quickly bobbing over the selection of bottles near the front of the store.

Sid fluffed out two bags while the cashier swiped her card. In went one bottle, then the next. The register spit out a receipt and only then did Brooke feel the weight of the world lift from her shoulders.

As Sid put the receipt in one of the bags and scooped them up, Ethan reached the counter.

"Hi there," he drawled, his charming smile putting a blush on the female cashier's cheeks. "I was told you have a bottle of 2010 Duckhorn Cabernet, but I don't see it on your shelves."

Sid placed the bags in Brooke's arms just as the cashier pointed in her direction. "Sorry, that lady just bought the last two."

Ethan's smile vanished. His gaze shot around, searching for *that lady*. The moment he recognized her, his face morphed into an angry mask of disbelief.

With the surge of victory warming her body throughout, Brooke returned his earlier salute with one of her own. "Nice try, slick," she purred.

Ethan chased after her as she headed toward the rear exit. "Ken only wanted one bottle, you know!"

Brooke graced him with an over-the-shoulder smirk. "I needed something to go with my macaroni and cheese tonight."

When Ethan reached the back hallway, Sid stopped him with a hand to the chest. "Sorry, no customers beyond this point."

"She's a customer!"

"She's an exception."

While Brooke listened to the exchange, Sid shot up to the top of her list of favorite people. With a hand on the exit door, she turned around and flashed her hero an appreciative smile. "Thank you, Sid. That first round will be on me."

Behind Sid, Ethan paced back and forth like a caged tiger as she slipped out and into the warm Florida air. "Everyone knows you don't drink a hundred-dollar bottle of wine with mac and cheese!" he shouted after her. But the last word was cut off when the back door slammed shut.

Cradling both bottles in one arm, Brooke popped the top button of her blouse open…and let the sunshine in.

The moment she placed the coveted bottle of wine in Ken's eager hands, Brooke floated back to her desk on a fluffy white cloud of victory. After such a tumultuous week, this win meant more than just the competition; it was a symbol that things were finally turning in her favor.

And, despite Ken's recent lecture about office romance, the first person she wanted to tell was Roger. There were still twenty-five minutes left for lunch, so she headed for the break room with a handful of quarters. As she fed them into the machine, the door swung open.

"That was my bottle," Ethan growled behind her.

Though his tone begged for a fight, Brooke was just too damned happy to care. "It was my money."

When he approached, his thunderous mood cast an electrically charged shadow over her perch on cloud nine. "I can't believe you spent a hundred bucks just to screw me over. It only proves how far you'll go to win."

She bent over to retrieve her package of sandwich crackers from the machine. "Don't even think of comparing a wine purchase with leaking information."

When she left the break room, he hounded her every step as they walked through the office. "Anyone who deserves that title," he persisted, "doesn't have to spend money to get it."

She gave a dry laugh. "It's no worse than making your patsy run offense for you."

"You're just upset because all your patsies were fired!"

The crackers crushing in her fist, Brooke halted, turned, and met his scowl nose to nose. "You're right. But in this case, it paid to have *friends.*"

She left him simmering by the reception desk as she continued down the long hall, her heart beating a mile a minute. With that last remark, she'd just scored another major point. Life was good and getting better with every breath she took.

When she reached the server room, Roger was there alone, surrounded by the warmth of humming hardware and working his way through a bag of chips. He looked up, stopped chewing as his eyes fixed on the opened top button of her blouse. A flush crept into his cheeks. "Wow."

Her smile widened. "You'll never believe what just happened."

They finished their lunch together, Roger listening in rapt attention as she relayed what went down at the liquor store. When she got to the macaroni and cheese part of her story, he threw back his head with an infectious whoop of laughter. Her body exploded with delicious tingles at the sound, his joy heightening her achievement like nothing else could. Leaning toward him, Brooke beamed. "I feel like I can accomplish anything. Oh, Roger, I've never felt so alive in my life!"

Just like that, the air around them changed. As thoughts of him touching her naked skin began to percolate in her mind, his look lingered long enough to make those thoughts a definite possibility. "I must say, I've never *seen* you quite so alive," he murmured.

Her heart skipped a beat. "Pissing off Ethan Wolf must agree with me."

"I so want to kiss you right now."

The shock of his words rendered her speechless for a moment. But, by God, she wanted him to kiss her, badly. He must have seen it in her eyes because he rolled his chair a little closer.

An image of Ken lecturing her from across the desk broke through her lustful haze. Brooke clung to it as if it were her only link to sanity. "It wouldn't be wise, Roger. Ken is watching us pretty closely."

He stared at her mouth. "There's always the darkroom."

Holy moly. The way his chest rose and fell beneath the shirt and tie made her desperate with need, all consequences be damned. Never before had she fostered such a strong desire to test her limits. "We can't—"

"Why not?" he interrupted. "No one's discovered it yet, no one would even think to look for us in there." She was silent for so long, he tilted his head. "Come on. Break a rule. Take that one last step over the edge...."

They both jumped when the server room door opened. The new systems administrator came in with a Coke in one hand and a half-eaten burger in the other. He spotted Brooke, lifted the burger in greeting, and then sat down at his desk to finish his lunch over an open binder.

Brooke returned her attention to Roger. Though they had company, he repeated his last request through the heat in his eyes.

"I'd better," she swallowed hard and abandoned the chair she'd borrowed for the last fifteen minutes. "Um...get back to work."

She could feel his intense gaze on her back until the door closed behind her. She was standing in the creative department with its scattered, individual work environments that defined the quirks of every artist there. Roger was right. Their old team of artists loved to express their creativity and took advantage of their unique opportunity to blow off some steam when the managing heads were turned.

This new team would be no different. For the first time, Brooke understood the need for such venting. She hadn't slept with a man since Brandon.

But the urges were there now more than ever.

Penny waved her little pixie fingers, snapping Brooke out of her ruminations. She waved back, gave the woman a wobbly smile, and then dashed out into the hallway. The alcove to the bathrooms was just a few feet away. Once there, a cool drink from the water fountain beckoned. As she sated her raging thirst, Brooke made a deal with herself. If Roger found her there within the next few minutes, she'd take him up on his offer. If he didn't, she'd go back to her desk and never give it another thought.

But in her current mood, she really, *really* wanted to break a rule. Eyes closed, she leaned against the wall next to the water fountain and fought to steady her breathing by counting down from one hundred. At ninety-three, she noticed a shadow dimming the light from the windows. She opened her eyes.

There stood Roger, his body braced with anticipation.

A zing of excitement shot through her core. With a slight curve of her lips, she pushed herself from the wall. "The darkroom," she said. "Five minutes."

ETHAN PACED OUT HIS FRUSTRATION IN THE stairwell. With today's win, Brooke now had a significant advantage. How had this competition turned to shit so fast? All he'd done was bring to light the possibility that she was leaking bids to the competitor. Was it such a fucking stretch? Did Ken not *want* to believe that she was out to hurt him or the company?

The man needed to open his goddamned eyes.

A noise alerted him that he was no longer alone in the stairwell. Ethan turned to find Shannon leaning against the door she'd just walked through and closed.

"You look like you want to drive your fist into the wall," she said with a strange lilt in her voice.

He did. But Ethan knew that what he really needed was to drive himself in and out of a woman…and here was one whose last offer echoed in the void between them.

I like it rough. I like to be tied up. And I like teeth marks on my ass.

"I have a lot of anger inside me, Shannon," he rasped, openly scanning her curves from head to toe.

Her hands flattened against the sides of her skirt.

And she smiled.

BROOKE WAS ABOUT TO DO SOMETHING SHE considered wicked and reckless. Something she had vowed never to do—which is exactly why she snuck into the storage room with a wicked smile on her face.

Her pulse hammering throughout her veins, she turned on the light illuminating the stacks of boxes and office furniture that blocked her path toward the back. Moments later, she stood before the black cylindrical door that was built way back when to keep out even the faintest sliver of light. Now would be the time for that inner voice of reason to come out and tell her that this was wrong.

But she couldn't hear it. She didn't want to. Hell, Roger was probably already in that darkroom waiting for her with his clothes undone. With a steadying breath, Brooke flattened her hands against the cold metal cylinder.

Do this.

The door began to rotate on its narrow track, creating a low, hollowed sound. When the chamber opened, she stepped inside. As she rotated it closed with one hand, she opened the buttons of her blouse with the other. Now she was in the pitch-black abyss that was the darkroom. Brooke stepped out of her capsule, feeling much like a heroine in one of those sci-fi movies exploring strange new worlds with unimaginable bravery.

"Roger?" she whispered. Nothing.

Since he wasn't there yet, she felt around the wall and located the light switch. She flipped it on only long enough to get an idea of her surroundings. The film-developing equipment was still arranged the way it had always been, relatively undisturbed since the darkroom had been decommissioned, but various things had been piled around it, like some outdated fax machines, some old waiting-room chairs, and a shelf stacked with boxes of forgotten computer cables and keyboards.

The smell of sex was gone at least, replaced by a bottled-up odor of old plastic. With the room memorized, she turned off the light and kicked off her shoes. As she ripped the elastic band from her low ponytail, voices began to reverberate through the walls from the conference room on the other side.

Damn! One of the other account specialists had brought in a client. She heard the click of the conference room door and identified Regina Sandusky's voice as she offered them coffee, water, or anything from the soda machine. Brooke was horrified by the sound quality, knowing that if she and Roger so much as grazed against anything, it would be heard on the other side of the wall.

But somehow, the danger only heightened her excitement. Flipping her hair upside-down, she knotted it on top of her head where it would stay out of the way. In a hurry to disrobe before she changed her mind, Brooke pulled down her skirt and finished unbuttoning her blouse.

The revolving door began to turn, sending shockwaves of excitement throughout her body. More than five minutes had passed since they'd made this deal, and now Brooke stood in her bra and panties unable to wait any longer. She touched the door and felt it move beneath her hands. Once the opening came around, she reached in, grabbed Roger's shirtfront, and pulled him against her.

In a frantic bid to keep him quiet, she covered his mouth with hers until he could figure out the situation for himself. While the conference room voices hummed around them, his lips opened. Their tongues met for the first time. Brooke felt an immediate, overwhelming connection, one that had remained untested between them for days now. The kiss built with scorching intensity, her sigh of pleasure whisper-soft. The fact that there was a meeting going on right beside them ramped up the naughty factor and made the game that much more exciting.

Her sense of daring soared out of control. While her hands explored his chest, his traveled up her bare arms, clamped around her shoulders, and yanked her against his lean, hard body. With trembling fingers, she loosened the first button of his shirt and then another. While she worked on getting his clothes off, his fingers hooked her bra straps and slid them down her arms, exposing her breasts to the chilly air. Her nipples instantly hardened, coming alive with a tingly yearning to be touched.

She ripped her mouth away with a gasp. He softly shushed her, kissed her neck and shoulders as he cupped both her breasts in his large, warm hands. She arched into him, finally able to tear the shirt from his shoulders. Before she could do more, he grabbed her hands and forced them behind her back. The heat was so encompassing, all that mattered was the pulsing need between her legs. She needed him to enter her, needed him to fill her up, needed him to quench the fire until it no longer consumed her.

While they sipped from each other's mouths, she stepped backward, her bare feet moving along the cold floor until she bumped into one of the old cushioned chairs behind her. Thrown off balance, she fell back into it, making a bumpy noise in the process.

The voices next door stopped for a second. Someone asked what that was. Brooke waited, her breath suspended as the juices flowed from her aching body.

Despite the danger, Roger's clothes continued to rustle with movement as he removed them. Apparently, he would not be deterred in his quest to have her. Commanding herself to breathe, she waited for him, knowing that she was about to get laid for the first time in a long while.

By a man other than Brandon. And at work.

His zipper made a painfully loud noise. Her tongue skimmed her lower lip in anticipation. Then something unexpected happened.

In one smooth move, Brooke was lifted out of the chair and spun around. He forced her back down into the cushion, only on her knees this time. Bent over, she rested her cheek against the back of the chair, keenly aware that the mood had changed from sweet and cautious to something much more frantic. She heard a tearing noise and knew he was arming himself with protection at that very moment. His mouth came down and left an erotic trail of nips and kisses along her shoulders and back. All the while, he fondled her breasts, kneading them at first and then rolling her nipples between thumb and forefinger. She buried her gasps against the musty fabric of the chair.

Never before had she been handled this way. Brandon's gentle touch and dry kisses had always failed to elicit that ever-elusive climax. As a result, he'd accused her of being rigid and cold.

Or perhaps the asshole just hadn't known how to please a woman. As Brooke thought of that, she smiled. Here was living proof that, in the hands of the right man, she was far from cold. In fact when Roger sank his teeth into her right ass cheek, Brooke came alive with a mixture of surprise, pain, and fascination. Had he really just bitten her? And was it an accident that her body fairly gushed with heat in response?

While his hands moved from her breasts to the apex of her thighs, he bit her again—not too hard, not too soft—delivering a heady contrast of pain and pleasure as his fingers delved beneath her panties at the same time. She parted for him and arched her back, struggling not to make noise. God, he was torturing her, daring her to cry out and alert a whole bunch of people in the other room. He was incorrigible. He was fighting dirty.

And she loved it.

With one knee, he pushed her legs farther apart. Then he reached down and moved the crotch of her soaking wet panties aside. His fingers parted her exposed folds and found all the places that begged for his touch. As he slid them in and out of her, swirling his rough fingertips in circles around her clit, Brooke fought the need to scream out her pleasure. In response, he bent down and took a huge portion of her ass in his mouth. Oh, yes, the message was clear. He'd bite her again, harder this time if she didn't keep quiet. The anticipation—the unbearable pleasure—built until her body was singing with the need to explode.

Roger stood up and replaced his fingers with the firm tip of his erection. Brooke tensed and waited.

When he entered her, it was hard and fast. She threw her head back, her hands balled into fists before her. His fingers dug into her skin as he stilled for a moment. Then he pulled out and drove into her again. She bit her lip to keep from screaming. He held her firmly at the waist, forcing her to meet each thrust with equal momentum. What had begun as painful slowly morphed into a torturous kind of pleasure as her body stretched to accommodate him. Then she began to notice his many techniques, the way his cock skimmed along her folds as his fingers had done before.

A burst of laughter came from the neighboring room, reminding them that the workday carried on around them while he fucked the living daylights out of her in secrecy. The reminder took her pleasure to a whole different, foreign level. It must have had the same effect on Roger because he gripped her shoulders and pulled on them so that she arched backward, giving him full access to what felt like the depths of her soul.

Sweet God in heaven, the desire to tear into him the way he was tearing into her was almost too much. The fact that she couldn't heightened the need. All her untapped desires melted together until her body began to convulse around him. As her inner walls tightened, pleasure burst outward and enveloped her in the sweetest, most sensational pool of pleasure she had ever felt. He cupped her jaw, twisted her around, and shushed her cries with his mouth as he continued to pound into her from behind. Finally, he tensed, slowed, and then let loose with a violent tremor that told her he was coming too. When it was over, he continued to move inside her, his breath mingling with her own as he slowly brought them both back down to earth.

Never before had Brooke felt anything like it. She had tried so hard to come for Brandon, but she'd also heard that many women couldn't have orgasms so she'd assumed that she was one of them. That sense of failure had stayed with her since he had left and saddled her with the belief that she'd been the problem.

Now Brooke actually found herself in a state of post-coital bliss. Did Roger feel as good as she did at that very moment? As she wondered about it, he lifted his body off of her and pulled out. As she gingerly exited the chair, there was a rustling of clothes and the pull of a zipper. Still shaky and weak-kneed, Brooke felt around until she found the roll of paper towels she'd seen earlier. She tore off a few and started to dry the moisture between her legs. Before she had a chance to even begin dressing, the revolving door whispered with movement.

Was he really leaving? Already? Not even a tender touch or a parting kiss to say goodbye? Then she remembered the conference going on next door. Perhaps Roger wasn't as turned on by the danger of being overheard as she'd originally thought. Of course, he'd want to leave ahead of her since they couldn't exactly be seen leaving together.

Yes, she'd catch up with him later and tell him just how wonderful he'd made her feel. Perhaps she'd even suggest doing it again someday.

ETHAN SQUASHED THE URGE TO RUN TO THE men's room and wash the scent of woman from his fingers. Though he'd just quite possibly had the most pleasurable sexual encounter of his life, he was terrified by the fact that it had been with Shannon.

Because instead of "getting it over with," he'd just dipped his toe into something he'd only want more of.

Shit.

Regrets. Silence. Bathed in the white light of the men's room, Ethan leaned against the sink with both palms and let the water run while he waited for the inevitable dread to come crashing through. He'd just fucked his sister's best friend, something he said he'd never do. Besides that, Shannon was an enigma, a complication he couldn't afford. So why had he done it?

Because he'd let his anger for Brooke get the best of him. Over a year of abstinence didn't exactly work in his favor either, and there was a cute, curvy blonde in the stairwell, offering herself up at his greatest time of need.

I'm here for you, Ethan, she'd said. *Waiting, wanting, and ready to take it from behind.*

Good God. After the way they'd left things at the bar, Ethan had expected some sort of retaliation, but she'd actually come through for him. She'd actually met him in the darkroom like she said she would.

And the sex...holy shit! She'd all but attacked him straight out of the rolling doorway, her need for him dissolving every ounce of common sense he possessed. In all his thirty-two years, he'd never felt a connection of that magnitude. Not with the groupies, or the short-term relationships, not even with the girlfriend of four years. How could two people—as fucked up as they were—find an impossible rhythm like that?

When Ethan finally faced his reflection in the mirror, his brow relaxed. The regrets he expected to see weren't there, only the less-harried face of a man who'd just ended a long drought. A sense of calm came over him, one that told him to lighten up. So what if he'd enjoyed being with Shannon? When it was all said and done, she was his friend, and he should be grateful she'd been there for him.

He reached for the jacket and tie he'd flung over a stall door and began to put himself back together.

Good mood restored, Ethan walked past the reception area with his hands in his pockets and a whistle on his lips. Letreece gave him an instant smile that said she liked what she saw.

"Why, Mr. Wolf, you look much better than the last time I saw you."

He returned her smile with a wink. "Why, I feel much better, Letreece, thank you." Then he decided to stop and talk for a while, give himself another few minutes to regroup.

While they chatted, Brooke showed up from seemingly nowhere. Ethan—still riding that sexual high—was hunkered over the reception desk, perfectly at ease when their eyes met.

Damn if the woman didn't look different. Her luminescence practically shined brighter than the sign behind the reception desk. If he didn't know the reason for it, he'd swear that it was afterglow.

With emery board in hand, Letreece sat back and gaped. "Why, Miss Monroe, you look much better than…well…ever."

Brooke stopped in her tracks, looked down at her clothing as if she were afraid something was out of place. When she realized Letreece had paid her a genuine compliment, she cleared her throat and smiled back. "Oh, thanks."

What? No gloating over her latest victory? Not even a hint in her tone or in the brief look she bestowed on him in passing? With a furrowed brow, he watched her sachet down the hall toward the administrative department.

"Was her top button undone?" Letreece asked, her eyes following the same woman.

Ethan remembered seeing it open when he'd confronted her in the break room. Despite how angry he'd been, he'd still noticed a hint of creamy cleavage peaking out from underneath. He shifted from hip to hip, uncomfortable all of a sudden. "Yup."

"And I think her hair is a bit messier than usual," Letreece added. "Now why would that be, I wonder?"

Ethan envisioned her jumping for joy in the parking lot. His look turned droll. "Because sticking it to me really agrees with her."

When he pushed off the desk to leave, he caught sight of Letreece's intense gaze boring a hole right through him. She slowly smiled as if she were privy to some kind of secret.

Ethan stopped in his tracks. "What?"

"Nothing." The emery board scratched across the tips of her glossy red talons. "I'm just glad to see you two so...*agreeable*."

Her tone dripped with a suggestive nature that he didn't like. Ethan pointed a finger. "Don't even go there." Because if he was right about Brooke leaking information, it was as good as wiping any attraction he'd ever had for her clean away. "By the way, did you see Shannon come through here yet?"

"A while ago," Letreece answered, her smile fading into a pout. "She was acting weird too, all puffed up and satisfied with herself."

I'll bet she was. The woman had every right to be satisfied with herself. With his optimistic side in check, Ethan gave Letreece a wave of gratitude and left the reception area.

He finally ran into Shannon around two o'clock on his way back from the fax machine. Her office door had been closed for the most part, but when she emerged, it was with an armful of files and a fresh coat of lip gloss. Four feet from his desk, they faced each other for the first time since the darkroom.

Brooke was away from her desk, so they had room for some low-spoken words. "Have a drink with me after work," he murmured. "We should talk about what happened."

As the afternoon sun filtered through her shaggy mane, Shannon's brow went up. "Will I be safe with you, Mr. Wolf?"

Ethan glanced away with a suppressed smile. "That remains to be seen."

"Then I'll have to decline your offer."

When she attempted to pass him, he blocked her path. Damned if he'd let her play hard to get now. "How well do you know me, Shannon?"

She looked down at his hand on the sleeve of her satin crepe blouse. "I used to know you quite well. A lot has changed since then."

Why did he get the feeling she was afraid of him? "Yes, it has," he agreed with a softer tone. "Despite that, we've been friends for a long time. Don't make it awkward now."

When her gaze returned to his, it was still a bit closed off. "Alright. What do you want to talk about?"

This was not how he'd expected things to play out. As he thought this, he noticed Brooke heading back toward her desk with that same afterglow on her cheeks. Damn. If her good mood hadn't been acquired at his expense, he'd be tickled by it.

"Come on," he said, nudging Shannon backward. "In your office."

"But I—"

"You can do that later."

Once behind closed doors, he was finally able to think straight. Shannon backed up against her desk but refused to relinquish her armload of files. "So why do I get the feeling you're avoiding the subject," he said with his hands on his hips.

She shrugged. "If you tell me what the subject is, I'll follow along better."

"Don't play coy with me. What happened in that darkroom deserves a little recognition, don't you think?"

Her laugh came out a bit smokier than usual. "I have no idea what you're talking about."

What the hell? Since he'd known her, Shannon had never been shy about the subject of sex. Something was off. He'd sensed it during his private reverie in the restroom, but figured it was all part of the shock and awe. His look narrowed. "The *darkroom*. You suggested we meet there, remember?"

A gleam of recognition entered her eyes. "Oh…yeah. About that."

Just then her phone rang. In no mood to wait, he dove for it as she moved toward the handset. "Let voicemail get it," he snapped. "Talk to me."

Her slender face masked over with disbelief as she pulled her hand out from beneath his. "Jeez, Ethan, I'm sorry if you're pissed, but a girl has a right to change her mind."

"What do you mean by that?"

Hugging the files closer to her chest, an air of faux innocence surrounded her. "Maybe I decided you were right about us after all. Why should we complicate things with sex when there are plenty of others out there willing to play?"

A sense of dread unfurled within him, swallowing him whole in the time it took to flinch. His gaze moved over her clothing, desperately searching for clues that they'd been shed once already that day. "Tell me this change of heart came *after* the darkroom," he said with deathly calm, "because if you're saying you never showed up, we're dealing with more than just a simple misunderstanding."

But he didn't need her to voice it when the truth was in her eyes. The threat she'd made at the bar siphoned through his brain.

Fuck you, Ethan. Some day you'll come crawling to me and I'll treat you like an asshole. See how you like it!

She'd set him up. For the love of God, how could he have not known whom he was having sex with?

Locked in a trance, Ethan ran a hand through his hair and backed away from her. The need to commit violence was roiling below the flow of memories that plagued him. Whispered moans, warm curves that felt like silk, a hint of lavender as he ran his tongue over those curves, downward, and between parted legs, an insane need to join while voices surrounded them, a torturous mixture of agony and delight when he'd first slipped inside.

"Shannon," he whispered, his eyes glazed over with alarm. "Who the hell was I with?"

When the awkward silence finally registered, he noticed that Shannon was experiencing her own jolt of disbelief. The woman slowly put down the folders, covered her mouth with a slender hand. "No way," she whispered back. "You actually had sex in there, didn't you?"

Ethan noted the genuine dismay in her countenance, but she definitely knew more than he did. After all, what were the odds that another woman would be waiting for him in the darkroom at the same exact time? In measured degrees, his anger boiled to the surface despite the voice in his head that told him to cool down. "Who was she?" he asked through gritted teeth. "Who did you set me up with?"

"I didn't set you up." Her voice wobbled a bit like a child fearful of punishment. "All I did was...." A burst of insane laughter broke from her chest. "I can't believe this. How could you mistake her for me?"

"*Who?*" When his outburst forced her to back away, Ethan relaxed his fists and took a moment. Then another flash of reality hit, burning the truth into the back of his eyes like a hot poker. It was the picture of Brooke emerging from nowhere with messy hair and a suspicious afterglow.

I'm just glad to see you two so...agreeable.

Yes, Letreece definitely believed they'd had sex together. Why wouldn't she? Now that the pieces were fitting into place, Ethan realized Brooke's afterglow wasn't suspicious at all. It mirrored his own, from his improved mood to his flushed face.

"No!" It came out a desperate sort of roar as he mentally made the comparisons between Shannon's slender form and Brooke's. They had a similar-enough shape, especially in the pitch dark. Shannon's breasts were a little bigger. Brooke was a little taller. Their hair was completely different, but it had been tied up, and the room was totally dark. Then he realized that there had been no perfume or lip gloss to distract him from the natural scent and textures of woman.

And Brooke didn't wear any of those things.

"She was there to meet Roger," Shannon offered from a safer place behind her desk. "I heard them making plans and I—I stopped him before he could go. Ethan, I never thought you would—"

"Shut up!" Ethan snarled. He had to think, figure out what to do. He had to get out of there before he killed her. On his way to the door, he turned and pointed. "I advise you to steer very clear of me, Shannon. Do you understand?"

When she didn't answer right away, he sent her a look that forced a reaction. Her eyes welled up and she nodded. "Yes, I understand."

Later, Ethan found it impossible to focus with Brooke's happy humming floating through the air. Knowing just how much he'd contributed to her happiness forced him to relive every moment of that darkroom tryst. *She* was the one he'd screwed. *She* was the one he'd tasted. *She* was the one who'd gasped when he bit her.

And she'd loved every moment of it.

But he was supposed to have been Roger. The whole thing was so fucked up, Ethan couldn't get past it enough to even pick up the phone. How could Brooke have confused him with Roger? They may be similar in height and size, but Ethan was in way better shape. Roger couldn't *find* a muscle beneath that doughboy exterior, let alone flex it.

But as much as he wanted to hate her for it, Ethan knew that Brooke had been just as duped as he'd been. She'd ignored obvious clues, just as he'd done. The only difference between them was that he was painfully aware and she was still living in blissful ignorance.

But what really messed with his head was that he wanted her again. Despite the attitude, despite the lies, despite his suspicions of her...his dick responded with every relived moment they'd spent together.

"Hey, Brooke, you have a moment?"

That was Roger's voice. Just as Ethan registered what could be happening, Bill Knight showed up at his desk with a confrontational look.

"Ethan." Their lead illustrator threw a stiff, puny shadow. "We need to talk."

Ethan strained to hear the conversation next door.

"You can tell your Romcore client to kiss my ass."

"Huh?" he responded with divided interest.

"My time is not a bargaining chip. If Ken expects me to do his cover art for free in order to keep his business, I'll take my talent elsewhere."

It was the same song Ethan had heard before, and Bill's complaints couldn't have come at a worse time. Just as the man dropped his little bomb, Roger left. Frustrated and angry, Ethan shot from his chair, making Bill jump backward. He leaned in with a snarl. "I'll look into it," was all he said before storming toward the break room.

"And don't throw that commission business in my face," Bill yelled after him. "If you can't keep a client, it's hardly my fault!"

Since Bill was salaried, Master Ink owned the work he produced for them, not the other way around; therefore, Ethan couldn't give two shits if Ken decided to give his work away for free. Let Bill quit. There was other secret-weapon-caliber talent out there that would welcome Ken's fat paycheck.

Face to face with the vending machine, Ethan wanted to kick it. The few bits of conversation he'd picked up between Brooke and Roger revealed little, but it was probably better that way. If he could just take back the entire day...forget all about it...maybe he could enjoy a little blissful ignorance too.

An irritating blade of guilt wedged its way into his soul. He fought it back, told himself Brooke didn't need to know. Leave it up to fate. If she was meant to go on thinking she'd just experienced a beautiful thing, then he was perfectly willing to let her. Because if he had his way, she'd never find out it wasn't.

IT DIDN'T TAKE BROOKE LONG TO REALIZE THAT
she actually loved the lingering sensation of a man between her legs.
It was a raw kind of hurt that came after a long dry spell, but it was
sweet enough to nurture the dreamy kind of memories a girl would
want to relive.

Roger. Wow. Since when had he started lifting weights? She'd
definitely expected a softer physique, but not having seen him without
long sleeves, she just assumed he wasn't the type. And the biting! The
feel of his teeth grazing her skin had been incredibly arousing. It
seemed Mr. Kerrigan possessed a dark side that Brooke found mouth-
wateringly sexy.

As she wrapped up her last call for the day and shut down her
computer, she had a thought about the man who sat quietly in the
next cubicle. Ethan had barely uttered a word since their liquor-store
challenge, reinforcing her belief that he was a hopeless sore loser. She
didn't doubt that he would pull no punches next week in order to gain
the lead.

But she was ready.

She grabbed her purse and briefcase and turned off the light. As she passed his desk, she said jovially, "Have a wonderful weekend, Mr. Wolf."

His lack of a response piqued her interest enough to make her backtrack a few steps. Indeed, she found him hunched over his desk, steeped in a cloud of what looked like dejection. It was so unlike him. It was…weird.

But Brooke felt so good, she actually thought of offering a kind word without the attitude this time. She opened her mouth.

"Are you lost, Monroe?" he growled, his back to her.

Ah. There he was: the Ethan she knew and hated. "Not anymore," she answered, and then caught sight of the framed photograph of him, his family, and his racecar…or rather his shattered dream. Knowing something about those, Brooke decided to give the man a little slack, but only because she was in such a good mood. He was still a prick for accusing her of cheating, which had totally ruined any kind thoughts of him she'd developed after her conversation with Harper.

"Look, I know Ken is getting tired of the fighting," she said with a sigh. "Frankly, so am I. If you're willing, I'd like to get through next week without it."

"Better late than never, I guess."

His clipped response told her to go away. Rolling her eyes, she shifted her briefcase from one hand to the other and nudged him in the back. "I mean it, Wolf. Let's just do our thing and then have the decency to congratulate whoever comes out on top."

When he turned around, the burning fire in his eyes took her aback. He was quiet for so long, watching her, it seemed he wouldn't answer. Then he stood up, moved close and propped an arm on the partition beside her. "Tell me something, Brooke."

She blinked back a jolt of surprise. "What?"

"Would you really be able to work under me?"

His close proximity was messing with her concentration. She

swallowed, decided to throw out a compliment and see if it stuck. "If you're as good as everyone says you are, I guess I'd take it one day at a time." Her lashes lifted to find him studying her. A shade of whiskers tinted his lower jaw, giving him a rugged appeal she'd never noticed before. "What about you? Would you be able to work under me?"

Instead of giving her an answer, Ethan looked up and around. After a moment of quiet reflection, his gaze returned, hooded and somewhat cold. "Don't forget to bring a change of clothes on Monday."

Taking that as a no, Brooke backed up a step, her own expression carefully blank. "Thanks for the reminder," she said stiffly. "But when I make a deal, I honor it no matter what."

When she left him there, she sensed him watching her until she was out of sight. Why did she let him unnerve her like that, even when she was in the best of moods? The man was incorrigible, throwing out a reminder of her failures when she'd extended something of an olive branch. That impending car wash had haunted her for days. The humiliation she would endure while he barked orders at her from his lawn chair...how could she endure it?

The elevator doors opened just as a solution presented itself. As she watched a delicious scenario play out in her head, other Friday stragglers who'd collected in the lobby walked around her and got on.

"Going down?"

Her focus returned to find several faces watching her with blatant irritation. "Oh!" she blurted with a nervous laugh. "Yes, sorry."

Monday morning couldn't come soon enough. Though Roger had been adorably humble about their sexual encounter, she was a bit disappointed he hadn't tried to call her over the weekend. Then again, he knew all about her past with Brandon and probably thought he shouldn't push. She'd been notoriously against office hanky-panky despite Brandon's many attempts to get her into the darkroom. But now that she knew how good it could be, she wanted more.

Roger may be taking it slow, but she'd have him again soon, even if it meant adjusting her standards. This new feeling of freedom and empowerment was definitely worth the risk. He actually made her feel sexy, daring, and unafraid to try new things.

Amy had said it was just the orgasm talking. Even if that were true, who cared? Roger was the one who showed her it was possible to have one, and she'd make sure he gave her another—just not at work this time.

The plan was to take advantage of her moment of shame. Make a fine wine out of sour grapes. Monday after work when she was expected to wash Ethan's car before a crowd of spectators, Roger would be among them as her only cheering section. If she had to get wet and dirty, it might as well end up with him hosing her down in her own shower. To accomplish that, Amy and Miranda had taken her shopping for the appropriate "carwash" attire. Nothing too sexy or revealing, just enough to pique Roger's curiosity.

Finally, Brooke no longer cared if the coming workday ended in her favor or Ethan's. It would end with a bang, and one she was bound to feel good about despite Ethan's quest to humiliate her.

When she arrived at work, she left the elevator with her hair down and an unusually bright smile on her face. Letreece sat behind the reception desk checking messages with a yawn. "Good morning," Brooke sing-songed on her way by.

The woman frowned. "Unless you got a Friday in your pocket, I don't see what's so good about it."

Brooke only laughed and waved without breaking her confident stride. Even the sight of Shannon propped on the corner of Ethan's desk failed to stir her animosity, though it appeared she'd walked in on a tumultuous conversation. She put on her sweetest smile. "Trouble in paradise?"

Ethan, wearing a charcoal gray suit and tie that looked fantastically expensive, watched her closely. *Too* closely. Brooke stopped in her tracks. "Let me guess. You dressed for the occasion."

"What occasion?" Shannon asked with her signature phony innocence.

Ethan's gaze never wavered. "I even brought my lawn chair."

He was goading her. Not thirty seconds into their first day of the week, and the jerk was determined to spoil her mood.

Shannon brightened suddenly. "Oh, the carwash." Then she followed Brooke to her desk. "I hope you brought a change of clothes. You wouldn't want to get that outfit dirty."

Brooke looked down at the juniper-green pantsuit Miranda had picked out for her during their shopping spree. It was a form-fitting number that supposedly matched her eyes and complemented the reddish gold of her hair. "This old thing? It's washable."

"If I didn't know better," Shannon said with a tilt of her head, "I'd swear you actually look happy today."

Brooke tossed her hair over a shoulder, opened her briefcase, and took out a small mesh bag. "I had a busy weekend. Probably got some sun on my face."

Shannon sipped her latte as she continued her assessment of Brooke's appearance. "No," she said finally. "That's not it. You look like a woman in love."

The neighboring cubicle exploded with a round of choked coughs. Brooke stood on tiptoes and peered over the partition. "Something go down the wrong pipe?" Ethan nodded, still hacking into his hand. She brushed off his discomfort and tucked her small bag into the bottom drawer of her desk.

"You wore your hair down today," Shannon continued with ruthless determination, "and I believe that black stuff on your lashes is actually mascara."

"So?"

"So, I've never seen you in anything but that boring ponytail. And look at those shoes. Damn, girl, paired with those pants, they make your legs look a mile long."

"Shannon, didn't Ken want to see you first thing this morning?" came Ethan's voice as Brooke sat down and looked at her beige heels with the gem-studded design. They'd been a present from her mother who had always wanted her to dress better. This was the first time she'd actually worn them.

Shannon whirled around, saw Ken entering his office, and jumped. "Oh, right. I'll be right back."

"Don't hurry on my account," Brooke mumbled, turning on her light and computer screen. The woman had obviously been goading her since genuine compliments weren't in her wheelhouse.

Seconds later, Brooke was going through her scheduled meetings for the week when Ethan appeared in her peripheral vision.

"Tell me you at least brought a poncho," he said with wry amusement.

She answered without sparing him a glance. "I don't need one since I don't plan to get that wet."

"You can't spend more than ten seconds outside without getting wet."

She looked up at him with a sweet smile. "Guess it's a good thing I brought a change of clothes."

He put his hands in the air. "Just making sure you hold up your end of the deal."

"Don't worry, Ethan, you'll get your day," she said through her teeth. *And I'll get mine.* The thought of ending it in Roger's arms sent a delicious thrill throughout her body.

When five o'clock rolled around, it came with no small disappointment. Roger had been in training all day and Ethan had inched closer toward a victory since it appeared that he'd win Romcore's business after all. It must have taken quite a bribe to get Bill Knight to agree to the terms, but they were offering free cover art from the diva lead illustrator himself. They'd scheduled a meeting for Wednesday to go over the new proposal with Romcore's president. Until then, Brooke's chance of winning was bleak unless she could score a bigger client than Romcore.

All of that quickly dissipated when Roger finally appeared at her desk and helped her gather her things. "Hi," he said with a warm smile.

Brooke smiled back, removed her glasses with the pretense of cleaning them, and let him take her briefcase. "Busy day?" she asked his blurry form, satisfied knowing that he was scoping out the way her blouse flared open at the top. "I haven't seen you."

He nodded. When she put the glasses back on, it was to see he was, indeed, virtually salivating over her attire. "You look...stunning in that outfit," he said with a gulp.

Seeing the desire in his eyes made her heart trip with joy. It hadn't been her imagination after all, and the shaft of doubt telling her that she'd just been a quick distraction for him completely faded away. "Thank you," she whispered. "Wait 'til you see what I brought for the carwash."

His smile broadened. " I can't wait."

They started walking. Ethan was more reserved than usual when they passed by, especially for a guy who liked to gloat. Had he heard their whispered exchange? She quickly forgot the possibility, thinking that the man wouldn't give a hoot what she and Roger discussed. With purse and mesh bag in hand, she walked with Roger toward the hallway. "So that means you'll be there, right?"

Roger nodded. "I won't let you down, I promise."

When they reached the reception area, she indicated her briefcase. "I'm going to change in the bathroom. I can take that with me."

He jerked his head toward the bank of elevators. "We're parked beside each other. Give me your keys and I'll put it in your car for you, along with your other stuff."

How sweet was that? Brooke gave him a grateful smile as she shrugged out of her form-fitting jacket and handed it to him along with her purse and keys. "Thank you. I'll be down in a few minutes."

He took the whole load and disappeared into the elevator along with a handful of other employees. Letreece whistled behind her desk as she gathered her own things. "It looks like we have ourselves a couple of love birds."

Brooke felt her ears get warm. "We're just friends," she hedged with an artificial smile. "That's all."

"How many men you gonna be *friends* with, darlin'? In my opinion, you should have quit while you were ahead."

Brooke's smile faltered with confusion. "Excuse me?"

"Oh, right." When the woman skirted around her, she gave her a playful bump with her hip. "I'm not supposed to go there. *Sorry.*"

With her bag in hand, Brooke began to rethink things as she headed for the ladies room. Maybe she should tone it down a bit. If Letreece sensed something going on between her and Roger, Ken would too. But what the hell was that comment about being *friends* with other men? It almost sounded like the woman thought she was sleeping around.

Once inside the bathroom, she took out the pink halter top she'd purchased at Nordstrom and held it up against her shoulders. After a turn or two in the mirror, a wicked grin lit up her face.

Tomorrow. Starting tomorrow, she'd tone it down.

Moments later, Brooke breezed through the parking lot with her business suit thrown over a shoulder, high heels dangling at her hips, and a smile on her face. It was damned hot, the sun burning brightly from its 5:30 position in the sky. With the humidity, her skin instantly started to sweat, but she was dressed for it in her halter top and denim Capri pants.

As soon as she unloaded the rest of her stuff into the backseat of her car, and since Roger was nowhere around, Brooke made one last discreet inspection of her cleavage, fluffed her hair, and checked the status of her lip gloss in the rearview mirror. Satisfied with her appearance, she found her prescription shades and an elastic hair band and tucked both items into her pockets. Then she reached for the two extra sponges she'd brought because Ethan would probably only provide one.

And one simply wouldn't be enough.

When she finally made her way to the front parking lot, it was to find Ethan's car parked beside a yellow bucket. The Mazda's sleek paint was covered in grime with a thick layer of bug guts coating the grill and windshield. A garden hose was stretched across the lawn from behind a row of manicured bushes.

Not one, but *several* lawn chairs had been placed on the front walk.

She found out whom they belonged to when a group of men from the creative department appeared lugging a cooler between them.

So, Ethan had put a lot of effort into making her a source of entertainment, which was okay by her. She checked the time on her phone. Backup should arrive any minute now....

The sloshing of ice stopped. The cooler thumped to the ground.

"Holy shit!"

Brooke looked up to find the men staring open-mouthed in her direction. So unused to the attention, she glanced behind her first before realizing they were staring at her.

Just as Roger appeared from the building's double doors, a red Mustang pulled into the lot and parked nearby. While Amy and Miranda stepped out of it, Roger approached her with a look of approval. "Nice," he crooned. "You brought reinforcements." Then his eyes scanned her appearance once again, blatantly showing his appreciation for her choice of apparel.

Brooke extended her glasses in his direction. "Hold them for me?"

Since he was too caught up in her cleavage, she shoved her glasses inside his breast pocket. When she gave it a pat, it was with the hope of feeling that hard muscle she'd discovered in the darkroom. But he must have been wearing an undershirt or something because there was a lot more "padding" this time.

Roger backed away from her touch with an embarrassed nod. "Sure, uh...don't worry, I'll take good care of them."

Of course, she shouldn't be touching him like that in front of everyone, even though Ken Stevens had already gone home for the day. She donned her shades and looked through the crowd for anyone who might have noticed.

Ethan rounded the building with his lawn chair in one hand and his jacket draped neatly over an arm, though he still wore slacks and a dress shirt. He must have forgotten a change of clothing—or rather forgotten how hot it got in southern Florida, because his shirt was already mottled with sweat.

"God, he's such a tourist," Brooke muttered under her breath while

Roger greeted Amy and Miranda behind her. "I mean, look at him."

"Oh, I'm looking, alright," Amy said, wrapping an arm around Brooke's shoulders. Her platinum chin-length hair was pulled back by a pair of retro square sunglasses. "And I still say he's quite delicious."

When Ethan hooked his jacket over the back of the chair and finally sat down, he noticed them staring. Brooke knew then that he had figured out her plan because his brows lowered. "Hey," he barked. "No one said you could have help."

She smiled. "No one said I couldn't."

Roger headed toward the grass and Miranda joined them, her purple bikini top and cutoffs bursting with her curves. "Why, I do believe your tourist is the only one not happy to see us."

"Don't take it personally," Brooke replied with a barely contained smile. "His focus will shift soon enough. Speaking of which, how can I ever repay you guys?"

Amy made a dismissive "tssk" and ran a hand over her hair. "Are you kidding me? We look like Charlie's fucking angels. How could we say no?"

Even though Brooke thought of herself as the less attractive angel, she felt like a million bucks. If not for them, she'd have been seen as a complete laughingstock over this whole car-washing bet.

"I still can't get over it," Miranda murmured low, watching as Roger folded his arms and leaned against the brick wall. "Roger Kerrigan, an amazing lover. Who knew?"

Brooke, remembering the feel of him against her bare skin, freely stared at him through the dark lenses of her sunglasses. "I didn't know the darkroom had that kind of power. To make people completely let go like that...."

"Oh, it wasn't the darkroom," Amy said through a grin. "I happen to know he got quite familiar with Cheryl Smarker in there, but I never heard any compliments from her—ow!"

After the jab that finally shut Amy up, Miranda took a breath and sent Brooke a look of apology. "What she's trying to say is that it must have been you who released the beast in him. It's a compliment."

"Hey," Ethan yelled from his lawn chair. "This isn't the library, ladies. Let's have less whispering and more washing. It's hot out here."

"So says the cocky turd in the suit," Brooke shot back. "With all that harping about a change of clothes, one would think you'd have come prepared."

A wave of "oohs" came from the crowd on the grass. "I didn't expect a big production," he volleyed back, clearly more amused with their verbal sparring than she was. "Perhaps I should have brought popcorn too?"

"I vote you lose the suit and join us," Amy added with a wink. "I'll show you just how warm it can get in these parts."

Now it was Brooke's turn to shut Amy up. She pulled her away from the front lines and murmured, "Aren't you laying it on a little thick?"

Amy shrugged. "What do you care? You got yours last Friday, it's my turn."

With *Ethan?* Just whose side was Amy on anyway?

The sun was beating down on the parking lot with brutal intensity. The spectators lounged in the shade, passing cold sodas that Brooke suspected were actually beers in disguise.

Tossing her hair upside down, she yanked the hair band from her wrist and wrapped it several times around her locks to form a loose knot. Then she handed a tube of sunscreen to Miranda. "Shoulders please."

Miranda squirted a healthy dose into her palm. "I thought this was going to be Roger's job."

Brooke sighed, dabbing a little on her nose and cheeks. "Too risky, Mr. Stevens has a strict rule against office romances."

"So did your father," Miranda murmured as she rubbed her hands together and applied the lotion to Brooke's sun-sensitive skin. "But that didn't stop us from riding the flagpole on occasion."

"Only because we had the resources to do it," Amy threw in. "I'm going to miss that darkroom."

Brooke stifled a laugh that quickly dissipated when she noticed all the men staring at them with lecherous grins. When she realized why, she shot out from beneath Miranda's hands.

The woman chuckled and wiped the remaining lotion on her shorts. "I thought the point of us being here *was* to cause a distraction." "Yes, to distract them from *me*." Everyone except Roger, of course, not that Brooke needed to worry. Every time she looked in his direction, she found him scoping her out.

Amy was busy scoping out Ethan's car. "God, what a sexy little beast," she purred, running her hand across the trunk as she sashayed around it.

Brooke barely gave it a glance, refusing to be impressed. "Hate the color."

"*Love* the color."

"It looks like a baby school bus."

"With a matching roll bar even," Amy said as she peered through the windows. "I bet she goes fast."

"Yes, I'm sure Ethan likes his cars as fast as his women."

Amy followed that comment with a droll look and picked up a wet sponge. "This is why you drive a boring sedan. No sense of adventure."

As they washed, conversed, laughed, and had fun, Brooke noticed she wasn't the only one with a man in her sights. Amy proved quite efficient at multitasking, which involved a lot of bending over the hood and making eyes at Ethan. The fact that he enjoyed every moment of it made Brooke want to throw up.

He jerked his chin in the blonde's direction. "You two always do her dirty work for her?"

Amy stopped scrubbing and lowered her lashes. "Oh, we volunteered for this one, sweetie."

"In that case, can I request a wax and a buff?"

As more laughter trickled through the audience, Brooke's scowl deepened. Why did Amy's wanton behavior piss her off so much? Why should she care that her friend was willing to sleep with the enemy?

While scrubbing the headlights, Miranda lowered her sunglasses. "Hey, is that Shannon?"

Following her gaze, Brooke spotted Shannon Webber—still in her work clothes—standing by Roger. Despite the fact that she sported a pair of armpit stains, the woman watched with a wicked smile and raised her cell phone.

Amy straightened. "That Elizabeth Shue wannabe just took our picture."

But Roger was watching Brooke, and that was all that mattered. "Ignore her," she said. "Lord knows I've been trying to."

"Wait a minute...," Miranda's efforts slowed as she perused the scene. "Something's up."

"What do you—?"

Before Brooke could get the words out, her entire backside was doused with luke-warm, dirty water. She sputtered in shock as some dude from accounting backed away with an empty bucket.

Her assailant put his hands in the air and laughed. "Hey, don't shoot the messenger. This was a paying gig."

Brooke looked down at her new clothes. They were filthy and wet, her hair sticking to her face in gross hanks. Shannon fell into a fit of laughter, as did most of the folks on the grass. "Even on a clear day, you manage to end up soaking wet," the woman yelled.

The only person not laughing was Roger, who suddenly appeared to be battling a case of indigestion. Ethan also managed to keep a straight face, even though he was the one who probably orchestrated her dousing. He'd seen her wet more than once and had always mocked her with an annoying smirk. He'd done it with a salute. And now he'd done it with a bunch of witnesses.

Amy came up and whispered, "Screw them, Brooke. You don't need this shit."

Her friend was right. With a clenched jaw, Brooke picked up the hose and threatened Ethan with it. If he was worried, he hid it well.

"Amnesty row, remember?" he reminded her with a dare in his eyes. "You agreed not to get anyone wet or you owe me another wash."

Brooke lowered the hose as she weighed her pros and cons. Making a decision, she handed the hose to Miranda. "Make it hurt."

Ethan jumped in his seat. "Don't even think about it!"

Miranda grinned like an armed gangster ready for bloodshed. With a loud whoop, she squeezed the trigger and opened up on the crowd. Men scattered. Ethan fell backward in his haste to escape the spray.

Brooke casually pointed. "Don't forget the Elizabeth Shue wannabe."

Miranda adjusted her aim. Shannon screamed as water hit her back, soaking her before she was able to outrun it.

"It's about time you had a bath!" Brooke shouted, unable to contain her glee. "Oh, go ahead and get Roger too. Maybe we'll get a glimpse of his hot body."

"Ooh, I love a man in a wet shirt." While Miranda chased Roger around with the high-pressure stream, Ethan and a handful of others recovered enough to start charging. The girls panicked and took cover behind the sports car with the hose at the ready, but the doused men were beyond caring at that point.

Screams and shouts ensued as an all-out water brawl commenced in the parking lot. Sponges flew, women squealed, and everyone was laughing, but it was no longer at Brooke's expense. Shannon had retreated into the building. Roger was nowhere to be found. She spotted what's-his-name from accounting and let her thirst for revenge lead the way. When he got a face full of wet sponge, he let out a dramatic battle cry and took chase. Brooke, who was nearly crippled with laughter at that point, couldn't run to save her life. He caught her, twirled her around while shouting quotes from World of Warcraft, and then put her back down to move on to the next queen of the forsaken.

Before she could fully recover, she spotted Ethan amid the chaos. His hair was slicked back and his light blue shirt was now dark and clinging to every hard muscle of his body.

And he was coming for her.

Brooke's throat suddenly went dry. If Letreece could see him now, her ovaries would explode. Ignoring the butterflies in her stomach, Brooke pointed and backed away. "My finger wasn't on the trigger."

The man was clearly pissed, but he was also something else...something hot and confusing. As he closed the distance between them, it was with a lethal grace that told her to drop the sponge and run for the hills.

When she tried it, he caught her arm, whirled her around, and pulled her hard against him. "Just like I thought," he growled. "When shit gets real, you cut and run."

Stunned by the close proximity, she flattened her hands against his chest. There was no mistaking the sinewy muscle beneath them. "You don't scare me," she answered, struggling to keep her voice steady. "You're all wet and I couldn't be happier."

Chaos continued around them, but for some reason, it faded as time seemed to stand still. In his arms, her chest constricted with a strange feeling of familiarity. Her pulse quickened. His jaw tensed. Then his grip tightened around her arms before he shoved her away.

Suddenly, the shouts returned, and Brooke was left in the middle of all the chaos, watching his hasty retreat with a sick feeling in her stomach.

AS ETHAN STORMED THROUGH THE BUILDING'S
front entrance, Roger's voice reached him from the lobby. "Man, you
just went from turd to chump the moment you put out that hit on her."

Shit. Kerrigan was the last person he wanted to run into, but the
man followed him down the hallway.

"How much was that suit, anyway?" Roger persisted. "Two
hundred, three hundred bucks?"

"Try nine hundred and fifty," Ethan snarled. "And I didn't put out
that hit."

"Then who did?"

His bet was on Shannon, but all he said was "Ask the hit man."

Roger walked away and Ethan was able to brood in private. He
had to get to a bathroom before anyone else noticed the erection he'd
been fighting since first spotting Brooke in that halter top. Despite his
efforts, he hadn't been able to take his eyes off her. She was wet, sexy
as hell, and laughing with her friends. He'd never seen her so carefree before, and he was suddenly fighting back the memories of her

bare curves beneath his hands. In the darkroom, he hadn't known the woman he'd fucked was Brooke.

But he knew now.

Was he disgusted or annoyed by her open fascination with Roger? Those goddamned Capri pants were obviously worn for that man's benefit, no doubt so that he'd take one look at her pert little ass and turn into a lovesick fool.

Now in the safety of the men's room, Ethan gave his face a good splash of cold water. When he stared at his reflection in the mirror he saw a man tortured by the truth. *He'd* been the one to bring that little witch out of her shell. *He'd* been the one to put that blush on her cheeks, the light in her eyes, the glow of happiness on her face.

And here he was, miserable and angry, lusting after a woman he didn't trust...and completely out of his element.

WHEN BROOKE RETURNED FROM LUNCH THE next day, a small vase of roses was at her desk. The card read: *12:45— From you know who.*

She bit her lip and looked around. Her schedule was full that afternoon, starting with a one o'clock meeting. Could she possibly meet Roger, freshen up, and still make her meeting on time? Did she want to turn him down when he only seemed interested in playing at work? She had to admit, she'd been more than disappointed when he'd bowed out of going home with her the night before. She'd known him long enough to see that the sadness in his eyes was genuine...that he really wanted to, but couldn't for some reason.

Over a lonely dinner of microwave pizza, she'd wondered why. Was he afraid that he'd find her lacking when the lights were on? Or that *she'd* find *him* lacking? Brooke knew that he hid a lot of sex appeal beneath the dress shirt and tie, and he made love with enough confidence for the both of them. So that couldn't be it.

Stumped, she'd gone to bed with a familiar worry from her past with Brandon—that she just wasn't good enough to satisfy him. The roses, however, seemed to prove that theory wrong. He must have thought about her earlier proposal and decided to make up for turning her down.

After a quick peek over the partition confirmed that Ethan was nowhere in sight, Brooke picked up the phone and dialed Roger's extension. When he answered she cupped her hand over the mouthpiece. "Can we make it 12:30?"

There was a short pause. "Uh…can we make *what* 12:30?"

"The appointment we had at 12:45," she said with a shake of her head. He was adorable. "I have clients at one o'clock."

"Ooooookay, I'll try?"

She hung up and smelled her roses again. Whether he could make it earlier or not, she'd be there at 12:30 waiting.

Finally! Over the last four days, her sexual frustration had built into an insatiable desire. Now that she knew how good it could be, her body yearned to be touched again, but only by the one man who'd made it sing before.

ETHAN RETURNED FROM LUNCH TO BE INSTANTLY waylaid by Letreece.

"Have you seen Brooke?"

He glanced behind him at the couple occupying the cushioned chairs by the windows. "No, is she late for a meeting?"

Letreece, chewed her lip, phone in hand. "Not really, her clients came early. I know that she's back from lunch."

"Maybe she's in the creative department," he suggested.

As she entered another extension, he stayed nearby for a verdict before moving on to his desk. It would be easy to relocate the clients to the conference room and let them wait there.

"No one has seen her." Letreece hung up and lifted her sultry gaze.

Ethan chuckled, accurately reading her silent request. "I'll handle it."

"Thank you!" she whispered.

As he led Brooke's clients to the conference room, he treated them as though they were his own: turned on the charm, offered some refreshments. He assured them that Brooke and the graphic artist in charge of their project would be there shortly. If not, he would be happy to help them in any way he could. The man seemed impressed but the woman seemed way too focused on Ethan's crotch, despite the fact that they wore matching wedding bands.

As soon as the conference room door clicked shut, a splash of color caught his eye. After a closer look he realized it was a small vase of roses. They were tucked deep in the corner of Brooke's desk as if she'd wanted them out of sight.

Mixed emotions swarmed through him as he approached her private domain. Who the hell sent her red roses? He searched for a card, but found none. There was no sign of it on the desk, so he opened a drawer.

Bingo.

Ethan tilted his head to get a better angle without having to fish the card out.

12:45—From you know who.

The message hinted at a private meeting that might explain her absence. The cryptic nature of it suggested secrecy. Having spent the last four days fighting demons he couldn't control, Ethan drew an instant conclusion that tightened his gut.

She's in the darkroom.

A bunch of scenarios jumped through his brain at once. The flowers had to be from Roger. If those two hooked up, the truth would be out before he could own it.

Was he ready to own it?

Hell no. Shit! Yes, he had to. He should have known better than to hope that the entire thing would just die down. And if Ethan was about to be busted, why the fuck shouldn't he just go get her? Drag her out of that room half-dressed and blast her for the goddamned fool she was? Then he'd shove her into Shannon's office, tell her the truth, and leave them alone to have it out.

The thought of doing just that fed an old mean streak he'd strived to get rid of. Yes, it was about time that Brooke Monroe shared in his secret hell. Let her feel the betrayal and humiliation of being duped, the torture of knowing that her body yearned for a man she hated more than anyone.

The set of keys he was still holding began to dig into his palm. Ethan threw them on his desk in passing, determined to see this whole thing end now.

But what if he was wrong? If he stormed into the darkroom to find it empty, would he be so gung-ho to tell the truth? Fuck yeah, the thought of delaying the inevitable didn't sit well anymore. This needed to happen, especially before she made a huge mistake with Roger. That doughboy wasn't right for her, and the only reason she wanted him was because she thought he was someone else.

Before he made it to the hallway, a flustered Brooke burst onto the scene. "Don't even think of trying to steal my clients," she snarled in passing.

Ethan stopped in his tracks and watched her storm toward her desk. The impact of seeing her and what she'd said to him left him floundering in a fog for a moment.

Oh, she'd been in the darkroom alright. She'd *heard* him with her clients through the paper-thin wall. The question, though, was what exactly had pissed her off? Was it the thought of him horning in on her territory, or was it because she'd just found out her "lover" wasn't whom she thought?

When Brooke made it to her desk, Ethan studied her carefully. Her face was flushed, and her brows were creased in angst. She disappeared behind the partition for a moment. There was a suspicious "thunk" before she reappeared with her portfolio tucked under her arm, and then she headed to the conference room. As soon as the door opened, her somber expression morphed into a dazzling, professional smile.

Since she would be busy for a while, Ethan decided it was a good time to get some answers. First, he needed to know what exactly had made that "thunk." He took a look at her desk and found that the flowers were gone. He moved her chair, pulled out the wastebasket... and there they were.

Yes, she was definitely pissed. Ethan decided it was time for a one-on-one with Roger to find out just how involved he'd become in the growing monster Shannon had created. When she'd approached him Monday morning in hopes of a little forgiveness, he wasn't exactly in the mood to oblige. He knew now it was because he was coiled up inside, waiting for the bigger shoe to drop, and that her only shot at forgiveness would be in how well she fixed her mistake.

His mistake. Hell, even Brooke's mistake. After all, the woman did choose to have sex in the workplace.

As Ethan pushed Brooke's chair back into place, he caught sight of Roger entering the administrative department. The man was on a mission, headed straight for him.

Ethan met him halfway and backed him up a few steps toward the break room.

"Get the hell off me, Wolf," Roger grumbled as he tripped backward through the swinging door.

"You wouldn't happen to be looking for Brooke, would you?" Ethan asked, blocking the only escape route.

Roger heaved a few breaths, clearly in a state of distress. "Yeah, so what?"

"She's with clients. Is there something I can help you with?"

"It's none of your goddamned business."

"Maybe, maybe not." Ethan stepped closer and saw the worry in the other man's eyes. "Were you in the darkroom with her just now?"

Roger squinted. "What? No."

"Are you sure about that?"

"Yes, I'm sure!" he snapped. "I tried finding her for some appointment we were supposed to have and I couldn't. I finally gave up looking, and the next thing I know she storms into the server room and tells me to go to hell."

Despite how good that made him feel, Ethan's suspicions only grew. "So you *didn't* send her the roses?"

"What roses?"

It was starting to smell like a setup. Ethan ran a hand over his mouth and began to pace. "Shit."

Shannon walked in with a handful of quarters. As soon as she processed the scene, she attempted to back out without a word.

"Hold up," Ethan growled, halting her retreat. "Why don't you fill in some blanks for our friend here before things get worse."

Shannon glanced at Roger. Roger glanced at Shannon. The signals were flying wildly enough for Ethan to get a clue. A disgusted laugh broke from his mouth. "He already knows, doesn't he?"

She moved a shoulder. "I filled him in last Friday after work."

Ethan whirled around and fixed Roger with an incredulous stare. The man glared back. "Don't judge me, Wolf. I didn't see you rushing to tell Brooke the truth."

"I was still reeling from the blow!" Ethan shot back. "You're her friend, what the fuck are you doing conspiring with Shannon?"

"I'm not conspiring. Shannon just wanted me to be informed so that I'd know how to deal with Brooke."

Quarters dropped through the coin slot. "It was the best way to fix the problem, Ethan," Shannon said from the vending machine. "That's what you wanted, right?"

The only problem was that Shannon's plan kept her from facing the consequences of her actions. "If you were so intent on fixing the problem, why did you send Brooke flowers that were supposedly from Roger?"

Roger turned to Shannon with his mouth agape. The woman fished her soda out of the machine and straightened up. "Look at it this way. She won't be after Roger anymore, will she?" The can opened with a wet smack.

Roger sucked in a breath as the pieces fell into place. "Only because she thinks I stood her up," he said loudly. "She hates me now! Why would you do that?"

"Because you've done nothing but fret about the whole thing since I told you," Shannon explained. "You obviously don't know how to deal with pressure, Roger. This way is better. Eventually, she'll forgive you and you can be friends again."

"That's bullshit," Ethan snapped. "You did it to get her back for yesterday." Shannon waved away the notion, which Ethan took as more of an admission. "Did you think she had no right to retaliate for that bucket of water you paid what's-his-name to throw on her?"

"What makes you think it was me?" she asked and took another sip from the soda can.

Ethan rolled his eyes. "Come on, you've been fueling this war between me and her from the start."

"Because I know what she's up to!" Shannon shot back in a sudden burst of indignation. "Even you know it, but somehow her crimes are less offensive than mine!"

"What the hell are you talking about?" Roger asked.

"She's cheating, Roger. She's sabotaging Ethan's high-end bids so that she can win VP."

Roger's face puckered in disbelief. "Brooke wouldn't do that."

"My God." Seething with attitude, Shannon headed for the door. "Whatever. Go ahead and be mad at me, but I refuse to feel bad for a few stupid pranks when she's *breaking the law.*" She turned to Ethan. "And if that cheating bitch is the reason you end up back in South Dakota, I hope Jackie Jackhammer makes your life a living hell."

In the wake of her exit, the room grew painfully quiet aside from the hum of the soda machine. Both men stood there, absorbing the impact of her words. "She's crazy," Roger mumbled in a daze.

Was she? At that point, Ethan didn't know what to believe. "She's just mad at me. I haven't exactly been myself lately. Well…for a while."

"Then you need to get her off Brooke's case. You've done enough damage having sex with her in the first place."

Ethan noted the lack of resentment behind Roger's words. "You don't sound pissed enough for a guy who wants her for himself."

"Are you fucking kidding me?" Now the bitterness emanated from Roger in acrid waves. "Any chance I had was blown to shit when you moved in and performed like some god in the sack. I'm not about to try and follow that. And don't get all cocky about it because she hates you, remember?"

Ethan wiped all expression off his face. "I wasn't getting cocky."

"Bullshit. I can almost see the testosterone oozing from your pores."

"I don't take joy in the fact that I had sex with Brooke," Ethan explained, his patience wearing thin. "Shannon duped *me* too."

Roger snorted. "Yeah, I'm sure you hated every minute of it."

"Fuck you, Kerrigan. I thought she was someone else; it's not the same."

Roger jammed his fists into his pockets. "You know what I think?"

"I don't really care—"

"I think you'd do it again in a heartbeat."

"What?" How many times had he denied that very thing over the last four days?

"I'm not blind, man," Roger continued ruthlessly. "You were ready to chew glass when she was making eyes at me yesterday."

It almost sounded as if the asshole was accusing him of being jealous. "Did you think that could just be good old-fashioned rivalry?" Ethan said with sarcastic flare.

"Do you always get a boner from good old-fashioned rivalry?"

He swore under his breath. "Every guy with a pulse had a boner, Roger. There were *three* women draped over my car."

"But only *one* you'd been intimate with."

"Lay off!" His itch to throw a punch must have shown because Roger backed up with his hands raised. Ethan took a few breaths and calmed down a bit. "When I tell her the truth, she'll be disgusted enough with the both of us, and then I'll be lucky to leave with any junk to spare."

Roger's look turned sour. "You're seriously going to tell her the truth?"

"I have to."

"No you don't. It's been fixed, remember?"

The man was unbelievable. To think that Shannon wouldn't keep milking the situation just proved how incredibly clueless Roger was.

"Wow," Ethan said. "With friends like you, who needs enemies?"

"She'll hate me for keeping quiet," Roger groaned.

"She already does hate you, remember?"

The slump of his shoulders indicated defeat. "Then let me do it."

Really? And make it look like he had no balls whatsoever? "This is more between me and her, don't you think?"

"Yeah, but she'll believe me over you."

"Why *wouldn't* she believe me?"

Roger's face went deadpan. "What are you going to say? 'By the way, I'm the one who rocked your world in the darkroom last Friday.' She'll laugh in your face!"

As much as Ethan didn't want to admit it, Roger was right. Brooke, as stubborn as she was, would never believe or own the fact that she'd responded to him the way she had.

But there was one surefire way to prove it. "When I'm done explaining," he growled, "she won't be laughing."

PITCH BLACK SURROUNDED HIM ONCE AGAIN.
Ethan waited for Brooke by the revolving door with the intention of
leaving if she was even two minutes late. It was hard enough getting
her to agree to meet "Roger" in the darkroom with the string of texts
he'd sent her from the man's phone.

Roger: *Meet me in the DR in ten minutes.*

Brooke: *Drop dead.*

Roger: *I'll be there this time, I swear.*

Moody little shit: *Enjoy the crickets.*

Roger: *Just one more chance. I need to explain.*

Enough time passed to leave him steeped in doubt. Then finally:
Last chance.

Ethan was ready to get this over with. Let the competition between
them continue without any more drama. The thought that this was
the wrong way to go about it entered his mind more than once, but it
was the quickest way. Once she could no longer deny the truth, he'd
reveal it in a very calm, rational manner.

Bullshit. You just want to prove that she has no effect on you.

Yes, that too. He'd been just as wronged as Brooke, so why shouldn't he get some closure?

The conference room was empty this time, which meant that they could whisper without drawing attention; however, raised voices and screaming were out of the question, so they would be forced to handle things with some measure of civility.

When he heard a noise beyond the darkroom, he briefly considered that it might not be Brooke. Then the revolving door began to spin. He braced himself as he waited for the opening to come around. When it did, he searched her out, pulled her into the darkroom and into his arms. The silky mass of hair in his hand confirmed that it was indeed Brooke, so he pulled her head back and kissed her.

As soon as their lips met, she pushed him away and whispered, "I don't want this anymore, Roger. You said you'd explain."

Frustration shot straight into his groin. "So, let me," he whispered hoarsely. Before she could argue, he crushed his mouth to hers and kissed her with desire and demand. Within moments, she let him in and he tasted the sweet flavor of her mouth.

Not sweet, he reminded himself. *Venomous, that's what she is, full of venom.*

But then she moaned and softened in his arms, erasing all bad thoughts from his mind. When she brought her hands up to his chest, his body instantly rose to the occasion, filling him with a kind of alarm that was completely and utterly foreign to him.

Come on, you have more control than that.

It must be the heightened emotions. Yes, that was it. Their natural propensity to tear into each other was a turn-on and the reason his dick was so hard right now. It wasn't the way her body molded against his in a perfect fit. It wasn't the soft sounds that came from deep within her throat. It wasn't the feel of her inner thigh touching his own.

He squelched the urge to reach down and explore that bare inner thigh with his hands. Her skirt was short and would have been easy to reach under, but that wasn't what he'd asked her here for.

Suddenly in a desperate hurry to confess, Ethan broke their heated kiss. "There's something you should know," he whispered.

"I don't care, just keep going," she whispered back.

It wasn't until he felt the cool air on his chest that Ethan realized she'd unbuttoned his shirt. What the hell, a few more kisses would only strengthen his case. He dove into her mouth one more time, claiming her with a breathless kind of urgency. Somehow, his tie came off. Then his shirt was peeled down his arms. Her soft hands roamed his naked skin, sending goose bumps all over his body.

Fuck! Why the fuck did she feel so good? This needed to stop before—

Ethan ripped his mouth away from hers, regaining enough sense to see that he'd already undone the first three buttons of her blouse. The urgent need to feel the weight of her bare breasts in his hands had put him on autopilot, which would only end up with her bent over that chair again.

"Brooke," he rasped in desperation, "you don't want this."

"If you stop now, I'll implode," she whispered back. Her soft palm skimmed across his belly and then moved downward to cup his aching erection in a firm hold.

Well, he couldn't let her *implode*. That would be…ungentlemanly. His zipper went down.

No!

He grabbed her wrist, backing away with a groan. "I'm not who you think I am."

"I know you aren't Roger." Her fierce admission stunned him for a moment, long enough for her to move in again. "But we've done this before, right?"

"Yes," he hissed, arching back when her teeth clamped onto his nipple.

"Then you're who I want you to be." She whorled her tongue around the sensitive spot, sending him deeper into that sea of pleasure. Her words were like a drug. They meant she wanted him. She didn't want Roger; she wanted what only he could do for her.

And he wanted her more than anything, which was why he pushed her away in a desperate bid for clarity. He found the light switch and flipped it on.

"I'm the last person you want me to be," he panted, hating himself for depriving them of the opportunity they both craved. But he had a feeling, despite her words, that he'd be branded the villain if he didn't.

When he opened his eyes, it was in time to catch her look of horror. "I don't believe this!" she whispered, buttoning her blouse with trembling hands.

Ethan yanked his shirt up over his shoulders, fumbled with his own buttons. "I tried to tell you—"

"Well, you should have tried harder," she hissed.

"I couldn't get a word out with your tongue down my throat," he argued.

"You hate me as much as I hate you! How could you let it go that far?"

Ethan's anger rose at the implication that he was the only one at fault. "A man has no sexual integrity when a woman has her hand on his dick. As an adult, you should know that by now."

"You have no integrity of any kind, do you, Ethan?" She jabbed the bottom of her shirt into the waistband of her skirt. "You tricked me into thinking you were Roger, you piece of shit."

"Yeah, well, I didn't expect you to get so violently aroused."

"Oh, please, you attacked me as soon as I walked through the door."

He grabbed his tie off the floor. "I was trying to tell you the truth."

"An email would have sufficed!"

His fly went up. "You would have never believed me and you know it!"

"You could have tried me! It would have been better than..." she gestured toward his crotch, "*that!*"

"From what I hear, you've been dreaming about," he gestured toward his crotch, "*this* since we did it the first time!"

A vivid color of mortification stained her cheeks. Brooke walked up to him and punched him in the gut. As he doubled over, she stormed over to the rotating door, stepped through it, and spun it closed.

So much for civility.

Ethan took a deep breath, straightened his hastily donned tie, and followed her.

AFTER STORMING INTO THE CREATIVE DEPARTMENT, Brooke heard the storage room door open and close behind her. Ethan was hot on her heels, but the last thing she wanted was to give him an opportunity to defend himself. All she wanted to do was march right into Ken's office and scream sexual harassment so loud that all eight floors would hear it.

Whispers followed her into the hallway along with the sounds of hurried footsteps. "Brooke!" Ethan hissed behind her.

He was too close, so she made a quick detour into the ladies room. Three women chitchatted at the sinks and she pushed through them in a sudden, desperate need to wash her hands. The door flew open behind her. The women gasped. Brooke spun around, scattering water and soap as her eyes widened in shock. Ethan loomed in the doorway, an imposing figure of stormy rage.

The women gawked and watched in fascinated silence until Ethan finally ordered them to get out. Without question, they filed past him and into the hallway.

As the bathroom door slowly closed, Brooke yanked out paper towels, her chest heaving with fury. "Of all the vile...low...*awful* things to do to a person."

Now that they were alone again, he turned the lock and faced her in a clear effort to pull it together. "I didn't *plan* for things to go that far," he murmured as he approached her. "And that first time, I thought I was with Shannon. I didn't know it was you until later."

"*Shannon?*" She tossed the paper towels in the trash and grabbed her breasts. "You confused *these* with Shannon's?"

He closed his eyes and swore. "It was dark enough for you to confuse me with Roger, so let's not go there."

God, he was right. Still..., "You and Roger aren't that different. Shannon and I are *nothing* alike."

"Well, it's quite clear you haven't been feeling Roger up lately, so I'll let that pass."

"You expect me to believe you've never felt Shannon up before?" she scoffed.

Ethan straightened up at the implication. "For your information, I haven't. All I know is what I see outside the clothes." His eyes moved downward and locked right onto her chest. "Except for you of course."

As if on cue, her nipples hardened, remembering the pull of his mouth on them four days ago. She groaned, turned around, and headed for a stall. He grabbed her arm and pulled her back. "No, we're going to talk this out, something I should have done last Friday."

Friday? He'd known since Friday? "But you didn't," she reminded him, yanking herself out of his hold. "Instead you let me believe...." All of the dots began to connect until she put her face in her hands. "Roger knows about this, doesn't he?"

Ethan inhaled deeply and moved toward a sink. The water came on. When Brooke peeked between her fingers, she saw him staring at his reflection while he washed his hands. It was clear then that he was suffering as much as she was. "Roger was told not to say anything."

"Why?" she sneered at his back. "So you could mess with me? Set me up and humiliate me like you did with those flowers?"

He turned the water off and looked for a paper towel. "That wasn't me."

"Oh really? And I suppose the texts weren't from you either?"

"The flowers were from Shannon. The texts were from me."

Even worse! "You two are in on this together," she concluded with a short laugh.

"No!" Ethan tossed the paper towel and ground his palms into his eyes. "Let me start from the beginning." He took a deep breath. "Last Friday I was in pretty bad shape. Shannon was mad at me for something I did to her before, and she used the opportunity to get even. She set us both up in the darkroom, letting us think we were with other people. When I found out, I was every bit as mad as you are right now."

More dots fell into place. Brooke crossed her arms, remembering a certain conversation that had left her in a resentful mood. "Is that why you were such an ass when I tried to extend that olive branch?"

"Pretty much. At that point, I was determined to keep the truth to myself, which I admit was wrong. Then I found out that Shannon sent you those roses and I realized she wouldn't stop harassing you unless I did something about it. The darkroom, the bucket of water, Roger keeping quiet...that was all her."

The humiliation of being played so easily by that pretentious bitch was almost worse than being the only one in the dark for so long. "So, Roger just *agreed* to play along?" she asked with narrowed eyes. "You expect me to believe that?"

Ethan produced a sound of disdain. "Oh, come on. The wimp wouldn't know what to do with a hooker, let alone a willing woman. There you were all lovesick and clingy—"

"*Lovesick?* Don't be absurd!"

"—pining after the man, it was getting pathetic."

"I was not pining. The sex wasn't that good."

The moment the words left her mouth, Brooke wished to take them back. Ethan squared his shoulders and closed the distance between them with a challenge in his eyes. "This isn't grade school, Brooke, and I'm not a fool. I know when a woman loses control, especially when it's for the first time."

He wanted her to try and deny it again, to give him an excuse to prove her wrong. The intent was written in the hard lines around his mouth as he watched her. "How—" Brooke cleared her throat and tried again without a tremor in her voice. "How could you possibly know that?"

"Because I practically had to gag you before someone heard your screams of pleasure."

She gasped at the insinuation. "I was faking. Women do it all the time."

Ever so slowly, his head dipped a little bit more. She watched his mouth as it hovered close, threatening to descend on hers at any moment. The breath froze in her lungs as she struggled to keep her anger alive.

"You're a terrible liar," he said with a touch of humor. Then he headed for the door. Halfway there, he threw out, "And, according to Roger, you think I'm a god in the sack."

Brooke could only blink at him, speechless for a horrified moment. When he flipped open the lock and walked out, she managed to find her voice. "I just said that because it's what men like to hear!"

"Liar," he said calmly as the door swung closed behind him.

WHEN BROOKE REENTERED THE ADMINISTRATIVE
department, it was with a crippling sense of paranoia. Many eyes
watched her, and she knew one pair belonged to Ethan Wolf. Over
the past twenty minutes, she'd just reviewed the last four days through
his and Roger's point of view: how she must have looked to both men
as she'd carried on during the carwash, how Ethan must have laughed
at her, how Roger had clearly avoided her. The humiliation of it all
was simply too much to bear.

And despite her initial reaction, she couldn't go to Ken. When it
all came down to it, she'd broken a very strict rule that would most
likely get her fired. Until she figured out Shannon's role in all of this,
she needed to take a step back and use her head from this point on.

When she reached her desk, she found Roger Kerrigan sitting in
her chair. Brooke drew up short as his betrayal slammed home once
again. He was supposed to be her friend. Instead, he had played right
along with Shannon's game, and now that the truth was out, the Judas
was in a clear state of distress.

Brooke told him to follow her to her old office despite the fact that she was banned from it until the end of the competition. Let Ethan say whatever he wanted. Privacy was the luxury she missed so badly—one she would kill to have again. As she entered her corner office, warm sunlight bathed her face. Roger shut the door behind him while she crossed over to the windows. There was the corner view she so cherished, the bayside scene through the leaves of her giant Ficus.

But it offered little joy compared to the hurt in her heart.

"Brooke—"

"You knew about this," she interrupted, bracing herself for a string of lies.

When Roger answered, he was standing notably closer than before. "Yes."

Her forehead hit the glass. "You've been laughing at me this whole time."

"No!" He grabbed her arms and forced her to face him. "I wanted to tell you, but we thought it was better not to."

Brooke pressed her fingertips into Roger's chest, desperately searching for some firm muscle in hopes that this was all a bad dream. "How could I have ever thought there was a real man under there?"

Pain slashed across his face. "I'm not the bad guy, Brooke. Shannon on the other hand…I think you had better watch your back with her."

She pushed him hard. "Gee, do you think so? Really? Because it would be nice to know that I have friends who watch my back too!"

"I do!"

"Then why are you conspiring with the enemy?"

He threw his hands up and appealed to the heavens. "I wasn't conspiring. Shannon heard us planning to meet in the darkroom last Friday. She stopped me from going, that's all. I had no idea that she tricked Ethan into meeting you until well after the fact."

"Yeah, I got that," she spat out. "What I don't get is why you let her continue to make a fool of me."

"Because I figured that what you didn't know wouldn't hurt you.

Ethan was beyond furious with her, Brooke, and he was embarrassed. I didn't want to even *think* about how you would react."

She made a choking sound. "Embarrassed? He didn't seem very embarrassed a half hour ago!" Brooke stopped herself short from confessing that she'd nearly slept with him again. If there was a god in heaven, Ethan wouldn't want that bit of gossip going around either. Roger took a breath and headed toward her leather chair with the six-point massage.

"Don't even think about it," she warned with a growl.

He aborted his attempt to sit down with a helpless droop of his shoulders. "Look, as soon as we figured out that she was messing with you, Ethan and I both wanted to tell you."

It sounded reasonable, but Brooke didn't trust anyone now. "What makes you think they aren't *both* messing with *you* to make a fool out of *me?*"

He shook his head emphatically. "No. Not a chance. Wolf was fighting a genuine case of the heebie-jeebies over sleeping with you."

For some reason, tears stung her eyes. Roger came to her and grasped her by the shoulders again. "I'm sorry, I didn't mean that as an insult. If it makes you feel any better, I've always wanted to do you."

"Ugh!" She socked him in the chest. "You suck, Roger!" Brooke shoved him aside and flung the door open. A handful of people standing outside it suddenly scattered, one of them Shannon. All doubts about the woman's guilt vanished into thin air. Although Brooke wanted to call her out right then and there, she decided that stealth was the only course of action to take. Because if Ethan *was* innocent in all this, he wouldn't know what Shannon was really after. *You want my corner office for yourself, you skanky whore? Come and get it.*

The moment she got home, Brooke hopped in the shower to wash the lingering sexual tension from her body. It had haunted her the rest of the day, a merciless reminder that she'd been duped in the worst possible way. But as the soap touched her skin, Ethan's face flashed in her mind. The instant jolt of desire that followed had her gasping with horrified shock. No! No way in hell did she want *him* to touch her.

After her shower, she walked through the townhome in a state of disconnection. In her upstairs studio, surrounded by awards for her graphic design achievements, she sat at the desk to pursue her newest hobby: a clandestine online campaign to keep an eye on Shannon.

But as Brooke faced the most advanced hardware her money could buy, she couldn't focus long enough to accomplish anything worthwhile, so she went back downstairs.

Her bright Tuscan-style kitchen yielded little comfort. What good was a five-thousand-dollar fridge without a single grape popsicle in the freezer?

Twenty minutes later, Brooke was huddled on the couch with a microwave meal getting cold on the coffee table. The TV was on to distract her, but that proved to be quite ineffective. In a state of misery, she picked up her cell phone and dialed Miranda's number. The Latin beauty's finesse had landed *her* plenty of relationships, including the problems that came with them. She would know how to handle Brooke's situation, if anyone could, that is.

When Miranda answered, a flood of noise drowned out her greeting. "Hey, hon."

Brooke sniffed. "Where are you?"

"Playing mini golf with Cordero. What's up?"

Miranda's on/off relationship with the dashing Spanish man who lived in her building must be on again. "I have a big problem."

"You need me to come over?"

Then again, the date might not be going well. "I wouldn't want you to—"

"I'll be there in twenty minutes."

Brooke stared at the blank screen of her phone and thumbed out a text: *Bring popsicles.*

When Miranda arrived, Brooke gazed at the grocery bag in her hand with tearful appreciation. "Who needs men when I have you?"

Miranda's mouth drooped in sympathy. "Uh-oh. That doesn't sound good."

They walked to the kitchen. "I didn't mean for you to ditch Cordero," Brooke said as she took a popsicle from the box.

Declining one for herself, Miranda put the box in the freezer and went right for the wine rack. "No biggie. I was losing anyway and he was being a prick about it."

Brooke settled at the kitchen island with her popsicle. Miranda chose a bottle and held it up for inspection. Seeing the pricy Duckhorn label, Brooke shook her head. "Not that one. It's my trophy."

So Miranda chose a Zinfandel, popped the cork and looked for two wine glasses. Brooke wasn't sure she wanted to drink on a work night. "Maybe we should call Amy."

Miranda placed a full glass in front of her. "Amy will only drag you to the hookah lounge and shove you at the first man sporting a set of high-end car keys."

Brooke took a sip and wrinkled her nose. "You mean the valet?"

Miranda choked on her wine. "Funny. Now drink up and tell me what's wrong."

Brooke took another sip and related the entire sequence of her day, beginning with the vase of roses on her desk. "I don't know what to do, Miranda. I'm sure the whole office knows about it by now. Ethan and I did enough arguing to alert the *Naples Daily News*."

With a sympathetic pout, Miranda refilled both their wine glasses. "If I see it in the paper tomorrow, I'll let you know."

Brooke released a tearful laugh, her head swimming with a mixture of alcohol and misery. "That does it. I'm calling in sick tomorrow. There is no way I can show my face there after what they did."

Miranda waved away the notion. "Ethan didn't cower at home, and it sounds like he was as much a victim as you, at least the first time around."

Brooke held up a finger. "But not the second."

Miranda shrugged. "He told you the truth before it went too far, didn't he?"

Yes, he had. And, indeed, Brooke had the awful feeling that she had known it was him from the first whisper. She covered her face with her hands to block her friend's knowing look. "I figured out on my own that he wasn't Roger," she admitted. "But I didn't want him to say it."

"So you *knew* it was him?"

More miserable than ever, Brooke plunked her hands back down on the granite countertop. "I *suspected*."

"Do you mean before or after it got too hot to stop?"

The answer was in the slump of her shoulders. Miranda released a throaty chuckle and got up to wrap Brooke in a tight hug from behind. "It's okay, sweetie. We can't all choose who we share chemistry with."

Brooke dismissed the notion. Was it chemistry when, according to Roger, she gave Ethan the heebie-jeebies? "Or maybe he's just a man-whore and I'm an easy target," she concluded with a sigh. "That's how everyone will see it, which is exactly why I can't show my face tomorrow."

"If you do that, you'll prove how messed up you are by it."

"So?"

Miranda let go of her and took her face in her hands. "Honey, the best way to humble a guy is show him how *unaffected* you are. Don't just go to work tomorrow; go with your chin up. If someone looks at you funny, smile and say, 'good morning.' Treat Ethan as you always do, claws and all. If you waver just one time, he'll be on to you in a nanosecond."

"What about Roger?"

"Well now, he can just fuck off."

They shared a giggle. Tipsy and glad of it, Brooke's eyelids began to grow heavy. "So, you're basically telling me to forget the whole thing."

"As best you can," Miranda answered through a yawn. "At least act like it never happened, and pretty soon it will be old gossip. I promise."

And that's exactly what Brooke did. Miranda stayed the night in the guest room upstairs, and she sent Brooke out the door the next morning with breakfast and a few words of encouragement.

With a renewed determination to win VP and get her friends' jobs back, Brooke showed up for work in her signature ponytail, beige flats, and buttoned-up blouse, determined to never again lose herself in lustful tendencies. There was a decent man out there who would want a professional, dignified woman, and when she found him, he'd love her, dull wardrobe and all.

It took a major effort to follow Miranda's advice, but she got through the first few hours of her day with her chin up, a few brightly spoken "good mornings," and even a break-room conversation with Letreece.

Since they'd neglected the two-inch file in lieu of the previous day's drama, Brooke even got through a half hour with Ethan, fulfilling her obligation as transitional assistant. She even sniped about the annoying noise he made every time he popped a candy corn into his mouth. He sniped about her tendency to bitch. It was all very, thankfully, normal since it appeared that he was just as determined to forget what happened between them as she was. She didn't care that he was "unaffected" too. In fact, it relieved her greatly.

Afterward, she camped at her phone, dialed numbers, and put a smile into her voice, working harder than ever to cajole a new customer into believing it was time for new marketing materials. One such client agreed to meet with her that afternoon. Unfortunately, Ethan had already booked the conference room for his very important meeting with Romcore's president.

This gave her a perfect excuse to use her former corner office. Brooke left her desk to search out Ken, since the man was still pulling double duty as acting project coordinator. On her way, she thought about who would be the best artist to assign to this new project in order to make Ken's job easier.

"Um...Brooke?"

She turned to find Roger approaching her desk. Remembering Miranda's profound advice, Brooke gave him her professional, unaffected attention.

He leaned in close and murmured, "I just wanted you to know that no one really has a clear idea of what went on yesterday."

She blinked. "Okay."

"I mean, they've been guessing, but no one actually overheard anything solid."

This time Brooke gave him a patient smile. "Thank you, Roger, but I really don't care what people think."

His face froze in confusion. "You don't?"

Her smile remained. "I'm over it. You should be too."

When she moved to walk around him, he caught her by the arm. "In that case, you want to have lunch with me today?"

"Not on your life."

Behind him, she noticed Ethan giving them both his undivided attention. It was the first sign that he'd even been curious about the effects of yesterday. Ignoring him completely, she headed toward Ken's office.

Ken Stevens was reclining in his desk chair with the lights out, the blinds closed, and a moist washcloth draped over his eyes. She rapped a knuckle against the open door. "Excuse me, sir?"

"Yeah?"

"I'll need to—" The man looked like a statue. Brooke took another step into the darkened office. "Are you feeling okay?"

"Yeah."

But he didn't sound okay. That's when she noticed the open bottle of ibuprofen on his desk. If Brooke understood anything, it was what pain looked like. "Is it sinuses or stress?"

"I have two coworkers constantly at each other's throats," he droned. "I'm going with stress."

Guilt over her part in his suffering softened her heart just a tad. Having put in a few hours running an office, she felt his pain in that too. However, if he'd only kept the old staff, perhaps he wouldn't be steeped in so much drama...as long as he kept a blind eye to the dark-room antics as her father had. Brooke pursed her lips. "Hold on, I'll be right back."

She walked to her desk and removed a few items from the top drawer. Then she headed for the break room where she took a mug from the cabinet and filled it with a small amount of water. As she searched the drawers for a plastic spoon, Ethan walked in.

Hands in his pockets, he studied the colorful buttons on the soda machine. *As if the selection has changed since yesterday,* she thought with an annoyed tilt of her mouth.

He broke the silence behind her. "Are you really over it, or just acting that way?"

A small flutter churned in her stomach. Resisting the urge to run from the room like a skittish cat, she said, "I'm not going to Ken if that's what you're worried about."

"I wasn't. You have as much to lose as I do."

Brooke marveled that it had taken him so long to voice that subtle reminder. Locating a wrapped straw in the back of a drawer, she straightened and scooped up her items. "If you're trying to goad me, it won't work."

"I wasn't trying to goad you."

She put on her most professional smile before backing through the door. "Then we can put it all behind us."

When she returned to Ken's office, she found that he hadn't moved an inch. Brooke unscrewed the cap from a small jar and shook a bit of red powder into her palm.

He lifted a corner of the washcloth and peered out from beneath it. "What's that?"

"Cayenne powder. It'll help with the headache."

"Correct me if I'm wrong," Ken sat up a little, "but I think sneezing should be avoided at all costs."

She dumped the powder into the mug of water and gave it a good stir with the straw. "Trust me on this. Cayenne is full of natural good stuff that inhibits pain and it works fast if you apply it right."

His look turned dry. "Let me guess. You've never taken an aspirin in your life."

It wasn't far from the truth. Brooke smiled a little. "I avoid pharmaceuticals at all costs." She soaked a couple of cotton balls in the mixture and dug them out with the straw, squeezing out some of the liquid. "Lay your head back."

"What exactly are you going to do with those?"

"Oh, don't be such a baby. This is how I manage all my headaches, just relax."

Still hesitant, Ken leaned his head back. She shoved the first discolored cotton ball up one nostril. He reared up with a guttural growl. "Ah! That burns, damn it!"

Brooke prevented him from batting her hands away. "That means it's working, Mr. Stevens, just relax."

"Do you really think I'm going to let you stick that other one up my nose?"

"Yes." She laughed. "You're a tough guy, you can take a little discomfort. Once it subsides, you'll notice a difference in your headache."

"My biggest pain is standing right beside me shoving foreign objects in my face," he griped.

"As long as you don't suck them up, you'll be fine. It'll only take a minute."

When the second one went in, a noise came from the doorway. Brooke looked in that direction and saw Ethan looming there.

"What the hell is going on in here?" He walked closer to inspect the scene. "Ken? Can you confirm that you are a willing party to this?"

"Dot really," he mumbled nasally.

Was Ethan following her? Afraid she'd rat him out despite her claims? "Go away," she said with annoyance.

Ethan flipped the lights on and graced Ken with a look of horror. "It's my job to look after my boss."

"He's fine," Brooke said through clenched teeth.

"He has carrots in his nose."

"They aren't carrots, they're cotton balls."

While she gathered her things, the two men shared a look—Ken's more of a plea for rescue. "I think he passed that stage when he turned three," Ethan claimed, a hint of humor having seeped into his countenance.

Ken sat up. The washcloth dropped from his forehead and right into his cup of coffee. With a loud curse, he dug the thing out and glared at Brooke, who offered the mug of orange water as a solution to his immediate problem. He plopped the dripping rag in there. "I thought you were here to ease the headache, dot bake it worse."

"You're absolutely right, sir." She grabbed some tissues and began mopping up the mess. "Ethan, leave."

Ethan stubbornly crossed his arms. "No."

"You're making his headache worse."

"God bless Aberica!" Ken ripped the soggy orange balls out of his nostrils. "Both of you just get out!"

The orange streaks beneath his nose completely ruined his air of stern authority. Hiding a smile, Brooke gathered up her stuff.

"Don't you laugh!" Ken grumbled.

A snort escaped. Doubling her efforts, Brooke curled her lips inward and bit down on them hard. Unable to speak without falling apart, she simply ran from the office with Ethan close behind. But it wasn't in her to let Ken off the hook that easily, so she went back and stuck her head through his door. "It worked though, didn't it?"

Ken masked his look of amazement behind a scowl, but not before Brooke caught it first. Her grin reflected a victory. "Oh! And I'd like to schedule a half-hour meeting in my office at 2:30," she added while Ethan began to tug on her arm.

"Fine!"

"And I'd like Penny to handle the graphics."

"Absolutely! Get out!"

When they returned to their desks, Brooke half expected Ethan to make some snide remark about her calling it "her" office. Instead, she was surprised to hear a similar snort to the one she'd produced. When she realized he was suppressing his own amusement, it brought back the image of Ken with a thunderous frown and comically orange nostrils.

Her stomach convulsed in a laugh that she promptly stifled behind her hand.

Which spurred another snort from the other desk. Brooke clamped another hand over her mouth in a concerted effort to keep it in. But then Ethan's quiet, wheezy laugh infused the air.

Unable to control it any longer, Brooke let hers loose, while trying to keep it quiet, which only escalated the problem. Within moments, they were both laughing out loud. She wiped the tears from her eyes and told him to stop it.

"What's going on here?"

Just like that, the moment faded. Shannon stood there with her Diet Coke, notepad, and a look of wide-eyed censure. Brooke could swear that the woman was jealous over finding them doing something as normal as sharing a laugh.

Shannon cocked her head and then turned to Ethan. "I have your bid ready. Let's talk about it, shall we?"

When Ethan got up and followed Shannon into her office, Brooke buried herself in her computer screen, vowing not to watch. It was none of her business what those two did behind closed doors. As long as it wasn't conspiring to cheat or steal her corner office using under-handed tactics, she wasn't the slightest bit interested in their business.

Not even a little.

"HAVE YOU SEEN ETHAN?"

Brooke turned to find Ken Stevens standing behind her, sans the orange nostrils. She looked at the time on her computer screen. It was just after two in the afternoon. "No, I haven't. You look like you're feeling better though."

"I am," he admitted as his gaze searched the room. "Can't say I'd shove that crap up my nose all the time, but it seemed to work when the ibuprofen didn't."

She knew it! The satisfaction of a personal win was as good as any other. With a confident smirk, she asked, "Is there something I can help you with?"

At first Ken shook his head, but the man was definitely struggling to make a decision. Finally, he said grimly, "Ted Troll with Romcore is in the waiting room for his two o'clock meeting. Ethan seems to have disappeared."

Disappeared? One thing about Ethan: He was never late for a meeting. And this was by far his most important meeting yet. "Maybe he got stuck in traffic on his way back from lunch."

It was well known that Naples was a city full of continuous road improvements—something else newbies would have to learn to navigate.

"I wouldn't know," Ken said, clicking out a text on the keypad of his blackberry. "I called his cell and it rang on my office's floor."

That didn't sound like Ethan either, unless he'd gone searching for the phone he lost. Then Brooke recalled the way Ethan had wooed her clients with his charms when she'd been in the darkroom waiting for Roger. If she hadn't shown up when she did, he might have snatched them right out from under her. It was something she would never do to a fellow account specialist, but perhaps a little payback was in order…a scare for a scare. Occupying herself with the email she'd been typing, she asked with subtle innocence, "Would you like for me to handle Mr. Troll until Ethan gets back?"

She could feel Ken's gaze boring a hole into her back. "There's enough tension between you two. Better not to exacerbate it."

Brooke typed her closing and hit send. "Mr. Stevens, I think we are all aware that Romcore is Ethan's client." She spun around in her chair to grace him with a dry smile. "It would be like trying to steal a lion from the zoo." When he still balked, she shrugged it off. "You're right. It would be better for you to handle it."

"I'm already late for my tour of the seventh floor with the building's manager." Ken checked his watch. "Go ahead and get Mr. Troll settled in. If Ethan doesn't show up in the next five minutes, you have my blessing to conduct the meeting in his stead. Bill Knight expects to attend also."

She hid her glee behind a respectful nod. Ken disappeared for a moment and reappeared with a file in hand, which he placed on her desk. "Look through it real quick first just in case. I won't be available for the next half hour, so I trust you to handle it on your own if Ethan doesn't show. Oh, and tell him I left his cell phone on his desk."

"Don't worry about a thing," she assured with a kind smile. "He's probably in the lobby with Mr. Troll as we speak. If not, I'll take care of it."

But Ken was already gone. Brooke picked up the file and, resisting the urge to prop her feet up, scanned the contents. Even if Ethan showed up at that very moment, he'd see her with it and explode. Cue her line: Paybacks are a bitch.

Thumbing through the paperwork, she found a copy of their original bid, the competitor's lower bid, and a new bid that would surely win Monroe Graphics the account. Offering custom cover art free of charge for the first textbook was a pretty sweet deal, but Brooke had dealt with clients like Ted Troll before. He'd balk and try to negotiate an even better deal, dangling all of their future business in front of Monroe's nose.

As far as Brooke was concerned, someone so reluctant to fork out the cash usually didn't have the backing to publish a textbook, let alone a whole series of them. She also found it odd that Mr. Troll hadn't just accepted the competitor's winning bid and left it at that, like most people would.

Brooke took out that particular bid and gave it a quick scan. Almost immediately, something strange caught her eye. She reached for her cell phone, thumbed through her address book and made a call.

Five minutes later when she entered the lobby, a tall white-haired man in golf apparel stood at the windows. A single white glove dangled out of a back pocket as if he'd just come from a game. His sunlit profile was a harsh one complete with hooked nose, bushy eyebrows, and a practiced scowl of discontent.

On her way by the reception desk, Letreece waved Brooke over and whispered, "Ethan's MIA and I will go Scarface on this guy if you don't get him off my ass."

Brooke stole a glance at the man by the windows. "Then I'm about to make your day." She cleared her throat and spoke loudly. "Mr. Troll?"

He turned around. Brooke walked over and extended her hand. "Brooke Monroe." They shook. "I apologize for the wait."

"Where's Ethan?"

The gruff manner in which he spoke was testament to his displeasure with Monroe Graphics so far. Brooke gave him her most professional smile and beckoned him to follow her down the hall of windows. "I believe he's stuck in traffic. I've been asked to fill in for him until he arrives."

The man didn't budge. "No offense, Ms. Monroe, but I'd rather deal with Ethan."

Her smile never wavered. "None taken. I'll just get you settled and you can review our offer while you wait."

Shoulders back, Brooke walked with a sway to her hips that bespoke of a woman with confidence, something Mr. Troll most likely didn't want to deal with. She allowed him to enter the conference room first and then chose to leave the door open.

As Brooke settled at the head of the table, Mr. Troll watched as if she were daft. "I'm thirsty," he snapped. "Mind getting me a ginger ale?"

She opened the file and chose the top page. "Oops. I completely forgot to offer you refreshments, didn't I?" She looked up and smiled. "Please sit down."

"Aren't you going to—"

"I'm a woman who likes to get down to business, Mr. Troll." She slid the page across the polished wood. "If this offer agrees with you, I'll get you that drink."

His look narrowed, but he finally pulled out the cushioned chair beside her and sat down. "Wasn't your lead illustrator supposed to be a part of this meeting?"

Brooke waited while he flicked open a pair of reading glasses and perched them on his nose. "Bill's time is fairly limited since his work is in such high demand," she said, propping her chin on her palm. "If you'd still like to see him after you look over the offer, I'll be happy to call him in."

He picked up the bid and scanned it. Slowly his sunburned face contorted with ire. "What the hell is this?"

"It's our offer," she replied.

"It's the same offer!"

"Precisely."

The glasses came off and he angrily shoved the paper back in her direction. "I don't like games, Ms. Monroe. If Ethan isn't available, I want to see your boss."

Brooke sighed and nodded in complete understanding. "I don't like games, either. They tend to muddy the waters until you can no longer see the bottom line." She straightened in her chair, back to her professional demeanor. "Unfortunately, my boss is also unavailable. I know how valuable your time is, so please allow me to explain why our bid hasn't changed."

He watched with a scowl as she fished another document from the folder.

A few minutes later, Brooke stood at the lobby windows with the file beneath her arm and her nose to the glass. "I am sooooo fired," she mumbled as she watched Ted Troll storm from the building's entrance and streak across the parking lot in a fit of rage.

Letreece came up behind her and scoped out the scene below. "What did you do?"

Mr. Troll struggled with the door handle of his silver Jaguar, his mouth moving with what was sure to be a string of colorful words. Brooke sighed. "I made an executive decision that wasn't really mine to make. Ethan won't be happy."

"Girl, you are brave for fanning that flame."

"It was the right call," she said with confidence. "Hopefully, Ken will see it that way."

"Wait a minute, what is that kooky old fart doing now?"

They both watched as he seemed to take his rage out on the clouds. Then he spotted them watching through the eighth-story window and pointed directly at her. Brooke reared back, wondering what sort of evil spell he was casting on her. But, no, it was as if the man was carrying on a conversation with another person. With a strange feeling in her stomach, Brooke looked above her at the paneled ceiling. "Does Ethan ever go up to the roof?" she asked.

"He takes the stairs a lot," Letreece answered as she made her way back to the reception desk. "Whether he goes up or down, I have no idea."

Chewing on her bottom lip, Brooke continued her surveillance of the man in the parking lot, but he'd already gotten in his car and was backing out. With nothing left to see, she decided to check the roof just in case. "I'll be right back," she said to Letreece. Halfway to the stairwell, though, something occurred to her. Better to be armed with some facts just in case. So she went back to Letreece.

"If he's up there, I have a feeling Mr. Troll left him with quite an impression. Can I borrow a pen?"

While she waited for one to appear, someone spoke her name from down the hall. She looked up and saw Shannon coaxing her shaggy blonde hair into place. The woman winked and disappeared into the alcove of bathrooms. As Brooke wondered what she was up to, Roger emerged from the creative department looking rather disheveled. When he spotted her, a flush crept up his neck. "Hey," he said with a guilty swallow as she approached him. "What's wrong? You look upset."

Her focus shifted to the misaligned buttons of his dress shirt. Numb inside, she pointed out the fashion gaffe. "Better fix that before someone suspects you've been banging Shannon in the darkroom."

His ruddy complexion losing all color, Roger's gaze shot down and his fingers fumbled with the gaping hole in his clothes. "I—uh—shit. Listen, Brooke—"

But she had already spun on her heel and was walking back toward reception. Luckily, he didn't follow, because Roger Kerrigan—her so-called friend—had absolutely nothing to say that she wanted to hear.

Brooke took the pen from a stunned Letreece. As she scribbled a message on a sticky note, the receptionist leaned in and whispered, "There's a darkroom back there?"

Damn. Guess she'd forgotten to whisper. Brooke handed back the pen with a stiff smile and left without answering.

File in hand, she made her way up to the roof one slow step at a time. As awful thoughts scrambled inside her head, she pushed them back in accord with Miranda's advice. Luckily, she was very much *unaffected* by the fact Roger had just screwed another woman. It was his *choice* of woman she had a problem with. Wasn't he the one who'd warned her that Shannon was up to no good?

Guess betrayal had no face in the dark. Brooke had a wry laugh over that one and pushed her way through the rooftop door.

"You *bitch!*"

She whirled around and saw Ethan approaching with rage in his eyes. His jacket and tie were off; his shirt was darkened with sweat and flared open. Though she tried to focus on something else, her attention zeroed in on that sculpted torso of his, which was lightly dusted with hair and glistening like an athlete's in a Gatorade commercial.

The fact he wanted to kill her right now seemed almost mundane.

"It wasn't me," she said automatically, holding out the file.

Ethan snatched it from her and forced her back a step. "So much for putting it all behind us." He stormed through the door she still held open and slammed it shut in her face.

Effectively locked out, surrounded by warm, colicky air, Brooke sighed and faced the wind. Thank God she hadn't worn heels that day.

ON HIS WAY DOWN THE STAIRS, ETHAN PRAYED for rain, a real toad-soaker that would wash Brooke Monroe straight out into the undertow. He wasn't pissed because she'd locked him on the roof. That was no worse than the shit he'd pulled on her. But she'd gone far beyond an acceptable level of payback by actually sabotaging his biggest account while he baked to a crisp in the brutal Florida sun.

The woman either had fewer brains than he gave her credit for or a well-hidden set of elephant balls. Either way, he now had a legitimate reason to cry foul in this competition of theirs.

Ethan buttoned his shirt only enough to make himself decent

before he burst into the air-cooled lobby of the eighth floor. Chest heaving and head swimming with heatstroke, he sank into one of the chairs and caught his breath.

"Damn," Letreece said from behind the desk. "How long were you up there?"

He pried his eyes open a crack. "Long enough to turn my lungs into bread pudding."

She looked from him to the stairwell door. "Where's Brooke?"

"In hell. Don't worry, I won't let her stay home too long."

The woman got up, circled around her desk and stood over him with her hands on her hips. "Did you even look inside the file?"

"Why?"

"She wrote something for you in there."

Letreece took the file from his grasp, opened it wide, and held it up. Ethan squinted, still catching his breath as he sat up a little straighter.

A signature at the bottom of the competitor's bid had been circled and the word "forgery" had been written beside it. Ethan grabbed the folder and read the sticky note next.

If you want an explanation, come back and get me.

"Shit." The word tore from his mouth before he could stop it. Could this day get any worse?

Having also read the note, Letreece straightened up with raised eyebrows that suggested he should act now. Ethan slowly rose to his feet. "Am I really that predictable?" he asked while heading toward the door he just came out of.

"Mmm-hmm," she replied with attitude.

It was the longest flight of steps he'd ever taken. When he finally reached the top, he opened the door to find Brooke lounging against the nearest ledge using his discarded jacket for shade.

"Hurry up," he said. "I'm thirsty."

She sauntered toward him with a haughty lift to her chin. When she passed by, he took his jacket from her outstretched hand and glared. "Am I really that predict—"

"Yep."

Now why had he bothered for a second opinion from a woman who hated his guts? "Come on, how did you know that I'd—"

"All I had to do was think like a child."

Her bitchy response echoed in the windowless tunnel of stairs. Still suffering from heat exhaustion, Ethan wasn't sure of his own mood, let alone hers. "And what would you have done if I didn't get your message?"

"I would have let myself back in."

"How?"

She produced a wry laugh. "Something you may not have heard, Ethan, but I've worked in this building for a long time."

Ignoring his body's thirst for cool air and something with electrolytes, he grabbed her arm to keep her from entering the lobby. "You know what I think?"

Her green eyes dulled behind the wire-rimmed glasses. "Yes, I know what you think."

"Who locked me up there if not you?"

She shrugged. "Gee, I couldn't guess. Certainly not the woman who's been pulling morbid pranks on you lately."

His look narrowed. "Shannon's not the one who just ran off my biggest client."

Her eyes growing cold, she dislodged her arm from his grasp and pushed into the lobby. "Your reaction is exactly what I would expect."

A small Asian woman occupied one of the waiting room chairs. Brooke blew at the loose hair that had escaped from her ponytail and, once again, broke into a professional smile. "Mrs. Higashi, how nice to see you again."

As he watched her greet an old client, a part of him wanted to strangle her. Another part of him admired her stamina. She was obviously shaken by their private talk. She was also windblown, hot, and smelled of copper, yet she managed to pull off the demeanor of Princess Di at a charity ball.

Both he and Letreece watched the pair stroll down the hall of windows.

Letreece also watched *him* from beneath her glossy black bangs. "Hey, Ethan?"

He barked out a gruff "What?"

"Did you know that there's a darkroom in here somewhere?" When he went still, she cocked an eyebrow. "I hear it's quite the place to get some workplace freak on."

"Who told you that?"

"Brooke."

Before he could regroup from the fact Brooke had told an avid gossipmonger about their private affairs, Letreece broke into a huge grin and said, "When she busted Roger and Shannon coming out of it, she ripped into him loud enough for me to hear. Boy, was she pissed."

Ethan's jaw went slack. "Roger and Shannon?"

She made a face. "Yeah. I know, right? It's like feeding a cute little bunny to a piranha."

Having suffered several cases of whiplash already, Ethan rubbed his forehead to sort it all out and walked away.

HIS BODY TEMPERATURE BACK TO NORMAL, ETHAN
sat before Ken's desk, a half-empty sports drink in one hand, the
Romcore file in the other. "So Brooke thinks Ted Troll had this signature forged?"

Ken sat forward and steepled his fingers beneath his chin. "The
signature on that bid is from a Ms. Marion Dailey."

"I see that. Does Brooke know this lady?"

"Not well. Design Solutions is a relatively small firm in Estero, but
they've attended some of the same tradeshow events in the past."

"So how could she know her signature?"

Ken turned his computer screen around and pointed to a news-
paper article covering a 2013 awards banquet. There was a picture of a
middle-aged man wearing a garish, orange tuxedo holding his award
in the air. "Because Marion Dailey of Design Solutions is a guy."

Ethan closed his eyes, rubbing at the sudden tension between them.
There had to be an explanation. Ted Troll was the president of a fairly
large company. Why would he resort to forgery?

Ken continued from across the desk. "Brooke knows the project coordinator at Design Solutions. She called and confirmed that they never bid a project for Romcore."

"Son of a bitch!"

"She thinks Mr. Troll was able to get his hands on our bid before it was actually shown to him. He came prepared with a forged bid on Design Solutions letterhead that looked like the real deal."

"Can he go to jail for this?"

"Maybe for the forgery," Ken said with a thoughtful roll of the eyes, "but that would be more Marion Dailey's problem. Right now I have someone looking into whether Romcore actually owns the copyright to the textbooks he wants to print. Even if he provided proof, who's to say that those wouldn't be faked too?"

Brooke stuck her head in the door. "You wanted to see me?"

Ken gestured to the chair beside Ethan. "Shut the door and have a seat."

When she appeared from behind him, Ethan sensed her stress. Their working relationship was in such a state of limbo, even he didn't know what to think. He stared at her profile as she kept her attention solely on Ken.

"How did your meeting go?" Ken asked first.

"Fine," she answered. "I was a little late." Her eyes darted sideways in accusation.

Ethan kept his visage carefully blank. If his suspicions were right, Brooke was anything but a victim.

Ken leaned back in his chair, his expression extremely serene for a man whose headache should have returned in force. "Ethan and I were discussing timing," he said.

Brooke cocked her head. "Timing, sir?"

"Yes. He found it strange that his unfortunate incident on the roof occurred just before his Romcore meeting."

"There's a brick by the door to keep it open," Ethan said. "Someone nudged it out of the way and locked me out."

"How do you know it didn't just slip?" she asked, keeping her attention on Ken.

"Because I heard someone coming up the stairs before the brick was moved," Ethan answered tightly.

Ken held up a silencing hand in Ethan's direction. "Letreece was away from her desk around that time and can't verify who entered the stairwell."

"Are you accusing me?" Brooke asked outright.

"Not at all. More like ruling you out."

She turned to Ethan, her green eyes cold. "I told you it wasn't me. I was at my desk after I got back from lunch."

"You understand," Ken sat forward, regaining her attention, "with this competition between you two, Ethan would naturally suspect you first. We're just trying to get the facts."

"I understand."

"Do you have reason to believe someone else would want him to miss his meeting? One of the other account specialists, perhaps?"

"I'm not exactly close with many of the employees here yet, sir," she answered, her back ramrod straight. "But no, I haven't heard or seen anything suspicious. Why don't we consider other possibilities?"

Her transition from suspect to Sherlock Holmes left Ken with a barely contained smile. "By all means."

"Maybe this was more of a move against me. As you said, I'd be the first suspect, especially since I'm the one who took Ethan's place in that meeting."

"Why would anyone bother?" Ethan asked.

"Maybe they want me fired," she shot back.

It took a moment for Ethan to realize that maybe she was accusing him of framing her. Of all the...

"In this case, it worked out in everyone's favor," Ken broke in. "If Brooke hadn't caught that one discrepancy, we would have eaten a lot of money and possibly earned ourselves future legal problems."

"Easy for you to say," Ethan grumbled. "Without that client, I'm screwed." Not to mention that Brooke now basked in the glory of sainthood. "Why don't we go over how Mr. Troll could have possibly gotten his hands on our bid?"

Now that the tension was effectively crackling, Ken blew out a breath and pinched the bridge of his nose. "It would have had to come from an internal source, someone with access to Shannon's computer files or Ethan's."

"Wouldn't it be obvious to suspect Shannon first?" Brooke's suggestion came out quickly and with a hint of condescension.

"She wouldn't do something like that," Ethan said before downing the rest of his sports drink. He could feel her cutting gaze.

"Are we even discussing the same person?"

"Brooke," Ken interrupted, "it's just that we've known her for a very long time, much longer than you."

"Of course. After all, you had no problem accusing me."

Ethan capped the empty bottle. "You have motive and you also have Roger."

She turned in her seat to face him squarely. "Roger has nothing to do with this, so leave him out of it."

Defending a man she'd just caught screwing her worst enemy? "You sound very sure of that, Brooke."

"Are you really that blind, Ethan? Or just that worried I may actually beat you?"

"Only if you beat me unfairly."

"Alright!" Ken began to massage his temples. "I can see more orange cotton balls in my near future."

Their shared laughter over the orange cotton balls earlier that day was all but a distant memory. Now that they were back at each other's throats, Ethan couldn't help but feel a loss over what could have been construed as progress in their tumultuous working relationship.

Ken rose from his chair and headed toward the blinds. "Why don't you two call it a day?" he said as he closed them, blocking out the afternoon sun.

Ethan's head snapped up. "I need every hour I can get, Ken, especially now."

"You can make it up tomorrow," Ken snapped. "Both of you go home. That's an order." When they both stood up with reluctance,

Ken indicated the switch by the door. "And turn off the lights on your way out."

BROOKE DIDN'T KNOW WHAT WAS WORSE—THAT Ken suspected her of spying or that Ethan did. For one brief moment, they'd let their guard down around each other. They'd shared a laugh. To Brooke, it had been a sort of turning point, proof that they might actually like each other under different circumstances. Apparently, she'd read way more into it than he had.

If only she hadn't offered to take Ethan's place during that meeting. What had started as a harmless quest to make a point had come back to bite her in the ass. Even though she'd caught the forgery, doubt would linger in everyone's minds as to whether or not she participated in some sort of sabotage.

She shoved her notes from the last meeting into her briefcase to work on at home. Hands shaking with the tumult of Ethan's accusations, she shut everything down, turned off the lights, and gathered her things.

As she passed by Shannon's door, she heard her name. Brooke stopped in mid-stride and backtracked to see what the woman could possibly want with her now.

Shannon crooked a manicured finger, her expression sparkling with mischief. Brooke entered the office with caution.

"I hear you've been a bad girl," Shannon whispered.

The woman's hypocrisy knew no bounds. It was almost as if Shannon wanted her to throw out a challenge.

Brooke whispered back, "I know you're the one who locked Ethan on the roof."

"It sounds to me like it was you."

But the truth was written on Shannon's amused countenance. Brooke knew no one would believe her without proof. Shannon was out to effectively make her a villain in the eyes of those who counted. Instead of rising to the bait, Brooke smiled. "Isn't it funny how every time you interfere, I end up getting Ethan off one way or another?"

The woman's smile disintegrated into a look of disgust. Brooke left her that way and made it to the door. "Oh, by the way…," she looked back. "I want to thank you for preventing me from making a big mistake with Roger. Guess you actually fell on that sword, huh?"

GREAT, WHAT A HELL OF A FUCKING DAY. HE GETS locked on the roof, loses his biggest account, and is forced to go home as punishment for daring to turn the spotlight on Saint Brooke.

Ethan shut down his computer and stared at the black screen for a while. Until Brooke could come up with some proof she was telling the truth, there would never be peace between them. That's all there was to it.

"I hear you have to go home," Shannon said behind him.

Ethan straightened up and scanned the main work area for the woman on his mind. "Guess I'm grounded."

Shannon put a hand on his arm. "Is there anything I can do?"

Shrugging off her touch, he grabbed his suit jacket and briefcase. "You can stay away from me."

"Look." She blocked his path. "I've told you fifty times I was sorry for tricking you into that darkroom. But is it really my fault things went that far between you and Brooke?"

No, it wasn't, which is what pissed him off most. Shannon may have done the shoving, but it was into a pit of quicksand he didn't seem to want to get out of. Brooke was a dangerous woman who could very well be out to destroy him—would do anything to get the top position she felt entitled to. But did he really believe that? Did he want to?

"How far did things go between you and Roger?" he asked.

Her face melted into a knowing smirk. "It didn't take her long to tell you about that."

"Brooke didn't say a damn word. But it really makes me wonder what else you'd do to get one over on her."

Shannon rolled her eyes. "Ethan, I told you—"

"Would you share sensitive information with a client to frame her for sabotage?"

She reared back as if he'd slapped her. "How could you ask me something like that?"

He wasn't sure anymore. Perhaps the humidity was getting to all of them. "I'm giving you a chance to come clean with me without consequence—one chance. If you lie now and I find out later, you'll be done at this company."

Shock turned to hurt. "I love this company. You know that." He watched her, waiting for her answer. Sure enough, a sliver of defeat entered her eyes. "I didn't share sensitive information," she said with conviction.

"But?"

"I—I may have locked you on the roof."

Her honesty delivered a slap of its own. Ethan's iron control faltered for a moment. "Why?"

"Because I knew Brooke would try to steal your client. I figured if we could expose her as a cheat, she'd be gone, and this contest wouldn't matter anymore."

Ethan swore and grabbed his keys and briefcase.

"You should have never agreed to it, Ethan," she said in a wobbly voice. "How could you put yourself in such a vulnerable position?"

He kept walking.

"Ethan!" She caught up to him. "Will you tell Ken?"

"I said I wouldn't," he growled.

But that didn't mean he'd throw Brooke under the bus for something she didn't do.

Ethan slammed into his sister's condo, threw his crap on the foyer floor, and went straight to the fridge. The moment he twisted the cap off a longneck, Harper entered the kitchen in her swim gear.

"Adrianna's napping," she said while he downed half the bottle.

He closed his eyes and let the beer settle. "Sorry."

Ice rattled as she took a sip from a nearby glass. "You're home early. Bad day?"

"You could say that."

"Want to talk about it?"

His twin was the only person he could truly open up to, but Harper had been Shannon's closest friend since grade school. "Not really," he answered, staring down at the bottle's sweating label.

"Is it about this competition between you and Brooke?"

He took another long pull. "You're on a first-name basis with her now?"

She shrugged. "I hear her name enough from you."

Until then, Ethan hadn't realized how much he unloaded on his sister every night. He'd sure miss her when she and Adrianna boarded a plane back to South Dakota in the morning. Ethan's own voice sounded distant to him. "I think she's out to get me."

"What did she do besides poison your candy corn?" Harper asked with a hint of amusement.

"She took advantage of an opportunity. I just don't know how far she went to do it." Still, he owed Brooke an apology for one particular accusation he'd made that turned out to be false. The thought burned him up inside and made him want to strangle Shannon more now than ever.

"That's too bad." Harper ripped an elastic band from her wet hair and picked up a brush. "You two would make gorgeous babies."

Ethan choked on the last of his beer. He wiped his mouth, placed the empty bottle in the sink, and went to the fridge for another. "You're a real fuckin' hoot, Harper."

She shrugged as the brush worked through some tangles. "I'm just saying you can tell me if you're attracted to her. I won't hold it against you."

The cap came off another longneck. "How did we get on the subject of attraction?"

She flipped her long hair down and back. "I can sense a little of it between you and Brooke."

He shifted uncomfortably, pretty sure that she'd picked that up from the many times he'd vehemently complained about the woman.

"I have a confession to make," Harper said. Ethan looked up and noticed that she'd been watching him. "Before we left the office last Friday, I told her about your accident."

He'd suspected as much. "Nice going. I was kinda hoping to leave the brain injury jokes back in South Dakota."

"Has she made any jokes?"

Despite her many opportunities, Brooke had somehow restrained herself. He hoped that it wasn't out of pity.

"That's what I thought," Harper continued with half-lidded eyes. "She doesn't strike me as the type who'd do that, even to you. In fact, I think she was impressed by your resilience."

"Doubtful."

"I'm pretty good at reading people's expressions, Ethan, and she was definitely battling some feelings for you other than resentment."

That was before their first time in the darkroom, before the liquor store challenge. "You were wrong," he said just before tipping the bottle over his lips again.

"Does that mean I'm wrong about you too?"

"Probably." Bullshit, she was always right about him and vice versa. It was some sort of twin thing they shared.

The same thought was reflected in Harper's eyes. "So, you don't have any attraction for Brooke whatsoever," she pressed.

Ethan's focus blurred as the image of Brooke in her sexy carwash clothes came to the surface. "Not even a little."

Saying it out loud helped somewhat, but he couldn't ignore the fact his thoughts were continually plagued by darkroom memories. His dreams were littered with sensual replays so real that he'd wake to a painful need to have her again. More than once he'd been tempted to just give her that damned corner office and leave Naples altogether just to outrun his tumultuous feelings for her.

But quitting wasn't in his DNA. Now that Brooke had a real shot at winning, he needed to try one more time to convince her that she wasn't qualified for the job.

Tomorrow. He'd catch her in the parking lot before work. Maybe then there would be peace in the office. Peace in his soul.

He put the unfinished beer in the sink and strolled toward his bedroom. "I need a shower."

And then he needed to get the hell out of there. Maybe hit the highway and head toward Fort Myers where he knew of a scheduled street race that was to take place that night. If Harper knew he'd been following the local message boards, her first lecture would be about law enforcement and the big possibility they watched those same message boards.

Don't get sucked in, Ethan. They throw people in jail down here.

But he didn't give a fuck. What choice did he have now that the track was off limits? He needed the noise, the rush, and to hang with likeminded people. He needed an outlet or he'd go bat-shit crazy... and nothing else would do the trick.

BROOKE SAT ON THE FLOOR BETWEEN THE COFFEE table and couch, staring into the deep plum depths of her wine glass. She turned the stem in her fingers, her thoughts far from where they should be. Shannon was out to get her fired, which was plain to see. As soon as Brooke got home, she'd marched straight up to her studio and spent a dangerous amount of time searching for the evidence to prove it, an act that would surely get her fired if she was discovered hacking Monroe's server. Her efforts turned up nothing. At this point, if Ethan gave Ken Stevens an ultimatum, there was enough stacked against her for him to win by default.

Neither of them wanted to openly use the darkroom disaster for ammunition, but it was certainly the catalyst for their suspicion of each other…and the building anxiety between them that seemed to trump any progress they made, no matter how small.

She closed her eyes. How could she have let herself go like that? Now she was stuck in an impossible war with the only man her body seemed to want. Even now, her thoughts veered toward a place she hated to go: his touch, his devouring kisses, their mutual urgency to join.

But that had been with the lights off. Never would she want him with the lights on. Yes, just knowing whom those hands and lips and tongue belonged to would send her libido straight into a nosedive.

"Earth to Brooke..."

Only then did she realize her eyes were still closed. Brooke opened them and blinked at the man who'd been rambling beside her. "I'm sorry, what?"

Sid watched her over his own wine glass. "You're a million miles away."

Her friend and liquor store hero had finally called to collect on that drink. She'd just happened to have a hundred-dollar bottle of wine she no longer viewed as a trophy. A half a glass through it, her head was beginning to swim, but the wine had failed to erase her troubles.

"I guess I have a lot on my mind." She removed her glasses and rubbed at tired eyes. "You were probably expecting better company."

"Want to talk about it?"

Sid was a good guy. He was much taller than she was and had an okay body, but his strong-yet-playful personality was mostly what made him attractive. They shared some things in common, like the fact they were both gingers with green eyes, they had a mutual interest in software, and they listened to the same music. He was exactly her type and seemed to show some genuine interest in her.

But the most important quality about Sid was that he was far apart from the mess at work. Though he may be able to help her find evidence against Shannon, she had no desire to tie him into something illegal. She smiled. "I'd rather forget about it."

He tipped his wine glass and took a drink, his eyes never straying from her face. "That may be something I can help you with."

When his gaze moved down to her mouth, Brooke knew he was going to kiss her. She wanted him to. This was not Roger or Ethan, but a genuinely decent man with no hidden agenda.

He slowly leaned forward. Brooke moved in to meet him halfway.

They shared a sensual kiss that was tentative at first and then deepened into something more. His breath smelled good, like rich Napa Valley wine. His lips were firm yet soft. The way he moved told her that he knew how to please a woman.

Despite all that, her heartbeat notably failed to pick up its pace. The doorbell rang. Brooke wasn't sure if it was an annoyance or a blessing. She backed out of the kiss, leaving him with an unfocused look that told her he'd enjoyed it way more than she had. "It could only be Mrs. Costa from next door," she explained as she got to her feet and put her glasses back on. "She always comes over when her computer acts up. I'll tell her to hold off for now."

Sid appeared in no hurry to leave his spot on the floor. He drew a knee up, but not before Brooke saw the suspicious bulge in his Bermuda shorts.

When she opened the door, a shockwave of alarm washed through her. Ethan stood there leaning against the doorframe in jeans, a black T-shirt, and an intense focus on the welcome mat. All she could do was stare in abject surprise at a man who couldn't possibly have sought out her address.

Words escaped her. The silence stretched as he too seemed to wonder what the hell he was doing there. Finally, he looked up. His eyes darted past her and over to the man at her coffee table. Slowly, their blue-gray depths changed into something turbulent.

Her hand slipped from the knob as he stepped over the threshold. He stood so close she could feel his body heat. His voice was rough, barely above a whisper. "We need to talk."

Now her heart was beating fast enough to power a small locomotive. Dazed and confused, she stepped back and turned to find Sid standing right behind her. "Sid...do you mind if we do this another time?"

The man stepped closer, caressed her back in an intimate way. "Isn't this the guy you were arguing with the other day?"

"And we've done a lot of that since then, haven't we, Brooke?" Ethan chimed in, sounding dangerous. "Well...not all of it was—"

"Ethan, shut up," Brooke snapped.

A quick look confirmed that Sid was following along just fine. As he nodded at his adversary, the pulse at his freckled temple began to thrum. "I get it." He turned to Brooke. "Are you sure you want me to leave?"

She took one of his hands and gave it an apologetic squeeze. "Yes, I'm sure. Another time would be better, when I'm all here."

Sid hesitated a moment and then pursed his lips as he began to leave. When Ethan moved aside to give him clear access to the doorway, Sid stopped, leaned over, and deposited a tender kiss on her temple.

"I'm only a phone call away," he said, his voice laden with meaning.

She closed the door behind him, swimming in mixed emotions. Why the hell had she just done that? And why the hell was Ethan Wolf standing in her living room? Brooke cleared the uncertainty from her throat. "I don't want our problems inside my home," she said.

When she turned to confront him, he was taking a good long pull from the open bottle of cabernet. Her anger rose to a fever pitch as she realized he'd just swallowed about twenty bucks worth of wine in one shot, no doubt to make a point. She moved toward him and was about to tell him to leave when he set the bottle down on the coffee table, turned, and immediately drew her into his arms.

Suddenly she was fully involved in a scorching kiss that completely rendered her senseless. It was not tender or sweet, but rough and demanding. All of her irritation melted away along with her reasons for not wanting him here. She'd been geared up to welcome Sid's touch. Surely that's why her body was thrumming with a need so strong, she clung to Ethan as if he were the only thing keeping her upright.

"You drive me insane," he hissed against her mouth, closing his eyes against the inner struggle she understood all too well.

Brooke dropped her head in a desperate attempt to find sanity. This wasn't possible. How could he turn her insides into molten lava like that when the mere sight of him pissed her off so badly? When she backed away, he let go of her waist and did the same. A moment of silence followed. "You said you wanted to talk," she said finally.

Ethan turned his back and jammed a hand through his hair. "Give me a second."

"Why should I?"

"Look." When he faced her again, aggravation laced his words. "I don't want to be here either. In fact I'm still trying to figure out why I'm not in Fort Myers."

"Because you'd rather harass me, apparently."

"Because no matter how hard I try with you, I can't get my bearings—which scares the hell out of me. We've been taking one step forward and two steps back since the start of this competition, and for what? Because we hate each other?"

"Yes!" she threw out in a desperate attempt to believe it.

His brow smoothed out with a look of wonder. "Really? Why, Brooke? What makes you want to skin me alive and me want to shake the living shit out of you?"

"You, for one," Brooke said with pointed finger, her chest heaving with emotion, "have looked down on me from the moment we laid eyes on each other."

"*What?*"

"I was a total stranger to you. I was wet and miserable and vulnerable and you took that opportunity to laugh in my face. So, yes, after Ken introduced us, I knew I couldn't work under a man of such poor character."

A choked sound escaped his throat. Then he was laughing. "You set out to upend my entire life because your feelings were hurt?"

His words mocked, but his eyes held genuine amusement. Brooke waved away his accusation. "Don't be absurd."

The more he laughed, the more he tried to control it, shaking his head as he moved to the alcove of windows. "The absurd part is, you got it all backward. When you entered that restaurant, I wasn't laughing at you. I was *flirting* with you."

"Oh, please." Like he *wasn't* laughing at her now?

"You see...," his amusement finally waning, he turned toward her again and propped himself against the windowsill. "You were no stranger to me. I'd already been in your office. I'd seen your pictures. I was *glad* I didn't have to wait until Monday morning to meet you. That lasted all of two seconds before you stuck that entitled little nose up in the air."

Brooke thought back, struggling to remember their first encounter word for word. Surely, he was blowing smoke, telling her what she wanted to hear. "If you expect me to believe you were attracted to me—"

"No." His interruption was accompanied by a blank, soulless look. "It's way too late for that, isn't it? We're stuck in this war you started, and I'm not sure we'll ever trust each other enough to get past it."

The air surrounding them grew heavy with the truth. "That's why you came, isn't it?" she asked quietly. "To throw more accusations at me?"

"I came to talk some sense into you." He stood up and approached her. "If you're doing what I think you are, the only way you'll survive is if you forfeit. Because if you try and ride it out...you'll get caught and you'll be fired."

She forced a bitter laugh. "Wouldn't that fit right into your plans?"

He kept his voice low as he reached out and took her by the shoulders. "You're missing something here, Brooke. I don't want you fired. I think you've been dealt some pretty shitty cards, and I can understand the desire to play a dirty hand in order to win. I get it. I sympathize with it. But if you follow through with that desire, I won't let it be at my expense."

She lifted her chin. "And if we find out Shannon's the one behind the leaks?"

"She isn't."

Damn. Of all the things Brooke had thought him guilty of, being blind wasn't one of them. "Unbelievable," she mumbled.

He gave her a little shake. "I know her, Brooke. Shannon may have pulled some childish pranks, but she's no criminal. Selling bids is a serious offense, and she's equally suspicious of you. All she's trying to do is flush you out."

In keeping with the respectful tone they'd adopted, Brooke asked, "When I come up innocent...what then?"

His gaze scoured her face. "Then I guess I'll be in trouble, won't I?"

Because he'd have to admit he was wrong? Or because he doubted she'd be of a forgiving mind? Fearing the latter, Brooke swallowed hard and backed out of his reach. "Then I guess we're still at an impasse. I'm sorry you wasted your time."

Ethan stared at her for a moment before looking away. "And I'm sorry I ruined your date." He moved toward the door.

Brooke watched him with a sinking feeling, knowing that if he left now she would never get a moment's peace. That kiss still lingered on her lips, a brutal reminder of just how much she wanted him despite their turbulent exchanges.

His hand froze on the knob. Shoulders stiff, Ethan stood there for a quiet second before he swore beneath his breath and turned back to her. "The hell I am," he rasped as he closed the distance. The look in his eyes told her there was no escape...and Brooke had no desire to try.

WITH A FEROCITY THAT SURPRISED HER, ETHAN
reclaimed her mouth, demanding a response that she couldn't possibly
deny. When Brooke grasped those solid shoulders, he held her just as
tight, moving both hands down her back until he took hold of her ass
and pressed her hard against his erection. It was thick and long and
rigid as steel behind the barrier of his jeans.

Then she felt herself being lifted. Succumbing to the heady
demands of her own desire, she wrapped her legs around his waist.
He backed her up against the wall and removed her glasses before
sweeping her into an erotic world of torturous pleasure. Her shirt
came off. Her bra was unclasped and slipped down her arms. She
flung it aside, arched back, and let him taste her skin, along her
collarbone and further down until his mouth closed over a rose-
tipped breast.

The feel of his tongue moving over her nipple and the sounds of
their erratic breathing pushed her lust into a whole different realm.
She forgot all about the competition and the misery that went with it.

All she wanted was for him to quench the longing that burned deep inside her, completely out of her control.

Ethan ripped off his T-shirt. "Where's the bedroom?" he rasped.

She pointed and then held on tight while he carried her past the kitchen and through a set of double doors. Throughout the short journey, she kept her forehead pressed against his, her eyes shut tight in order to not allow any sort of reality in. He was a man. She was a woman. This was the most natural outlet for the pent-up needs that plagued them.

He lowered her to the bed, curled his fingers around the waistband of her shorts, and pulled them off. Then he came back and repeated the process with her panties, all the while studying their slow progression down the length of her legs. Brooke stretched, feeling languid all of a sudden as she watched him unbutton his jeans. They came down, and in the dim light of dusk, she saw his erection standing at full attention. Somehow it seemed bigger than she imagined. But, of course, now she had the benefit of sight.

Ethan moved between her legs, parting them as he crawled onto the bed. They said nothing, just watched each other as he lowered himself on top of her. She opened her mouth in invitation. He delved inside it, kissing her with matched hunger. Then his lips were once again roaming down her body, slowly following a path down its center until they came to the valley between her thighs.

Brooke gasped when his lips grazed the tender flesh there. His breath moved over her folds, teasing until she tensed in anticipation of where they would go next. Then she felt his hot tongue flatten against her sensitive clit and everything around them melted away.

As she drowned in sensation, he wrapped his arms around her legs and pulled her closer against his firm, demanding mouth. After that first taste, he burrowed his tongue deep, moving from the bottom of her slit to the top and then repeating the process as he lapped at the essence flowing from her body. Her pulse raced. Soft moans of pleasure escaped from her throat. How could something feel so good? How could anything be so sinful and wonderful at the same time?

Closing her eyes, she let the mounting pleasure carry her away. She felt his fingers explore her entrance and then slip inside. She moaned and moved her hips against them as he licked and sucked. Soon her moans turned to gasps and then to high-pitched sounds of ecstasy. His fingers and tongue brought her to the brink of an orgasm that was different from the first—more focused and heavily concentrated in one spot from the inside out. As it intensified, she held her breath and waited for it to crown. When it did, the feeling of surpassing all boundaries had her writhing beneath him, grabbing his hair in her fists, and letting everything else fall away.

As the wave subsided, he slowed down, his tender ministrations gently bringing her back to earth. Though her body was well sated and thoroughly depleted of strength, she was left with a sudden need to be filled again.

She heard the tearing of foil, opened her eyes, and watched him roll on a condom. The sight of Ethan touching himself that way, preparing his cock, and knowing he used that break to take in every detail of her naked body filled her with a feeling of sensual wellbeing. Then he lowered himself between her legs again and positioned his engorged member against her slick entrance.

"Look at me," he whispered.

She *was* looking at him. His face loomed close above hers, his handsome features dark and fierce in the waning light.

"I want you to know who's inside you this time."

As the words sank in, he plunged. Her body took him in, stretching to accommodate his girth. In one instant, he managed to anger her and reward her, to satisfy that hungry need to join and to be filled so completely. As his hips ground against hers in deep, wide circles, her pulse began to race again. Yes, she knew exactly who was inside her, but he also knew whose body he took pleasure from at that moment.

His eyes bore into hers, refusing to let her escape. "Touch me," he demanded. She raised her hands, moved them over the contours of his shoulders, chest, and back. She felt all of him, the many curves and textures of his body, the scars that marred his skin's sinewy perfection, the dance of muscles beneath them.

"Ethan," she whimpered.

"That's right." Shifting to one elbow, he hooked an arm beneath her leg and drove deeper inside her. The angle changed the friction of each thrust, awakening a whole different part of her. Brooke panted as the pleasure built again, fast and furious.

Her lips opened wider with the knowledge that she was about to come again. A strangled sound escaped her throat as that familiar, exquisite tightening began deep inside her. When it consumed her, she threw her head back and the room was filled by her cries of pleasure. Ethan buried his face in her hair and roared out his own.

Once again locked in each other's arms, they gently came down from the incredible climax they'd reached together, enjoying the lingering intimacy of it all.

After a while, Ethan rolled off of her. "Would you hit me if I told you I'm not sorry that happened?"

He sounded dazed. She turned her head, stared at his profile as the air conditioning cooled her glistening body. "I would hit you if you *were* sorry."

He breathed in deeply and exhaled. "Then it's a fucking miracle. We agree on something." Then he turned his head, stared into her eyes for a moment. "Do you want me to leave?"

Brooke marveled over the fact that a man she had an ugly relationship with was lying naked on her bed. He was beautiful, his body long and lean with the natural physique of a born doer—a man who would ruin a shirt in order to tinker under a car hood for a stranded coworker. "I don't know," she whispered. "Can we do this for long without fighting?"

The bed moved as he rolled toward her, propping his head on his hand. "Wouldn't it be something if we could just...take a break: no fighting, no doubts, no cares?"

She smiled. "I don't know how we'd handle something like that."

He also smiled, but it faded in thought. "Maybe if we understood each other a little more, we'd find a way to survive the week."

"What do you have in mind?" Brooke asked with a fair amount of caution.

"We can ask each other one question. Just one, so it has to count. Nothing about work and nothing too sensitive."

That didn't sound too bad. "Okay," she said with a sigh. "You first."

"How did you get to be twenty-nine years old without ever having an orgasm?"

If they weren't trying so hard to get along, she might think he was making fun of her. "What makes you so sure I haven't?"

Annoyance deepened the lines around his mouth. "Still playing coy, are we?"

"I don't know." Brooke gave a helpless shrug. "I guess I didn't think I could."

"You are an incredibly capable woman," he said matter-of-factly. "It's not something you have to work hard at if you have the right partner."

Brooke frowned at his practical outlook on the subject. Were they talking about sex or square dancing? "Yeah, well...I've never been good at picking the right partner."

He gave a short laugh. "Something tells me your priorities were a little skewed."

She smiled, not offended and completely at ease. "I've always been very career oriented. Shocker, huh?"

"I'm stunned," he quipped back with a smile of his own.

"Okay, it's my turn." Her fingertips lightly grazed the scar over his left ribcage. "Is this from your car accident?"

He grabbed her hand and went still, his smile slowly fading. When she thought she'd gone over that "too sensitive" line, he brought her hand up and placed it over a part of his head. "Feel that?"

Brooke rolled toward him and carefully probed his scalp just above his left brow line. Beneath his thick hair was a scar, but also something else—a larger area that felt...different. "Yes," she whispered.

"It's a metal plate. My helmet came off."

"Jesus." A shudder ran through her. "That must have been one hell of an impact. How long ago did it happen?"

"Not as long ago as you think."

"You seem to have recovered okay."

"My vision is bad. I'm banned from racing."

Though he seemed nonchalant about it, Brooke wasn't fooled. "You must miss it."

He finally looked away, breaking the intimacy of the moment. "I'm dealing with the withdrawal one day at a time."

"Your sister is afraid you'll do something stupid." When he didn't answer, she pressed further. "She says you need a new hobby, a new distraction."

"My sister worries too much," he replied with irritation.

Brooke scrutinized his face and decided the stubborn crease on his brow was a sure sign of guilt. "Something tells me it's a legitimate worry."

Ethan looked at her as if he was surprised. "Why would you say that?"

"Your car has a roll bar on it." He rolled his eyes, prompting her to dig further. "You mean you've never been tempted to open it up on a back road? Or race someone in a dry riverbed like Danny Zuko?"

His sudden laughter filled the room, easing any tension that her line of questioning might have caused. "Seriously?" he choked. "Out of all the epic racing films out there, you pick a reference from *Grease*?"

"It's one of my favorite movies," Brooke argued with a pout.

He shook his head. "Why does that not surprise me?"

"That moment when Greased Lightning jumps the ramp in slow motion, it makes my heart go pitter-patter every time."

He snorted again. "You're hopeless."

She shrugged and yawned. "Why? Your idea of racing and mine can't be that different. A fast car is a fast car is a fast car."

Before the last word left her lips, Brooke realized just how much the tumultuous day had caught up with her. Now that the stress was gone and Ethan was lying beside her and they were exchanging their first-ever round of easy banter, the pull of sleep beckoned.

"Take a drive with me."

Her eyes widened. "What?"

"Take a drive with me," he repeated. "I'll show you the difference."

The suggestion alone drove the sleep right out of her weary body. "You're banned from racing, but you want to test your limits with me in the passenger seat?"

With a heavy sigh, he sat up, slid off the bed, and extended his hand. "I would never do that," he said softly. "Just trust me for once."

THE RIDE TO FORT MYERS HAD BEEN DEVOID OF conversation since they both seemed unwilling to break the amiable silence. It had not, however, been quiet. Much to Brooke's chagrin, that prevailing, vibrant whine still hummed in her eardrums even after the engine was cut. She supposed such power under the hood had a way of burrowing into one's soul, and she could see how a man would embrace it. Now parked in a shadowy corner of a mall parking lot, she sensed Ethan's restless mood as they watched a gathering in the distance.

Though it was way past her bedtime, her eyes were clear and her mind was sharp. "Do you know those people?" she asked.

"Nope," Ethan said, his wrist still draped over the steering wheel. "But I know why they're here."

So did Brooke. "It looks like they're shopping."

"They're looking for a compatible car," he explained. "They'll ask questions, compare specs, and make a bet."

"And then they'll race each other?"

"Yes, but not here, too many cops. They'll pick a desolate road somewhere and mark out a quarter-mile stretch."

She smiled. "You sound like you've done this before."

He shook his head and ran a hand over the stubble covering his jaw. "Not really."

But his intense focus on the unfolding scene said otherwise. "Bull," she challenged with a little laugh. "You said you were on your way to Fort Myers before you came to my house."

"That had nothing to do with this."

"And you just happened to find these guys through telepathy?"

"I just spotted them from the road," he said easily enough.

She shook her head. "You're lying, Ethan Wolf. You've probably raced half of them already."

He raised a brow. "That would be reckless and irresponsible of me. Besides, street racing wasn't my thing to begin with. These guys risk some hefty punishment because there's no other outlet available when the need hits."

"And you don't ever feel the need, huh?"

He gave a casual shrug. "Nope, and before, I had the track any time I wanted."

"Why is that?" she asked. "Because you were so good no one could deny you?"

"Because my sister married the owner."

It wasn't the answer she expected. Brooke's smile widened. "It wasn't an arranged marriage, was it?"

Ethan broke into a chuckle. "Don't tell her. She's in love, and Grant made me an offer I couldn't refuse."

He was joking, of course, but Brooke detected a hint of truth behind the story. "You were friends with Grant first, then?"

"Close friends. He builds cars, I drive—*drove* them. As soon as I was back on my feet after the accident, we finished the modifications on this car that we'd started a year before."

"Even if you couldn't race it?"

He rolled down the window and exhaled loudly. "You sound like

Harper. She thought that Grant was dangling a carrot under my nose. They fought about it a lot, I guess."

As the warm night air moved in and cleared the fog from the windshield, Brooke heard music and people laughing and talking in the distance. There were only a few women in the mix, probably girlfriends, not the tawdry-looking groupies she expected to see. Before, there was no sign to indicate that Ethan fit in with a crowd like that. It amazed her how easy it was to imagine now. "Watching this, listening to you right now," she paused, searching for the right words. "You don't seem like a man who would settle for a desk job."

He dismissed the notion with a grunt. "Racing was just a hobby… well, until it wasn't. But there was a nice balance between the office and the track."

Another two-door car pulled into the lot, purple with a spoiler that looked like a dual-blade razor. Ethan swore lightly and sank down in his seat a bit.

"What?" Brooke studied the new arrival with keen interest. "Do you know that person?"

"Nope."

The car had stopped just long enough for the driver to converse with some folks in the crowd. Then the engine revved and the wheels began rolling right toward them.

Brooke watched with fascination as Ethan propped an elbow on the window and stared straight ahead with a look of discomfort. Sure enough, the purple car came to a stop right beside them. A man of Polynesian descent sat behind the wheel with a mass of black hair hanging down his beefy shoulders in tight, orderly waves. "Well if it ain't the hotrod himself," he said in a gravelly voice.

While Ethan gave the man a sheepish smile, Brooke cocked her head. "So you *do* know each other?"

"Not really."

The other driver scoped her out as if assessing the situation between them. "Name's Kale, by the way."

Ethan tapped his fingertips on the windowsill. "Kale, your timing is unbelievable."

"The car sticks out, man," he continued. "You're kinda making the guys nervous. Are you here to run or not?"

"Nope. Just watching."

Brooke noted his prolific use of the words "nope" and "not really" with amused interest.

Kale stuck out a hand. "Why not? I'm sure your date wouldn't mind."

It was his use of the "D" word that had them both scrambling to set the man straight. "Uh...no, he isn't—"

"She isn't—"

"We aren't—"

"And this is definitely not..."

"That's cool, that's cool." Kale's teeth flashed bright white in the dark of the parking lot. "But instead of lurking, why don't you come on over and show the guys what you got. I know I'm curious."

Ethan jerked a thumb in her direction. "Nah, I should probably get her home."

But Brooke was enjoying herself way too much to end the evening so soon. "Actually, Ethan, I'm kind of curious too." When he shot her a look of misery, she said, "This is why you brought me here, right?"

"To get busted?" he mumbled. "No." Then he opened his door and stepped out. When Brooke followed suit, she watched from across the top of the car as the two men clasped hands. Kale towered over Ethan, who spoke in a low voice. "Didn't expect to run into you, what with the Alabama tags and all."

"I get it, man," Kale muttered back. "The lady doesn't approve?"

"Oh, he couldn't care less what I think," she broke in. "As long as I don't tell his sister."

Ethan's eyes reflected only a mild level of concern before he brushed off her comment. "Speaking of busted," he said to Kale, "how'd you make out with the black and white?"

"I shook him after a half mile or so."

Both men looked when headlights sliced through the dark. "Glad to hear it," Ethan said, hands on hips as two cars approached, one a bright green sport coupe with an elaborate graphics scheme and the other a smallish, older model four-door. They parked with their headlights trained right on them. As the drivers got out, Brooke noticed a group of people approaching on foot who must have decided to come check them out as well.

"Wassup, bruh?" said one of the drivers, a short man with baggy clothes and plenty of bling. Brooke watched them warily, uncertain of their intentions as they swaggered over to Ethan, who appeared tense.

Kale stepped in. "He's cool, man."

The driver of the four-door jerked his chin, a cigarette burning in one hand. "Never seen you around before." The guy craned his neck to get a better look at Ethan's plates. "South Dakota, huh? Fuck, dude, you're a long way from home."

"I just moved here." Ethan shook the man's hand when it was offered.

"What's your name?"

"Ethan."

"How'd you find us?"

He glanced at Brooke, a small smile on his lips. "Message boards."

Her brows popped up in mock surprise. As they were joined by the rest of the group, she was reminded that she and Ethan were the intruders, crashing a private gathering of an elite crowd. A woman in a cropped top and skinny jeans eyed her from the sidelines and showed no interest in being friendly. But as the men talked and more information was exchanged, tensions seemed to fade.

"Fuck, I heard of you, dude," someone said above the others. "You drove a white BMW, right? Didn't you wipe out in last year's Majors Tour with that guy from Omaha?"

Surprised, Brooke glanced at Ethan, sensing his uneasiness. "You follow it, then?" he asked the man.

"Anything in club racing." A hand was extended, as the guy seemed truly impressed. "You definitely got skills, man. I'm Jules."

Ethan shook it and several others as introductions were made. Jules, who spoke with a thick Spanish accent, indicated the yellow Mazda. "Hey, I thought that wreck ended things for you. Fucked you up pretty bad, didn't it?"

"I'm above ground," Ethan replied with a cautious edge.

"Yeah," said Kale with arms crossed. "And taking to the streets. You even supposed to drive?"

Ethan met his look. "I have a license, if that's what you mean."

"That ain't what I mean."

As the silence stretched out and the moths swarmed thicker in the flood of light, everyone watched Ethan with an expectant air, including Brooke. Finally, he nodded. "You're right. I had no business taking you on that night. But I'm not here to run anyone, we just want to watch, if that's okay."

While Kale kept his imposing stance, Jules clapped Ethan on the shoulder. "Yeah, we get it. Shit like that don't just leave you, you know?"

As Brooke was left to wonder if Ethan should even *have* a license, Jules walked over to where she stood. "So this is your ride," he said, his attention divided between her and the Mazda's sleek exterior. "Something tells me there's a little more to her than a pretty face."

Ethan scratched at his stubble, a devilish twinkle in his eye. "A little attitude."

Which "ride" were they talking about exactly? Brooke narrowed her eyes and Ethan's mouth twitched in response.

The hood came open. Flashlights were produced from every pocket. "Holy shit," Jules muttered as he scoped out the engine.

"Okay," Ethan said, "a *lot* of attitude."

"She fast in the straights?" someone asked.

"The hell if it ain't," Kale answered. "Fast in the corners too."

"Never figured a Miata could look like a street racer."

"It's the fender arches," Ethan said, all business as he lost himself in the details. "They're modified to fit the wider wheelbase. Changes the whole look."

They moved aside as he pointed out features, answered questions, and talked specs. Brooke was left behind as words like supercharger, third generation, and ACT race clutch were thrown around. Not that she was interested, but she listened with acute curiosity as Ethan continued to mingle. He was in his element scoping out other cars, relaxed. And incredibly sexy.

"You his girl?" said a voice behind her.

Brooke twisted around to find the woman she'd noticed earlier. "No," she answered quickly, uncomfortable under such close scrutiny. "We're..." What were they, exactly? She recalled his earlier words when they were in her bed recovering from a round of impulsive sex. "We're just taking a break."

Ethan must have been following the exchange because she found him watching her with keen interest.

And he apparently liked her answer.

Later, they leaned against the Mazda's trunk, observing from the sidelines as the night exploded with the squeal of tires, the screaming of high performance engines, and the passionate shouts of money lost and won. Brooke wondered what the hell she was doing on a desolate road in the middle of the night surrounded by biting insects.

The road was one less traveled, aged with a patchwork of cracks, flanked by tall weeds, no streetlights in sight...and no cops, which reminded her that she was also in the company of a bunch of hooligans.

But the excitement was hard to deny. There was a certain freedom that came with breaking the law and the lack of concern for getting caught. One guy was on constant surveillance, keeping close tabs on the police scanner—something that Brooke found mildly titillating as the thing spat out a steady stream of violations through the speaker.

Another pair of cars lined up. Her heart accelerated along with the sound of gunning engines, knowing that the guy between them would throw down his hands at any moment.

"Right now, so much is going through their minds," Ethan shouted above the noise. "They're thinking about clutch, missing a shift, all the shit that can go wrong."

At the signal, the two cars jumped and then darted down the

narrow strip of asphalt, building up speed, cutting through the darkness, and quickly fading into the distance. Ethan continued to watch them, his expression a wistful one. "But when the hands drop, all is forgotten."

Brooke missed the outcome of the race because she was too busy staring at Ethan. He wore his passion for the sport like a second skin, and she began to understand Harper's concern.

He caught her watching him. "*This* is why I brought you here."

The tragic connotation of his plight overwhelmed her for a moment, but she answered him with a brave smile. "It's amazing." And she meant it. "They're like little glowing bullets fading into the night."

He nodded. "They bring it up to about five-thousand RPMs, and then it's all about punching gas and throwing gears. Danny Zuko would have been smoked."

Ah, yes. There was a lesson to be learned from all of this after all. "Definitely," Brooke agreed. "I'm very impressed, except for the flag-waver guy with the hairy legs and potbelly. Not exactly Cha-Cha DiGregorio."

They laughed over that one and Ethan tossed out a joke about the guy's ample bosom. "See? He qualifies."

Brooke laughed harder, hiding her face against his shoulder to stifle the sound. When she emerged, he was watching her, his smile fading. "People think it's about being a badass." His voice had gone husky, almost tender. "That it's about the pretty girls, the prestige, the money...but it's all about the cars."

The intimacy of their gaze grew with each lingering second until Brooke thought he might kiss her again. But instead, he shifted and looked away. She cleared her throat. "I've seen a lot of money change hands," she said.

"Yeah, but you know where it all goes?"

"Back into the cars?"

"Yup."

Taking a few breaths, Brooke ordered her heart to slow down.

Why did this feel like something more than a physical attraction all of a sudden? She and Ethan had been at war for nearly two weeks, yet in the thick of it, they'd managed to have the kind of sex that could easily be construed as making love. They were conversing like normal people and having fun together, sneaking looks and sharing past experiences. The only tension surrounding them now was the sexual kind, which she'd been struggling so desperately to keep in check. A deep-seated regret for her role in his troubles began to take root and grow.

She shifted her weight and toed a shape in the sandy earth beneath her shoes. "I'm sorry for what happened to you. I can see how much you love this."

The instant she said it, Brooke felt him close off. "You know better than anyone what it's like to have the rug pulled out from under you," he said in a stiff manner.

She flinched against the bite of his words. "I didn't mean I feel sorry for you, Ethan. You're too much of a survivor for that."

"From one survivor to another, right?"

"Why are you—?" As the engine noises drowned out her voice, Brooke covered her ears and waited. Their amiable truce was falling apart, and Ethan's mood was going downhill fast. The pause gave her time to regroup, especially since she was no longer interested in the plight of two cars and a stupid stretch of road. But this time, as soon as the hands dropped, one car shot forward instead of two. The one left behind lurched, sputtered, struggled to creep forward, and then finally died.

"What happened?" she asked.

Ethan shrugged. "Who knows? Could be the carburetor or a bad fuel pump." Then he looked right at her. "Or maybe someone cut the gas line."

The suggestion took her aback. "Really? Someone would do that?"

As another car passed them, its brake lights flashed red, illuminating the harsh lines around his eyes when he answered: "If they wanted to win badly enough."

His message hit home with the force of a slap. Brooke blinked at him, suddenly questioning everything they'd been through that night. She crossed her arms, looked down and fought to keep her voice from cracking. "Remember when Ken threw us in that corner office together and ordered us to spend an hour on the file?" When he didn't answer, she proceeded anyway. "I kept wondering why he never stuck around to make sure we were doing the work. And then I realized that the work was never his goal."

"He hoped we'd work out our differences." Ethan clipped out a laugh. "It was a waste of everyone's time."

"Was it? You don't think he got what he wanted?" Brooke watched as his expression became guarded. "When the job was taken out of the equation, we spent an entire hour without fighting. It may have seemed like a waste of time, but we learned two very important things: We actually have some common interests—the food for example—and we have it in us to compromise—the TV show." As she ticked off each point with her fingers, Ethan rolled his eyes. "It may sound mundane as hell," she continued, "but I think it was the first time I saw you as someone other than a complete asshole."

"What's your point?"

"My point is that we managed to pull it off again tonight. From the moment our clothes came off up to now, we managed to enjoy each other's company...at least I thought so anyway. But then I say something that triggers a reaction in you and I'm forced to consider the possibility it was all a setup."

Ethan pushed off the car and moved as if he were restless. "A setup, huh?"

"Well, you just made it abundantly clear that if I pull ahead of you and take the win, it's because I cut your gas line." She felt his sharp gaze even though she couldn't see it. "Analogies like that are just too clever for me to see coming, especially when I've been distracted by orgasms."

He must have finally picked up on the severity of her mood because he instantly stilled. "Brooke..."

"So thank you, Ethan," she said with a chill in her voice. "For reminding me how close to the surface our problems will always be."

Now that their "break" was officially over, he headed for the driver's door. "It's a long trip back," he said flatly. "We should go."

It wasn't technically that long of a trip, but it felt like a million miles as they rode back to Naples in stony silence. This time, she failed to admire the sporty black-and-gray interior that somehow still had a new-car smell, or how good Ethan looked behind the wheel. She was definitely no groupie and why she'd allowed herself to be put in this situation was beyond her. *Take a drive with me?* Was she insane? This was the man who had repeatedly accused her of some pretty despicable things, things he still wholeheartedly believed. By the time they rolled into her parking lot, Brooke was in a fine rage, thoroughly convinced he'd staged the entire night with one goal in mind: to get a confession from her.

He pulled up to the sidewalk and let the car idle as he waited for her to get out. Her knuckles tightened on the door handle. "You know, I understand why you want to believe it so badly. The end is close, and we both have a lot to lose. But I didn't deserve this tonight, Ethan. It was a prick move."

"You're right." When she looked back, it was to find him still harboring a foul mood in the glow of the dash. His eyes were trained forward. "I think it's safer if we just keep our distance."

He wasn't even going to try to deny it. "Agreed," she said, feeling worse than before. After exiting the vehicle, Brooke slammed the door, and as the Mazda drove away, she didn't look back.

All she wanted was to get home.

HAVING SEEN HARPER AND ADRIANNA OFF AT THE
airport the next morning, Ethan made it to work a half hour late. His
sister's parting words resonated in his memory and only grew louder
the closer he got to Monroe Graphics.

*You make it work here, Ethan. I'd hate to see you run back to South
Dakota because of some girl.*

Harper had picked up on his mood as soon as he made it back
home the night before. He'd confessed to going to Fort Myers since
the smell of exhaust fumes and burnt rubber was a little hard to mask.
But he'd also quickly allayed her fears by explaining *why* he went, that
Brooke had been with him the whole time, and that things had ended
badly with no resolution to their problems.

It was pretty much his fault, he knew. Sympathy always triggered
the asshole in him, and he should have denied her accusation of staging
the whole evening. He *hadn't* staged it; he hadn't even considered
going to her place until his car had magically appeared in her parking
lot. But it didn't change the fact that Brooke had failed to give him

what he wanted—the truth. He wondered why he thought he could get through to the woman in the first place.

Of course he knew there would be conflict, only the sparks between them had flown in an entirely different direction. When Harper had guessed as much, she seemed way too satisfied, to the point that he was instantly sorry. After telling her to go to hell, she'd laughed and thrown a couch pillow at him.

Finally, she'd said, *a woman who keeps you on your toes for once.*

When Ethan dumped his things at his desk, Shannon appeared from her office. She greeted him with a hopeful look, reminding him of the way they'd left things the day before, which only reminded him that he'd forgotten to apologize to Brooke for the false accusation of locking him on the roof. Shit.

"Have you seen Brooke?" he asked, ready to get it out of the way first thing so they could go on with this damned competition without any regrets.

Shannon's face instantly fell. "Break room, I think," she mumbled.

Sure enough, that's where he found her refilling her mug from the coffeepot. Letreece was also there, fishing a snack out of the vending machine. "Hey, handsome," she said, and ripped the package open with her teeth. "Come by the desk later. I have something to show you."

"Sure." Ethan watched the receptionist leave, thankful that he'd get a few minutes alone with the woman he'd sought out. Unsure of her mood, he turned to Brooke, who was watching him over the rim of her coffee mug.

"It's a new sign-out sheet," she offered before he could speak. "For people who go to the roof, just in case."

He could sense her struggling to stay cool and detached when she'd probably been awake all night staring at the ceiling as he had. He cleared his throat again. "Last night…"

"Ethan…I know."

She knew what?

"You'd rather forget about it," she answered for him. "And so would I." Then she attempted to brush past him.

He blocked her retreat. "I was going to say that the reason I came over was to tell you Shannon confessed to locking me on the roof."

"Oh, that's…good."

"But I also wanted you to know that it doesn't change anything. I'm watching, paying attention now more than ever."

As if his words had no effect, she skirted around him. "So you said. We also agreed to keep our distance, remember?"

Ethan wasn't fooled. Though she'd tried for an air of detachment, he caught the underlying hurt in her voice. The woman was definitely affected, but she also had to know where he stood, especially after the mixed signals he'd given her last night.

For most of the morning, things continued in a tense haze. They both spent most of their time on the phone, in the conference room, and out of each other's hair. But as a result of his ten o'clock meeting with Byron Chandler of Country Club Yachts, Ethan's mood finally began to turn around. Not only had he just bagged a two-hundred-thousand-dollar ad campaign, his position as VP was all but secured.

When they exited the conference room, Mr. Chandler—who sported an ascot with the club's moniker—took the unlit cigar from between his teeth and pointed. "Hey, don't forget to try that little Korean place in Old Town. I'll call ahead and make sure they treat you right."

"I'll do that, Mr. Chandler." Ethan clasped hands with the man, hoping to hide his extreme dislike of Korean food.

"Eh, call me Byron. I like you, kid. You remind me of myself when I was younger."

Knowing full well that Brooke was within earshot, Ethan made a hearty introduction when Ken emerged from his office. "Byron, I'd like for you to meet my boss Ken Stevens. He's the one who took a chance on this little graphic-design business."

The three of them cracked jokes and went through a brief over-view of the project. Five minutes later, when the elevator doors closed after the departing yacht club president, Ethan gloatingly made his way to Letreece's desk.

"Guess who just landed the winning account?"

An emery board scratched across the tips of her fingernails. "You da man," she crooned with notable disinterest.

Despite the receptionist's lack of enthusiasm, Ethan whistled all the way back to his desk. When he got there, however, he decided to tone it down out of respect for Brooke's feelings. She would be quite upset right about now, probably even near tears over the loss of her lead.

But when he sat down, he heard her laughter from across the partition.

"We were all pretty goofy that night, Zack," she said. When she laughed again, he was fully tuned in to her side of the phone conversation.

"Well, I guess she didn't get the memo that no dogs were allowed, even the ones confined to a purse. Oh, yes, I remember. That poor thing chewed a hole through the netting just to get at that tumbler of scotch. You know what they say about dogs and their owners." Raucous laughter spilled from the earpiece.

Ethan smiled as he pictured her holding the phone away from her ear. He picked up his coffee mug and took a drink.

"So, tell me again how many billboards we're looking at."

The coffee shot out of his mouth. He swore, wiped his face, and shook his dripping papers over the wastebasket.

"Two bulletins, three digitals, and a wallscape. The convention center? I believe there's room for twenty-four street banners, but I'll check to make sure. Don't worry about that, we'll build up quite a diverse portfolio for you to fill those eight months before the elections. I don't really do that anymore. Monroe is under new management, Zack, but we have a great team of artists. I guarantee you'll love what they come up with. Yes, we'll outsource the printing, but we'll stay within your budget. Well, aren't you lucky to have such an abundance of wealthy backers." Another laugh. "I'm far from wealthy, but my commission for this project will keep the lights on for a while....What a lovely thing to say, thank you. Yes, be here by nine o'clock sharp so we can get an early start. See you soon, bye."

What the fuck was that? As Ethan stewed over the distinct possibility that he'd just been cock-blocked by this Zack person, Brooke punched in another number. "Diana Plake please. Thank you. Hi, it's Brooke. I need a rough estimate from you." She read off the dimensions for three vinyl billboards and twenty-four street banners. Ethan waited with bated breath. "Can you have it to me by this afternoon…? You're a lifesaver. Thanks."

When she hung up, he heard Roger's voice next door as well. "I see you're feeling better today."

"I am, Roger, thank you."

Ethan's growing sense of unrest quelled a bit when he realized why she was feeling better. *It's amazing what multiple orgasms can do for a woman's disposition.*

"Did our telephone conversation last night help?" Roger asked.

"Yes, it certainly did."

Her chair rolled, and there was a rustling of fabric. With a frown, Ethan peeked around the partition to see them in a fond embrace.

"You know I can't stay mad at you," she said, her voice muffled over his shoulder. "You're my friend and I need your support." They parted, and Ethan ducked back into his cubicle before they noticed him.

"Thank God," Roger murmured. "I was so worried I'd lost you."

Brooke kept her voice equally low. "As long as we're always honest with each other, we're solid."

"Does that mean you'll have lunch with me today?"

"I can't. I'm having lunch with Sid."

"Oh."

Ethan sat back in his chair, completely dumbstruck. What the *fuck?*

"But if you're buying," Brooke said with a smile in her voice, "I'll take a rain check."

By 10:45, Ethan had been forced to hear Brooke's endless string of calls for her jackpot project. His high from earlier that morning was gone. His mojo was a no-go. And he would be screwed if he didn't find an even bigger client by tomorrow afternoon.

But what bothered him more than that was her rekindled trust in Roger. The guy had hooked up with a woman who'd wronged her in many ways, and it took her only twelve hours to forgive him. People didn't become VP by letting themselves get walked all over like that.

And, as if he could forget, Sid was the hard-up red-haired guy he'd run off last night. Apparently, she had felt the need to call him back as soon as Ethan left. Didn't she know that all he wanted was to get in her pants?

Leave her alone for two seconds...the woman obviously needed guidance and a stark reminder of just whose body she screamed for.

Knowing he shouldn't even consider what he was about to do, Ethan waited until he heard her gather her purse and keys. He let her walk by and then got up from his desk and followed. When she reached the lobby, he grabbed her elbow from behind and steered her away from the elevators.

"What—what are you doing?"

He pushed her into the stairwell and forced her up the stairs. She grumbled all the way. "Ethan, let me go! Quit pushing me!"

"Then walk," he growled.

"Unless you want to congratulate me, I don't have time for you right now."

When they reached the roof, he shoved her into the brutally hot sunshine, ignoring the fact that he'd vowed to never go up there again. "If this Zack guy qualifies as a new client," he said as he pushed the brick doorstop into place, "I'll give you all the congratulations you want. What I want to know is what happened after I dropped you off last night."

Her mouth gaped in astonishment. "That's none of your business."

"Bullshit," he snapped. "We have unbelievable sex and that prompts you to call every guy who wants in after me?"

"Oh, don't flatter yourself," she hissed back, her ponytail whipping around her shoulders. "The only reason you came over last night was to prove a point."

That hadn't been the reason, but it sounded better than the

truth. To admit that he lost control at the sight of her entertaining another man was unthinkable. He'd told himself it wasn't jealousy, but the green-eyed monster inside him now was pretty damned hard to deny.

"And since I went to bed with you," she continued, "I was forced to remember what you said about sexual integrity. I obviously have none, so why should I condemn Roger for the same thing?"

"So now *you're* proving a point by forgiving Roger for sleeping with Shannon and sticking it to me for sleeping with you."

"What? Wait…Roger may be weak, but he's not a player. And how did you know he slept with Shannon?"

Ethan squinted in disbelief. "You really expect Letreece to keep something like that to herself?"

She threw up her hand. "Well, *I* didn't tell her."

"No, you just forgot that the hallway has one hell of an echo." He took a step closer with pointed finger. "And if this vindictive streak prompts you to get back at Shannon, just remember she'd sell us out in a heartbeat if Ken were to question her about the darkroom."

Brooke swallowed hard and looked away. "I didn't mean for it to get out. But if she did say something about us, he'd never believe it. Even I don't."

Oh, please. Ethan could feel her desire raging from there. "I realize it's a hard pill to swallow," he said darkly, "but every time we're alone together, you break into a sweat."

"You're delusional," she scoffed.

"That's not a denial."

Brooke shook her head and held a hand up to block the sun. "Look. If you want confirmation, then yes, the sex was good. But we both know it wasn't anything serious, and I just want to move on."

Ethan barked out a derisive laugh. "I suppose you mean with the carrot top?"

"Sid is the exact opposite of you," she lashed out. "He's fun, he's decent, and he doesn't think I'm a criminal."

"That all sounds really sweet, but it'll never last without chemistry."

"We have plenty of chemistry!"

"Obviously, which is why you sent him home and fell into bed with me."

Brooke set her jaw, hiked up her purse strap, and stepped around him. "An unfortunate mistake that we both know will never happen again."

It was the same thing he'd told himself over and over again up until this very moment. But just who the hell were they fooling? "Oh, I think at this point it's a given."

His words stopped her in her tracks. She whirled around and got in his face with a scowl. "You aren't as irresistible as you—"

He shut her up with a kiss. The woman asked for it, daring to put her lips within reach of his, and frankly he was tired of the denials. It was time for her to own up to her attraction for him despite the risks, despite the consequences. When she attempted to back away, he walked with her until they reached the shaded side of the stairwell. There, he pinned her against the brick, refusing to relinquish her mouth until she stopped fighting him.

The moment she did, her purse and keys dropped to the gravelly floor. Sensing his window, Ethan let up a little and waited. Sure enough, she picked up where he left off, chasing his mouth in a bid to keep the kiss going. It was a victory unlike any other he'd experienced, because now she would never be able to deny again just whose body she yearned for.

"You can lie to yourself all you want, Brooke," he panted between kisses. "But the truth is I've never had a woman respond to me the way you do."

"Ethan...I don't want to want this."

"But you do." She whimpered and he spread his hands along her outer thighs and slowly lifted her prim skirt until it was bunched around her waist. The kiss deepened into a feverish, sensual dance of tongues, but he wanted more. "I want to taste you again," he whispered against her mouth. "Open up for me."

She moaned and broke away for much-needed air, but he was

ruthless in his quest to thoroughly demolish her walls and show her that she was his to mold however and whenever he chose. He plundered and teased until she was squirming beneath his hands, parting her legs and thrusting her hips into his touch.

"Do you know how wet you are?" he asked, feeling the moisture from outside her panties. "Do you want me inside you, Brooke?"

"Ethan…"

"Tell me now."

"Yes!"

He moved her panties aside and shoved three fingers deep inside her. A new wave of her desire came flooding down until his hand was coated with it. All he had to do was make a few circles with his thumb and she'd come for him, but he wasn't in the mood to give her pleasure. He wanted her to be miserable—to punish her for torturing him with another man. So he pulled out, brought his fingers up and grazed them across her lips. As her eyes opened, he bent down and licked the slick, glossy evidence from her skin.

"Mmm." The sound came from deep in his throat. "Tastes like one hell of a response to me."

And, though all he wanted was to rip off her clothes and make love to her on the rooftop, he had a point to make. So he stepped away and pulled a handkerchief from his breast pocket. "Enjoy your lunch with Sid."

He effectively left her there drunk with her desire for him. It was a mean thing to do, but he was feeling particularly nasty at that moment. As he loped down the stairs, drying off his hands, a pair of flashy high heels came into view. He screeched to a halt, shocked to find Shannon waiting for him on the landing with her arms crossed.

"You need to get a handle on your feelings for her," she said, confirming that she'd heard at least some of the turbulent exchange on the roof.

"I don't have feelings for her," he snapped, "at least not that kind."

Shannon unfolded her arms and jabbed a finger into his chest. "Yesterday you made me see how badly I've been behaving. I realize now that I may have ruined our friendship completely. But as a *friend*, it's my turn to hold up the mirror now."

Ethan shifted uncomfortably. "Don't turn this into a big deal. Brooke and I just let things get the best of us sometimes, that's all."

"And I've learned how to read your moods, Ethan. You're so scared right now you can't see the difference between love and hate, because as far as you're concerned, either one is worthy of your cruelty."

Feeling as if he'd just been smacked with a sock full of quarters, Ethan watched her disappear back into the lobby. He looked upward and noted that Brooke had not attempted to leave the roof yet, no doubt still recovering from his very cruel gesture.

No. He was *not* in love with her. Shannon was just being Shannon, delivering her meaningless jabs when she could since he'd shunned her friendship. The fact that she could on occasion offer kernels of adult wisdom had no effect here.

With a sudden surge of self-loathing, Ethan reentered the lobby and headed straight for the men's room.

"You forgot to sign the sheet!" Letreece yelled after him.

WHILE BROOKE WAS AT LUNCH, ETHAN BROODED
at his desk, trying unsuccessfully to block out his thoughts of her.
Shannon was right. He needed to back off and get his shit under
control. Let Brooke jump Sid's bones in the back of the liquor store
since he'd effectively left her in the mood for sex.

Harper would get a kick out of that one. Since sugar helped calm
his nerves, Ethan dug into his jar of candy corn and jammed a bunch
of them into his mouth at once. That's when Ken's shadow fell across
his cubicle.

"Ethan, do you know where Brooke is?"

In the back of some liquor store getting her freak on with Sid. "At lunch,"
he grumbled through the sugary mass.

Ken sat down on the corner of his desk with a look of perplexed
wonder. "I just received an interesting call from Zachary Parks, one of
the state's congressional candidates."

Ethan's gaze shot up and he swallowed. "Brooke's new account?"

Ken took a piece of candy from the jar, popped it into his mouth, and immediately made a face. "Ick. These things will kill you one day." While Ethan patiently waited, he finally continued. "Anyway, Mr. Parks's is a new client, but also an old friend of Brooke's family. He requested that I allow her to handle the designs for his campaign."

Ethan was taking in this piece of information, wondering if Zachary Parks' partiality would disqualify him as new business. "You mean *supervise* the designs for his campaign," he corrected absently.

"No, I mean *create* them." The two men stared at each other for a moment. "Turns out she was an artist here before she worked in management."

An uncomfortable feeling entered Ethan's stomach. "You're kidding."

"In fact," Ken continued, "he said she was the most gifted artist he knew and that I was wasting good talent by confining her to the administrative department. By the time we ended the call, I felt thoroughly chastised."

"Did you tell him she failed to mention anything about it?"

"I was too busy wondering why her father hadn't mentioned anything about it."

Ethan guessed it wasn't a crime to hide artistic talent while working at a graphic-design firm, but it *was* suspicious. As soon as Ken ducked back into his own office, Ethan checked the time. Brooke should return from lunch in about ten minutes, and it looked like he would spend his own break getting to the bottom of this new discovery.

It was then that Ethan realized just how much he enjoyed solving the growing mystery that was Brooke Monroe. The woman fascinated him like no other...obviously, since he couldn't seem to leave her alone. But why? She was dangerous and not above stooping to subterfuge in order to win his job right out from under him.

Yet she had fight and spark and bottomless eyes that could suck a guy in, chew him up, and spit him out as a different man. Her pull was greater since she was adorably unaware of this power. There was a vibrant, sensual temptress behind those puritanical walls of hers, and he wanted to set her free as he'd done before.

But—despite his suspicions of a woman who obviously kept secrets—what he really needed to do was apologize. There was no excuse for his behavior on the roof except what he wasn't willing to admit out loud. Part of him wanted to believe that Brooke was the vindictive, heartless robot he first thought her to be. It was an easy way out of the guilt trip he was now suffering from. The truth was, he'd probably left her humiliated and hating him even more than usual, which she had every right to do.

"Damn it," he muttered under his breath. What the fuck was wrong with him? He didn't want to act this way anymore, and he thought he'd made great progress over the last few months, despite what Shannon had said. Maybe it was the humidity or the heat. Was it possible to blame one's deplorable behavior on barometric pressure? Regardless, he had to man up and make things right.

BROOKE PULLED INTO THE SAME PARKING SPOT she'd left almost an hour ago. Instead of cutting the engine, however, she put her forehead against the steering wheel, directed the AC vent toward her face, and cranked it up high. As the cold air blasted against her burning skin, she took a deep breath. The smug bastard was up there somewhere, reveling in his power over her. And why wouldn't he? Every goddamned time he touched her, she went all soft and pliant like some shallow, adoring groupie.

But that would stop today. From now on, she'd conduct herself with the utmost professionalism and restraint; she would avoid Ethan Wolf completely. Next week, everything would fall into place since she'd have her office back and she'd be his boss...if she could keep from killing him, that is.

Her dignity in place, Brooke cut the engine, grabbed her purse, and stepped out into the sweltering heat. Halfway to the front door, her cold cheeks had already turned warm. The gardenia bushes nearby gave off their sultry perfume. She inhaled and let the exotic fragrance soothe the raging beast inside. Yes, it was working. Like magic, her calm was returning, just in time to show her face on the eighth floor.

She walked into the downstairs lobby, welcoming the cool air. As she waited for the elevator, the rest of her collective pride slipped into place.

Ding.

The doors slid open. Chin up, she walked inside and turned toward the panel of buttons...and there he was again: Ethan Wolf, lounging against the corner in his fancy gray business suit in typical ambush mode.

Just like that, a whole hour of meditative therapy flew out the window. "Hell no," she growled as a red haze overtook her.

He straightened and held up a hand as the doors slid to a close. "I wanted to catch you before you made it up—"

"No!" She swung her purse at him. He took it in the arm, so she did it again, this time with some shoulder behind it. He deflected the blow, which just pissed her off more. How dare he defend himself! "Put your damned arm down!" she yelled. Then, seizing the opportunity she'd always wanted, Brooke opened up on him with everything she had.

"Brooke, would you stop and let me—"

"You *asshole!*" she raged at him like a crazy woman. "Asshole, asshole, asshole!"

Finally, he caught her purse in midair and forced her against the wall. "I know!" he yelled back. Then, quieter as they panted against each other: "I know. I'm sorry."

She closed her eyes against the sincerity in his voice and groaned. "I don't want to hear it; I just want you to stay away from me." But even now, as he pressed against her, the powerful lust he'd built within her earlier surged with renewed force. "Get away from me, Ethan!"

He did, stepping back with his hands up. "I don't know what came over me earlier," he said, calmer now. "I just...I don't know, I guess I got a little jealous."

That one must have hurt. She figured it was more of a pride issue rather than jealousy. Somewhat placated, she straightened her hair. "You still suck."

"So take a few more swings if it'll make you feel better."

"Screw you."

Someone must have pushed a button because the elevator finally began to move. Ethan stayed on his side, though he still watched her. "Did you have lunch with Sid?"

Brooke wanted to say yes, that she'd molested the man in the backseat of her car or something. "No," she admitted instead.

The relief in his eyes was there and gone before she could fully grasp it. As it sank in, disbelief put a scowl on her face. Since the elevator had no alarm, she reached out and pushed the stop button. The carriage lurched to a standstill. "What the hell was that?" she said in the silence.

Ethan's gaze slid from the control panel to her face. "What?"

Leaving her purse on the floor, she approached him with a belligerent swagger. "You don't get to be *relieved*."

"I didn't say any—"

"Because I fully intend to invite him over later for a romantic dinner, lots of wine, and a long night of rigorous, feel-it-in-my-bones, fuck-you-Ethan lovemaking."

His visage hardened. "Do you even hear yourself?"

Toe-to-toe, she got in his face. "Lots and lots of hot chemistry-filled lovemaking."

He pushed her off with a dare in his eyes, but before he could speak, Brooke grabbed him with both hands and pulled him into a hot, wild kiss that came out of nowhere. As he floundered beneath the onslaught, a feeling of empowerment took over. She slammed him back against the wall, making her role as aggressor very clear. When she broke the kiss, it was with his bottom lip between her teeth. Ethan freed his flesh from her bite, dabbed at the blood she'd just drawn, and took on a feral look of his own.

While Brooke nurtured a voracious longing to tear him apart, they reached for each other again. This time they attacked with equal demand, equal hunger, foregoing the need to explore this time for an all-out assault that had only one purpose...to join. When a desperate moan escaped her throat, Ethan backed her into the corner, their breath mingling as she tore at the zipper of his trousers.

Her panties slid to the floor. He lifted her up. She wrapped her legs around him. He plunged. She gasped. With the ferocity of a wild animal, he fucked her against the cold metal while she clung to him for dear life.

They came hard together, suppressing their sounds of pleasure as best they could. Thank God. Brooke's eyes slowly opened. In the blurred reflection overhead, she saw him holding her there, half naked with her legs wrapped around him. They were trapped in a box with their pants down, still connected to each other while catching their breath. Maintenance would be by any time to check out the malfunctioning elevator...but no one seemed in a hurry to move. Ethan put his forehead against hers and kept her off the floor. "What the hell are you doing to me?" he rasped.

"I think we have a problem," she panted, finally willing to accept her end of it.

"You mean like an addiction?"

She nodded against him. "What else would you call it?"

Ethan's expression looked grim. "Something I've never felt before."

Brooke absorbed the impact of his words, knowing that they'd just knocked down an important boundary. As the air changed between them, her eyes welled up with tears. When one fell down her cheek, he wiped it away with his thumb and spoke with tenderness. "You scare the hell out of me, Brooke."

Her tears scared the hell out of *her*. Could she possibly be in love with the one man who stood in the way of her dreams? She swiped at her eyes. "Why?"

"Last night...it wasn't a setup. Everything that happened surprised me as much as it did you. I've never let anyone in like that, not since the accident. That's the main reason."

Feeling his words touch the depths of her soul, she closed her eyes. "And the secondary reason?"

"Because you have secrets, dangerous ones."

"I have nothing to hide," she vowed, knowing it was a partial lie.

"Then why didn't you tell Ken that you'd been a designer here?" It was posed without accusation, yet Brooke felt broadsided just the same. Ethan gave her a little shake. "Talk to me or we'll never get past it."

With a resigned sigh and her gaze trained upward, she replied, "It's irrelevant and no one's business."

"It's my business, Brooke. I need to know if you even *want* the position we're competing for."

A myriad of emotions coursed through her all at once. Though she questioned the wisdom of opening up to him, she needed him to understand. "I want this takeover to have never happened," she said in a low, strangled voice. "I want things the way they used to be. I want my freedom and my future back." She swallowed hard, desperately searching for a way to make him see. "That's something you, of all people, should understand."

His answer came after a thick silence. "I do."

Her eyes welled up even more. "Monroe Graphics was a part of me, just like racing was a part of you. *This* was *my* racing, Ethan. So the answer is no. I don't want your job. I want *Ken's* job, or the next best thing to it."

His expression dark and unreadable, Ethan asked, "How far will you go to get it?"

"Not far enough to leak information, if that's what you're asking."

There was definitely an internal battle brewing behind those enigmatic eyes of his. Brooke waited for the battle to continue, for the doubt and anger to resume. So when he leaned in and swept her up in a long, slow kiss, Brooke kissed him back with a mixture of hope and relief.

"You don't know how much I want to believe that," he murmured against her mouth. "But let's take this one challenge at a time."

"Meaning what?"

He leaned back again with a focused look. "First we finish the competition without any more games," he said firmly.

She smiled a little. "I'd like that."

"And then we face this thing between us."

The fact he acknowledged they had a "thing" sent funny tingles down her spine. Brooke nodded. "Okay."

"If all is good there, we'll have to face Ken and his strict rule against interoffice relationships."

And therein was the real challenge. If she were to lose, she knew in her heart that she could get past it, especially if he soothed her damaged pride with the promise of regular, mind-blowing sex. But Ken would never stand for it and probably force one of them to quit regardless.

And it wouldn't be Ethan.

If *he* were to lose, however, Brooke was pretty sure it would take a lot of trips to the darkroom to "lick his wounds" per se. Would he quit in order to build on this *thing* between them? It wouldn't be hard for him to find another job, maybe even a better one. He probably wasn't even tied down by a non-compete clause as she was.

But their office without him in it would be like the Tin Man without a heart. Brooke decided she didn't like that option either. She banged her head back against the corner in complete dismay. "Shit."

21

FOR THE REST OF THE AFTERNOON, ETHAN CARRIED on with business as usual, but with a ton of weight lifted from his shoulders. He'd ambushed Brooke in the elevator knowing full well he could suffer death by handbag, and with the full intention of taking his punishment. Her attack of a different nature surprised and thoroughly pleased him. Until then, he hadn't known just how deep his desire for her ran—something that was no longer a daunting chasm to explore.

They'd left the elevator on the fifth floor with immaculate clothing and a pact to spend the weekend together regardless of who won or lost. They'd get a nice room in the Florida Keys, cruise the sandy beaches, and possibly charter a fishing boat. After a few days of relaxation, romance, and a whole lot of exploration—mainly of each other—they'd face the coming week knowing by then if a relationship was possible.

With that in mind, Ethan worked hard to find the client that would secure his position as VP, knowing that Brooke was working just as competitively in the next cubical. However, the animosity was completely gone, replaced with subtle exchanges that reminded them of their private pact to rise above the competition. When they passed by each other, they'd steal a look. In the cramped space of the copy machine, they'd "accidentally" brush hips. When they committed their time to the two-inch file, their fingers happened to graze on occasion. He felt like a schoolboy who'd discovered girls for the very first time.

When they found themselves alone in the break room, anyone watching through the window would see two people going about their own business. It was the opportunity he needed to address a very serious issue, so he sat at the table sifting through the emails on his phone, doing his best to look inconspicuous while she washed out her coffee cup at the sink.

"Are you on birth control?" he asked.

"Mm-hmm."

He stole a look in her direction. "Because I wasn't exactly careful that last time."

She turned slightly, her lower lip between her teeth. "I didn't exactly give you a choice."

He hid his smile.

"How is your lip?"

His tongue skimmed over the tender mark she'd left. "Thoroughly digging those fangs." He couldn't deny the gratification that accompanied his new battle wound. Brooke was still the same starchy, frustrating woman who'd figured out what buttons to push from day one. He found that he liked her that way—yes, he definitely preferred the Brooke with the ponytail and glasses and upturned nose over the sexy seductress she'd pretended to be for Roger.

She dried her cup and put it back in the cabinet. "So do we leave after work tomorrow or Saturday morning?" she asked.

"After work. That way, whoever loses won't have a chance to change her mind."

With a smirk, Brooke rose to the bait of his subtle hint. "You remember that when I have to drag you out of here kicking and screaming."

He grinned. "You'll be the one screaming."

"I sure hope so."

As she walked past him and out the door, Ethan checked the sway of her hips, her sassy round bottom, and the long, shapely legs that wielded amazing capabilities in bed…oh, yeah. Screw the competition, he'd lost to her the moment she became the woman in the darkroom.

Through the closing door, Ethan's view was blocked by a beige suit. He snapped his attention back to his phone.

"Too late," Roger said on the way in. "I saw that."

Ethan ignored the remark, knowing full well he'd been busted.

"So, uh…," Roger fed some quarters into the vending machine, "how does it feel wanting a woman you'll never have?"

A smile curved his lips. "Still jealous, Kerrigan?"

Roger fished his snack out of the slot. "Not much anymore, but thanks for asking."

Ethan preoccupied himself with an email from Harper. "Does that mean you're sniffing up Shannon's skirt now?"

"You shut up about her, Wolf."

He looked up with raised brows. Guess that was a big, surprising "yes." Letreece's description came to mind and Ethan pictured a fuzzy cottontail floating in a tank of piranhas. "If the feeling's mutual, don't let Ken get wind of it," he said on a helpful note.

"Like you wouldn't rat us out?"

"It's none of my business."

Roger sat down next to him with a somber nod. "Thanks, man. Sorry I snapped at you."

Ethan gave the man a thoughtful look. "How many times have you defiled that darkroom?"

"You mean recently or all together?"

He grimaced and continued to thumb through photos of his niece enjoying the various benefits of first-class travel. "Never mind, sorry I asked."

The man shrugged and broke off a chunk of his candy bar. "When Mr. Monroe owned this place, it was sort of a secret mile-high club. Everyone wanted a piece of the action."

"But not Brooke."

"Hell no." Roger chewed loudly. "Not for lack of trying on her fiancé's part, though."

As Ethan suffered yet another shock of the day, he kept his eyes trained on the phone, no longer seeing the images there. "Fiancé?" he asked.

"Yeah. It was Brandon's way of trying to break through her 'no sex at the workplace' clause. But she hated the stigma of that darkroom and the fact that her dad turned a blind eye toward it; however, he did have some pretty satisfied employees."

As the man rambled on, Ethan absorbed this new information with a grain of salt. This Brandon guy was yet another important piece of Brooke's past that no one seemed to talk about, and she'd gone to great lengths to avoid using his name the night before. But that, at least, was easier to understand, especially if she was embarrassed about the breakup.

But *why* did they break up? The sex couldn't have been all that great if she'd never had an orgasm until now. Maybe the man simply didn't do it for her. Maybe he was a complete putz. The sudden urge to compare specs with the guy had Ethan regarding Roger with a sideways look. "So, uh…what did this fiancé of hers do for a living?"

"He was the systems admin at the time."

"Here?" When Roger nodded, Ethan asked, "Her father didn't mind her dating a fellow employee?"

"Brandon was the exception. Her parents loved him, at least until he started coaxing *other* women into the darkroom. But he taught Brooke everything she knows about running the systems department."

A sense of unease pervaded Ethan's bones. Had he just heard right? Brooke knew how to run the systems department too? Though he wanted to dig further, that would probably stop the flow of information, so he took a different approach. "She mentioned having her hands in everything," he said instead.

"Like what?"

"Like the creative department."

Roger must have decided the subject was safe enough because he leaned in and pointed toward the general direction of Brooke's desk. "That there is the most restless woman you'll ever meet. She gets bored easily, has to try this and that." He sat back once again, completely at ease. "Monroe Graphics was her baby, a place where she could dabble in everything and change it up when she wanted to. Toward the end, she was working on her dad pretty hard to add website design and security to our repertoire of services, which of course she'd head up. It was her new 'thing.'"

His sense of unease doubled. If Brooke were to entertain the idea of hacking into his or Shannon's files, she wouldn't need Roger when she was fully capable of doing it herself. Was that why she had so adamantly defended Roger? Because she knew for a fact he wasn't the one spying?

THAT SAME QUESTION STILL BURNED IN ETHAN'S gut when he found himself at Brooke's doorstep once again three hours later. They'd agreed to stay away from each other until Friday after work when they'd toss their packed bags into one car and head off to a whole weekend of unmitigated play.

But he had to know. Before he committed himself to such a scary thing as an actual relationship, he had to know if he could trust her.

When he pressed the doorbell, a Latin woman with long dark hair and a curious smile answered the door. "Uh…," he checked the brass numbers beside it. "This is Brooke's townhouse, right?"

The woman lifted a sculpted eyebrow. "You don't remember me?" she asked.

Ah, right. It was her friend from the carwash; funny how that particular face was pushed aside in favor of a certain redhead with a knack for pushing his buttons.

He grinned. "Is it Miranda?"

Her answering smile was brilliant. "Very good, Ethan." Then it dissolved into a dry look of censure. "What are you doing here?"

"Just need to see Brooke for a second."

"She isn't here."

Ethan checked his watch, wondering if he should abort his mission for answers since Brooke had company. "How long will she be gone?"

Miranda, dressed in a purple halter top and cutoffs, lounged against the doorframe. "As long as it takes to buy frozen pizza and popsicles."

He squinted with revulsion. "Sounds delightful."

Her ample chest shook with a throaty chuckle. "I take it you'd like to come in and wait for her."

"If you don't mind."

To his amazement, she moved out of the way, giving him access to Brooke's private domain. When she closed the door behind him, she asked, "Don't you two hate each other?"

This meant that Brooke had decided to keep their "truce with benefits" a secret. Didn't girlfriends talk about everything, especially when it pertained to men? Unsure of how he felt about that, Ethan scoped out the living room with a keener eye than the night before, searching for clues that he was in the domain of an artist. "I'm surprised you even let me in."

The bracelets on Miranda's wrist jingled as she ran a hand through her thick mane of hair. "I have this perverse love for drama," she purred. "Brooke and I are polar opposites in that regard—which is why we get along so well."

They made small talk while he familiarized himself with Brooke's home. The complex was modern, clean, and in a nice neighborhood. She probably shelled out nearly two grand per month in rent. The open floor plan and recessed ceilings made it look bigger than it actually was. He suspected that she'd made her bedroom out of what was intended to be the family room, and that the actual bedrooms were at the top of the stairs beside the kitchen.

What was up there? And how easy would it be to get Miranda to show him?

"It's her studio and guest room," Miranda said, breaking him from his reverie.

Ethan chuckled, again asking, "Am I that transparent?"

"As a starving lizard."

He followed her into the kitchen. "Sounds creepy."

She got a glass from the cabinet, filled it with what looked like iced tea and held it out to him. "Are you a creep, Ethan?"

"I don't want to be." He took her offering and, after a tentative sip, deemed it safe. "I actually apologized to Brooke earlier today. Something I don't do often."

A gleam filled her dark, exotic eyes. "Good for you, Mr. GQ."

Ugh. He hated that label and thought it was mighty judgmental. Did Brooke call him that behind his back? Probably. She *used* to despise him after all. "So, uh...she was a graphic designer for her father," he said.

"Mm-hmm. A damn good one."

"You said her studio is upstairs?"

"Yes, why?" she asked, tongue in cheek.

He gave a noncommittal shrug. "I'd love to see her work. We have a very spoiled lead illustrator who could use a good kick in the ass." In fact, if Brooke was good enough, he might convince Ken to send Bill Knight back to South Dakota. She could lead that department if he won VP, and the problem would be solved.

Miranda considered him for a moment over the rim of her glass. She must have detected the sincerity behind his request because she crooked her head in the direction of the stairs. "Come on, I'll show you."

Ethan smiled. "Even though she may not like that?"

"Sometimes Brooke can be her own worst enemy. I think it's time she let you in." He moved to follow. She pointed toward his glass. "Please leave that down here; she doesn't allow drinks upstairs."

He obediently set the dripping glass down on the island's surface. "Why not? Is she a neat freak too?"

"More like a geek. Too many electronics."

When she led him into the studio, he was a bit stunned to find a workstation topped by a bank of high-tech computer screens and equipment. On the other side of the room was a drafting table littered with rolls of canvas, textured papers, and open cabinets filled with a wide variety of art supplies. Next to the drafting table was a large-format printer, much like the ones in the creative department at work. He lifted a roll of paper from the shelf below it and held it up to find four complex graphic-design ads situated in a rectangular pattern. They all advertised various ways to use a popular local brand of rust remover.

"Those are hers," Miranda said, peering over his shoulder. "She used to bring her work home a lot."

"Why doesn't she still do this?"

"Her mother, who was a co-owner, developed a heart condition and had to retire. So her father needed Brooke to pull double duty for a while. She put in way too many hours if you ask me, but she didn't exactly have a personal life after Brandon left."

Her dour look indicated that she'd offered too much information. Ethan dismissed her concern with a glib, "You aren't the first to mention him."

On the drafting table, he saw a sleek poster for Learjet, some low-light motion graphics for a roller skating rink, and a serene underwater oasis for a local spa. "These are…incredible." He held up the underwater oasis. "This one's hanging in the office." Miranda nodded and he wondered how many more works of art in the office belonged to Brooke. "Did she go to school?"

"Nope. The other Monroe designers tutored her a little, but it's mostly just raw talent."

"What in the hell is she doing in the administrative department now? I'm sure Ken would pay her plenty as a designer."

Miranda plopped down into the desk chair and barked out a laugh. "Do *not* ask her that. She'll think you're dissing her management capabilities."

"I think I'll take that risk," Ethan said with a frown. Why should he give up his position to a woman much better suited for other jobs? "Miranda, I understand why she's pissed. I have a feeling it has more to do with her loyalty toward you and Amy and all the others who lost their jobs. She made that pretty clear from the start. But I'll bet money Ken won't let her rehire any of you regardless of her authority as vice president. He's not a pushover and he doesn't make those decisions lightly."

"Ethan...," Miranda sat forward and rested her elbows on her knees, "we aren't exactly holding our breath. Hell, Amy already found a job. We know Brooke's intentions are good, but we aren't her only excuse. She was unhappy in just one department. When her dad let her move around, she found this nice balance that kept things fresh. She got to feed her creative side, her techy side, her administrative side.... Her father gave her that freedom. Ken Stevens won't. Now she can't even start fresh with her own graphics business because of that non-compete clause in her contract. Unless she's laid off, of course, which would hurt your company more than help it."

This only strengthened her motive to cheat. Though Ethan desperately hoped that wasn't the case, he couldn't ignore the damning clues that kept surfacing. He looked past Miranda and drank in all the hardware beneath the bank of screens that was somewhat concealed by the shadow of the desk. Some of it was broken open and partially stripped. Strange contraptions were connected via USB ports to the only computer tower with a glowing power button. He walked over to get a closer look at some printouts scattered across the desk. Most of it was gibberish, but the corner of a notepad peaked out from beneath the pile.

"I don't think she'd appreciate you going through that," Miranda said behind him.

"She has nothing to hide." Ethan echoed her words to him in the elevator that were spoken with such conviction and emotion when they were truly connecting for the first time. He pulled the notepad out and instantly recognized her wild scrawl. Several things popped out at once.

Miranda began to pull on his arm. "Come on, I think you've seen enough."

He shook her off and kept reading.

Voices came from downstairs and a door slammed. Brooke was home and she wasn't alone. He looked at Miranda.

"Amy's here too," she explained. "We sort of ambushed her."

"Yeah." His voice was tight. "She tends to frown on that."

"Miranda!" Brooke called from below the stairs.

The woman winced. "If she finds you going through her stuff, *I'll* be in trouble." She ripped the notepad from his grasp, stuck it back beneath the papers, and forced him to follow. "Coming!"

Armed with what he'd learned, Ethan descended the stairs without an ounce of expression on his face. Brooke was waiting at the bottom, her eyes practically burning with guilt. It wasn't until then that Ethan knew for certain his suspicions about her had been well justified. The disappointment that coursed through him quickly turned to anger... then to betrayal.

The woman barely breathed as she watched him take the last step. She swallowed. "What are you doing here?"

He answered with a cold sort of detachment: "Learning more and more about you as I go."

Her terrified gaze darted to Miranda. "Why did you take him up there?"

"He wanted to see your work," the woman explained with a shrug. "I didn't see the harm."

In the kitchen, Amy unpacked the groceries with wide-eyed curiosity. Ethan acknowledged her with a nod and then turned toward the front door. "Don't worry, I'm leaving."

"Ethan, wait—"

"What, Brooke?" He stopped and turned with a desire to shake the life out of her. They stared at each other for a few tense seconds. She was dying to ask him something. When the silence stretched on too long, he gave her no more chances to come clean on her own. "See you at work tomorrow," he said coldly and headed toward the door with the weight of crushing disappointment resting heavily on his shoulders.

And this time she let him go.

FRIDAY—THE LAST DAY OF COMPETITION—BEGAN strangely quiet. Brooke reached her desk, put down her belongings, and noticed that Ken's office blinds were closed. Ethan was nowhere in sight. Shannon's lights were on, but she wasn't around either. The sense of unease that had haunted her since Ethan's untimely visit the night before grew into a pool of dread. He'd seen something in her home last night. Despite Miranda's denials, she knew it to be true. The mistrust radiating from him in potent waves had not been her imagination.

She picked up her phone and dialed Roger's extension.

"Systems."

"Is Roger in yet?"

"He's in Ken's office."

The pool of dread turned into a pit of doom. He knew. And now Ken would know. Roger didn't have the spine to keep his mouth shut when put under that kind of pressure.

Her brain raced to stay ahead of the game. Shit, shit, shit…everything she'd done for this company was about to implode around her. Ken and Ethan already suspected her; they wouldn't understand. She'd never convince them.

The problem was that she couldn't even blame Miranda. Her friend was a matchmaker at heart and was only trying to give Ethan more insight into what made her tick.

Now, with only nine hours to go and a healthy lead under her belt, Brooke had a feeling that the competition was already over for her.

Ken's door opened. Roger walked out of it and shut it behind him. Brooke stood with a nervous edge as she watched him approach. The look on his face said it all.

She swallowed hard. "You told them, didn't you?"

The apology in his eyes came with a helpless shrug. "I may have said something to Wolf yesterday. I thought he already knew."

Ken's door opened again. Ethan's head popped into view, his eyes immediately searching her out. Their blue-gray depths were cold, lacking the warmth she'd come to know the day before and even the cocky assuredness from before that.

"Brooke. Would you join us, please?"

So professional and by the book; how did it ever come to this? Just one month ago, she was so close to running the business her father had built from the ground up. Now these people she considered as invaders were about to throw her out as if she never had a right to fight for it.

She glanced at Roger. It was clear the man was oblivious to the serious nature of her predicament. His attention darted between them and then his lips parted as it dawned on him that she was actually in trouble. She swallowed back the lump in her throat and walked toward Ken's office.

Shannon sat with her back to the blinds. Ken was behind his desk, searching her face for answers the moment she walked in. Ethan stood by the window, his mouth stretched into a grim line.

Ken gestured to one of the empty chairs. "Sit down, please."

She smoothed her skirt on the way down and sat primly on the edge.

"Do you know why we called you in here?" Ken asked.

Brooke fought back an urge to throw up. "I think I can guess."

"Why didn't you divulge that you'd also been a systems operator here?"

"For the same reason I didn't divulge I'd been a designer. It had no relevance in my bid to secure the vice president position."

Ethan spoke: "Is it also because you wanted to spy on this company without drawing suspicion to yourself?"

"No."

Ken: "Did you spy on this company, Brooke?"

She swallowed and stared down at her hands. The sound of her heartbeat drowned out the accusatory thrum of Shannon's fingernails on her chair. Her worst nightmare coming true, Brooke answered with a quiet "Yes."

"I knew someone had been hacking into my computer!" Shannon burst out. "I started noticing discrepancies in the dates on my confidential files, ones I knew I hadn't opened that recently."

Ken's eyes raked over her from across the desk her father used to occupy. "Do you know anything about that?" he asked softly.

Brooke clenched her hands together to stop them from shaking. "I'd rather not say, sir." What she really wanted to say was *Yes. I took a peek, but not to leak what I found. It was to find out what was worthy enough to keep an eye on.*

It was what she would have done as systems administrator. But these three people would never understand that or believe her.

Ken released a loud breath and settled into a pose that meant business. "Ms. Monroe, since discovering your technical background, we checked your computer."

Her eyes closed.

"We saw you'd recently broken through security and bypassed our system altogether. In the process, you managed to avoid our internal monitoring software, which records your personal keystrokes, as well as your internet activity. Do you deny this?"

"No, sir."

"You realize that even though we can't see what you've been doing, the timing is what works against you in this case. Since yours is the only computer not being monitored, we have to assume you're the one who broke into Ms. Webber's confidential files. This provides me with ample cause to fire you."

Her heart breaking into a thousand pieces all over again, Brooke's answer came out hoarsely: "Yes, sir."

"Now is the time I ask if there's anything you'd like to add in your defense."

Brooke quickly glanced at Ethan, who stared at the floor in quiet condemnation. "Only that my intentions weren't to hurt this company," she said to him. Shannon made a sound of disgust. "But I realize why it would appear that way." She stood on shaky legs. "I assume you'd like me to clear out my desk now, Mr. Stevens?"

Ken sat back in his chair and regarded her with a look of professional detachment. Gone was any warmth he may have developed for her within the two measly weeks of her employment here. "I'm afraid so," he answered. "In the interest of our non-compete clause, you won't seek employment in this industry for the next year or have any business dealings with our current customers in that time. All of your accounts, including the Parks campaign, will be divided among the other account specialists."

She dared one more look at Ethan, whose only sign of emotion came from a slight pulse at his jaw. At this point, it would be best to leave as quietly as possible, so she only nodded and left the three of them to discuss her transgressions in private.

When she reached her desk, it was blurred by the tears in her eyes. The humiliation she'd just endured was beyond anything she'd ever experienced, including the sale of her graphic-design business. Her mind numbed over with needless worries. Who would take care of her Ficus tree? Was she allowed to take the coffee cup she'd used for years, or had Ken legally purchased that too? What in the world was she going to put her stuff in? A box, she needed a box.

Roger appeared, a wobbly distortion in her peripheral vision. "What happened?"

Brooke carefully lowered herself to the chair while keeping her gaze averted. "He fired me."

"Why?" he exploded. "Because you used to work in systems? That doesn't make any sense!"

"Because they found out I was spying on the company."

A deathly silence followed her statement. "You wouldn't do something like that," Roger said with a good dose of denial.

Her eyes welled up even more. "I did do it, Roger." She reached for a tissue, hoping she was still entitled to one.

"Brooke...," his hand touched her arm. "No."

"Ms. Monroe." Her eyes now dry, she looked over to find the security guard plunking an empty box on her desk. "I'm here to help you collect your things."

Of course, he was more likely there to supervise so that she couldn't take anything considered Master Ink property. It was the same practice that she'd exercised the few times she'd fired someone, only now the tables had taken a humiliating turn. She looked at her longtime friend with a plea in her voice. "Go back to your department, Roger. I'll be fine."

But it was a lie. He knew it. She knew it. She didn't even bother with the brave face. He took her hand, their fingers locking for a few moments. Then he squeezed it and let go.

Brooke watched him walk away, her heart pounding louder than ever in her ears. She felt a pair of eyes on her and turned around to see Ethan leaning against the conference room doorway with arms crossed.

"It's policy," he said in explanation for his observance.

Brooke knew exactly what he meant. He wasn't there to gloat; as vice president, he'd been appointed the job of supervising the exit of a terminated employee. It was quite clear that anything between them was over. He probably thought she'd been playing him all along; that her declarations of innocence were all an act; that her feelings for him had never progressed into something more.

How could she blame him? Sure, her intentions had been honorable, but as Ken said, they didn't know her. She'd hoped to catch the leak. In doing so, however, she'd pointed the finger at herself. The timing had simply not been on her side.

Brooke squared her shoulders and gathered her few personal items from the desk. Ethan quietly went through her briefcase to remove any company-related items. Once it was nearly empty, he looked up with the same professional detachment Ken had bestowed on her. "Is that it?"

She nodded.

"Nothing at home or in your car?"

She shook her head.

He closed the briefcase and handed it to her. Avoiding his gaze, she took it from his outstretched hand and added it to her other personal belongings.

Then she gathered her purse, took the box in her arms, and—amid the whispers and curious looks from the other employees of the administrative department—began her last journey toward the elevators.

With the security guard on one side and Ethan on the other, she passed by a stern-looking Shannon who'd positioned herself in the perfect spot to witness her walk of shame. Their eyes met and locked. Brooke noticed a touch of satisfaction on the woman's face. Careful to keep her expression blank, Brooke gave her nothing else to celebrate. All she could do was hope that some kind of proof would surface that Shannon was behind the leaks all along.

When they passed through the lobby, Letreece sat behind the reception desk with a frown of curiosity. The woman had become sort of a friend, but Brooke was too mortified to say goodbye. Besides, she was sure that Ethan would fill Letreece in when she was gone.

The three of them rode the elevator down in silence. She wondered if Ethan were reliving the wild memories they'd made in the very same corner in which she stood. If so, he showed no signs of it.

On the ground floor, the security guard walked with them only to the double doors. Ethan, however, continued to walk her to her car. She unlocked it, slid the box in the backseat...and then saw the small travel bag she'd packed for their trip.

Brooke froze, remembering now that she'd packed it with a strange sense that it would never be used.

"You saw my notebook, didn't you?" she asked. When he didn't answer, she turned to regard him. "Why didn't you tell Ken?"

Ethan looked off into the distance. "After we discovered you'd bypassed security, I didn't see the need."

Yes, that had been damning enough. But the notebook contained information she shouldn't know—specific details regarding high-end bids that belonged to other account specialists, details that could encourage Ken to file a lawsuit against her.

"Guess I should thank you then," she said.

"No, you shouldn't."

Brooke finally cracked. "Why did you do it, Ethan? Why couldn't you have just asked me last night? That's why you came over, isn't it? To find something damaging against me?"

"Because I don't believe that you would have told me the truth."

"Maybe it's because you wouldn't have believed me!"

Ethan swore, his face finally revealing the pain and frustration they both felt. "I blamed your fiancé for fucking up, but it was you, wasn't it, Brooke? He didn't want a wife who couldn't be honest with him."

His words, designed to inflict the utmost pain, forced her back against the car door. Ethan swore again and ran a hand through his hair. Sensing that he was about to apologize, Brooke reached for the door handle and pulled it open. "Take care of my Ficus."

When she got behind the wheel, he stopped her from shutting him out. "I shouldn't have said that."

"It doesn't matter," she snapped back, horrified by the agony in her voice. "You won the job, and you won't ever have to worry about my reasons for anything."

Resting a hand on the car roof, he leaned over and glared. "Regardless of what you might think, I didn't want to win like this."

"I'm smart enough to know I brought it on myself," she admitted with a heavy heart. "You were right, I'm too naïve for this job. Shannon wanted me out, and I practically helped her."

"Don't blame this on Shannon!" he yelled.

This was getting them nowhere. He would never believe the woman was guilty, despite all the shit she'd pulled. Brooke reached for the door handle and closed her eyes. "Goodbye, Ethan."

This time he let her close it. She started her car and backed out. He simply stood there, watching her leave the lot. She knew because she watched him too in the rearview mirror.

This was the best thing. If she'd delayed any longer, he would have found out the awful truth one way or another: that she was more than just naïve.

She was hopelessly, completely, and miserably in love with him.

ENSCONCED IN THE SAFETY OF HER HOME, BROOKE
dropped everything on the foyer floor, kicked off her shoes, and noted
the time with numb disinterest: 8:45 A.M.

She had spent an entire twenty minutes in the workforce that day.
She trudged up the stairs and entered her studio. Morning sunlight
sliced through the wooden blinds, casting a pattern across the desk.
She looked at her own private workstation through Ethan's eyes. After
a careless slip from Roger about her background, Ethan had come here
yesterday looking for answers.

On the verge of tears, she sat down in her chair, picked up the
phone, and made a call she'd avoided for weeks now. Her father's deep
voice filled the line. Still upset with his choices, Brooke fought the
now-familiar urge to call him Stanley and to control her tone. "Dad?
It's me."

There was a moment of silence. "I was wondering when you'd call.
There must be something wrong."

Her face fell. "How can you tell something's wrong?"

"I've been reading your moods since you were in diapers. Fess up."

The natural authority he exuded almost made her want to smile. God, she missed him. "I was fired today."

He cursed. "Why?"

She released a wobbly sigh. "I forgot that Monroe Graphics isn't mine anymore." Brooke put her face in her hand and fought to keep from thoroughly losing it. "And thanks to that non-compete clause, I can't even look for another job."

"Aw, hell. I was sure that after your initial disappointment, you'd settle in."

"Is that why you tricked me into working for Ken?" she sniped.

"Sweetheart, it was either that or stay out of the business altogether. I figured you'd eventually realize that my way was the better way."

Suffering from a sudden headache, Brooke undid the top buttons of her blouse and pulled the elastic band from her hair. "If it makes you feel any better, you were right."

"You like Ken, don't you?"

"Yes, I do," she admitted with a grimace. "Despite the fact that he fired everyone."

There was yet another pregnant pause on the line. "He only did that at my recommendation."

The blood promptly drained from her face. Brooke stared at the phone in horror. "What? You advised him to let go of our entire staff?"

"Something I never wanted you to know."

"Why would you do that?"

"Honey, Monroe Graphics was on the cusp of bankruptcy. It seemed that no matter what I did, we lost money."

She shot up from her chair. "I know that. I wanted to try and fix it, but you wouldn't give me the chance."

"Frankly, sweetheart, I didn't think you could."

Her pain doubled with those five words uttered by the man she looked up to more than anyone. "Thanks for the vote of confidence."

She heard her mother's voice in the background, pictured her asking who it was and the hope in her sea-green eyes when her father said her name. Then she heard a door shut in the background and knew he wanted a private moment. "The reason I advised Ken to start with new employees is because I strongly suspected we had a leak."

Brooke went still. Her lashes slowly lifted. "A leak?"

"Our high-end projects kept getting outbid by other firms. When I looked into it, I discovered a pattern that went back way farther than it should have. I didn't want to admit I'd let it go on that long, so when I sold to Ken Stevens, I told him about the problem."

Brooke ran a hand through her hair, her mind running wild with the only equation that made sense. "Why did you recommend that he keep Roger?" she asked, knowing that their old systems administrator was the only common link besides her.

"Roger is the one who helped me find the pattern," he answered. "I trusted him."

Then again, her father had just admitted to a certain naïveté of his own. Brooke let her new suspicions marinate for a while and then came up with a plan. "Dad…I need to go."

"But your mother wants to—"

"Tell her I'll call back later." She abruptly ended the call without even saying goodbye.

No wonder Ken suspected her. He knew about the leaks her father had just mentioned, so naturally he believed she'd used the same proven technique to compromise his takeover. And why wouldn't he, considering how vocal she was about the whole thing?

But she wasn't the only common link to Monroe's troubled past. There was another person who was much savvier than she when it came to cyber stealth. With a determination born from betrayal, Brooke turned on her computer. She plugged in her external hard drive, selected a file, and opened it. There, she found exactly what she was looking for.

She picked up the phone again and, taking a gamble, dialed the corner office's direct line without concern about how her call would be received.

"Ethan Wolf."

She closed her eyes and pictured him standing by her desk and enjoying the corner view of the bay marina. Only now, the image didn't hurt. It felt…right. "Ethan, it's me. Don't hang up, I'm about to do something completely out of character and admit I was wrong."

"I thought you already did that."

His tone was unforgiving still, but Brooke knew she'd reach him somehow. "I'm not talking about what went down in Ken's office. I admitted to spying, not leaking information."

He was silent for a moment. "I think it's best that we end this phone call right now."

"Wait!" she burst out in a rush. "I'm trying to help, and I think you know that."

"Do I?"

With a hand to her heart, it was all she could do to keep from crying. "Remember when you said you didn't want to win this way? It's because, aside from all the bullshit things we've done to each other, you're a painfully honest man whose loyalty runs incredibly deep. I'm not trying to score any points or get my job back. I accept that I am completely done with Monroe Graphics." She took a steadying breath. "All I want is to settle a score with a certain hack."

Her heart nearly stopped as she awaited his reply. When he finally spoke, there was hesitation in his voice. "You said something about being wrong?"

At least he was willing to listen. Shoulders sagging in relief, she twirled in her chair and faced the computer screen. "Yes. I've been focusing on the wrong person. I let my feelings for Shannon get in the way, and I completely overlooked the obvious."

"Why call me?" he asked. "Why not Roger?"

Her lips drew into a tight smile. "Because, in order to catch this person, we need to bypass the systems department altogether."

He let loose a muffled curse. "Not that I'm saying I'll go along with anything, but…what exactly do you want from me?"

Her smile faded. She stared at the icon on the bottom of the email she'd just composed, knowing just how absurd it was to even ask. "First and foremost I need you to trust me."

"God help me."

"I'm going to send a file to your personal email," she went on. "I want you to download it on your own machine, not an office one, and put it on a thumb drive. Then I want you to manually install it on Shannon's hard drive."

"I'm hanging up now."

Panic brought her to her feet. "Just hear me out! Then I'll leave it up to you to decide, and I'll never bother you again." When he refused to answer, she finally let go and did the unthinkable: She begged. "Please, Ethan. You don't even have to respond, just listen."

The continuing silence was killing her, but at least he hadn't hung up yet, so she rambled on and hoped for the best. "A good hacker will use a stealth program to spy on a targeted computer without being detected and without leaving an easy trace for the IT guys to find. What I'm about to send you is also a stealth program, but it's an anti-malware tool. The next time anyone establishes a connection with Shannon's computer, she should get a pop-up warning highlighting any suspicious activity. I'll need you to take a screen shot of that warning and email it to me so I can trace it."

"You realize what you're saying, right?" His voice nearly floored her with relief. He was there and he was listening. "You want me—a man you've despised from day one—to actually upload a stealth program to the computer of a woman you've also despised since the beginning?"

Brooke ran a hand down her face in abject misery. "That's pretty much it."

"You're a real piece of work," he accused her with bitterness.

"Like I said, it's entirely up to you. If you decide not to do this...I don't know, just keep in mind it's not only for me. It's for Ken. It's another way to keep an eye out, that's all."

"Brooke, if you're targeting a specific person, I'd like to know who it is."

Though it was tempting to say, it was something she couldn't bring herself to do. "No. I won't make any more accusations without actual proof this time. Besides, if I'm right, everyone will know." She was poised to hang up, but hesitated. "And Ethan?"

"What?"

"I don't despise you. Not anymore."

She placed the phone back in its cradle, preventing her from making an even bigger fool of herself. There was only so much humiliation she could take in one day. For now and for the sake of her sanity, it would be best to assume that Ethan wouldn't go through with it. If she didn't hear from him within a week, she would figure something else out. What that was, she didn't know, but at least she was now looking in the right direction.

With no human interaction to keep her grounded, the daylight hours may as well have been night and vice-versa. It was her own fault, but wallowing in a sea of self-pity and betrayal, Brooke had failed to answer her landline as well as her cell phone the many times they had rung over the weekend. Unless the caller ID displayed the number she was waiting for, she would continue to ignore them. The few times the doorbell rang, she ignored it and the voices behind it, knowing that it was in everyone's best interest not to answer. Though she kept careful watch for an email from Ethan, all others were ignored and trashed.

On Monday morning, Brooke rolled out of bed earlier than usual, determined to keep watch over her inbox now that the workweek had officially begun again. Any moment now, an email would arrive or her phone would ring and it would be Ethan sending her a screenshot of Shannon's desktop computer. Feeling like a mad scientist with her wild hair, bloodshot eyes, and cracked lips, Brooke waited as the popsicle wrappers accumulated on the island around her laptop. By 1:30 P.M., her inbox was cleaned out with still no word from Ethan. If he'd decided to use her program at all, wouldn't he at least have the decency to tell her? Was a hint or even a code word too much to ask for?

Still in her pajamas and more depressed than ever, she ate an afternoon breakfast of grapefruit and a buttered English muffin.

By Tuesday—the fourth day in a row with hardly any sleep—she was positive that Ethan hadn't used her program, since her hack would have certainly tried something by now. She finished the day in a deep state of depression with lots of alcohol to dull her pain.

On Wednesday morning, Brooke woke to the sound of pounding. Determined to ignore it as usual, she rolled over and covered her ears, sensing that she had yet to achieve even a couple hours of sleep. The word "police" spoken in a very loud male voice forced her to reconsider.

What the hell was going on? Was it a crime to want your goddamned privacy? After a brief moment of confusion over the amount of daylight filtering through the curtains, she stumbled out of bed, shuffled through the living room, and—under the weight of a crushing hangover—leaned heavily against the door with eyes closed. "I am still alive and no one is holding me hostage," she managed to croak out.

"Ms. Monroe, my name is Officer Warren and I'm going to need visual confirmation of that."

She opened her eyes long enough to check out her reflection in the ornamental mirror beside the door. "Believe me, you don't want a visual."

"I insist that you open the door, or I'll be forced to break it down."

What? Grumbling over the fact this was still a free country, Brooke fumbled with the locks. Everything was out of focus since her glasses were still on the nightstand, but she was afraid to get them lest the cop went commando on her door. Oh, what the hell. It was probably better that she couldn't get a clear view of his horrified reaction.

The last lock came undone. She opened up about five inches and stuck her face through the crack. "See? I'm still breathing."

"Yes," the blob in black said. "I can smell that. Your friends are concerned about you, Ms. Monroe."

Another blob moved behind him. Brooke blinked and squinted.

"Honey, it's me," came a familiar voice.

"Miranda?"

"I'm sorry to do this, but if only you'd answer your phone or your door once in a while...."

Brooke forced out a half smile for her blurry visitors. "Consider it answered. I'm going back to bed now."

"Wait a minute!" Miranda shoved her foot in the crack. "I went to a lot of trouble to check on you."

"You probably got this guy's phone number," Brooke replied with a deadpan stare.

"That's beside the point. You look and smell like something that fell out of a garbage truck. This is unhealthy behavior, Brooke."

She peered over Miranda's shoulder at the officer looming in the background. "Is it against the law to look and smell like a garbage truck?"

"Unless the neighbors start complaining about a strange odor, I'd say no," he said.

Funny. Before she could argue further, Miranda muscled her way in and spun around with a smile. "Thank you, Officer Warren."

His voice lowered to a seductive pitch. "Now, I told you to call me Shawn."

"Mmmm, I'll be calling alright."

Brooke rolled her eyes and shuffled back toward the bedroom as the locks clicked into place behind her. "Nice tactic, Miranda. You could have just asked me if I was okay."

The woman spun around again and kicked her way through the pile of belongings still littering the floor from last Friday. "How? You wouldn't answer my calls!"

Brooke yawned. "You called?"

"Everyone's called. Me, Amy, Roger, your parents...."

"Which is why I ignored it," she declared hotly.

Miranda followed her into her bedroom with the persistence of a bulldog. "I get that you're depressed, but you aren't allowed to blow off the people who care about you the most."

It was more like people she *thought* cared about her the most. "I'm going back to bed." Brooke paused at the entrance to her bedroom. "If you insist on staying, the TV remote is in the couch somewhere and the garbage disposal is clogged."

"Good to know," Miranda said with a dry smile and then promptly took her by the shoulders and steered her in the direction of the bathroom. "You are not going back to bed. You're getting in the shower where you will wash that disgusting hair and then you will brush those awful teeth. In the meantime, I'm stripping your bed sheets since I have a feeling those are the cause of my watery eyes."

"You don't have to take care of me," Brooke grumbled, "I'm fine."

Once in the bathroom, her pajama pants were yanked down to her ankles. Brooke yelped and covered her butt. "Jeez!"

"My God, these are one step away from compost." Miranda spun her around and, with a curled lip of disgust, yanked the purple-stained top up and over her head. "Grape popsicles do not constitute a meal. You are skin and bones, and the bags under your eyes are hideous."

"I can undress myself!" But Brooke was already naked and getting shoved into the shower stall. Miranda reached in and turned the knob. Frigid water blasted down from above. A choked scream echoed throughout the townhouse and probably across the Gulf of Mexico.

The shower door slammed shut. A towel and washcloth were flung over the panel of distorted glass. "If you even think of shutting this water off in under twenty minutes," Miranda yelled over the noise, "I will personally drag you out to the back yard and hose you down. Got it?"

"It doesn't take me twenty minutes—"

"Then soak! Stand under the stream and cry your eyes out like they do in the movies; just get over this damned funk already!"

And Brooke spent not twenty but thirty minutes following her friend's orders. Hot steam rolled upward and along the ceiling. As she washed and thought about her troubles, the tears started to flow. Then they came down in torrents. Now unemployed and no longer caring if the hack was caught, she considered the possibility of joining her parents in Texas. The thought of being pampered and babied for a few months wasn't such a bad one, though she was so damned mad at her father.

How could every single man in her life turn on her like that? Even Sid had lost his shine, since Brooke expected no less heartache from him. It was a given. The rebellious thought of becoming a lesbian briefly entered her mind. Girls were pretty, kind, and compassionate and weren't prone to bouts of chauvinistic cruelty.

But then she'd eventually be expected to sleep with one, which held absolutely no appeal for her whatsoever.

By the time she left the shower, Brooke's skin was pink and raw. Her eyes were the same, and her wet hair needed something industrial-strength to get the tangles out. Since all she had was a simple brush, she sat down at her vanity and spent another twenty minutes working at her hair until it was restored to its original, glossy shine. The humidity in there was stifling, and Brooke knew the moisture dripping from her body was as much sweat as it was water. But she wasn't ready to leave the confines of her bathroom. Miranda would force her to do some other healthy task like eating.

Actually, the thought wasn't as unappealing as before. Still wrapped in a towel, she got up and opened the bathroom door. Her stomach grumbled as the smell of butter and seared vegetables reached her nose.

Please, Lord, let that be an omelet.

"Get out here and eat some protein!" Miranda called from the kitchen. "Don't bother fighting it. I can almost hear you salivating in there."

Brooke emerged in a set of clean pajamas. "Nothing you say or do will get me in a pair of shoes today, so don't even try."

She ate her omelet alone at the kitchen's island with her laptop and coffee while Miranda cleaned her house from top to bottom. The washing machine was churning, the dishwasher was humming, and the surfaces had been cleared of the cumulative debris that was a mockery of Brooke's life. It was only 9:30 A.M., almost a respectable breakfast hour. She checked her emails with halfhearted interest. The first to be deleted were the handful from Roger with headings like "Call me" and "R U okay?" That and the fact that there was still no word from Ethan made her want to vomit the first real meal she'd eaten in days.

For the second time that morning, the doorbell rang. Brooke picked at her food and ignored it. It rang again. The stairs echoed with footsteps. "You and your closed-door policy are over," Miranda said.

Brooke frowned as she looked up. She was pretty sure that Roger had come by at least twice before to check on her. "Don't answer it! I don't care who—"

But the door was opened anyway. Voices soon came from the entryway, one of them painfully familiar.

IT WAS *HIM*. NOT THE TRAITOR WHO STOLE HER future, but the corner office bandit who stole her heart. If Ethan had decided not to use her program, what had possessed him to come over? Certainly not for a random booty call with the woman who'd left a bad taste in his mouth.

As she thought about it, Miranda came around the corner with Ethan in tow. "Look who it is, Brooke? Now aren't you glad I got here first?"

Brooke dropped her fork to her plate, swallowed, and tried not to notice how much she'd missed him. In his crisp suit and tie, Ethan was a picture of success, health, and abundant good looks. Even in a T-shirt and jeans, he exuded the self-confidence of a born leader.

Though she wanted to look away, his blue-gray eyes held her captive. His wavy hair begged to be touched. His mouth looked charming enough to eat. But his glare told her that he hadn't come for pleasure. With a jerk of his head, he indicated the need for a private word.

As she slowly rose from the table, she crossed her arms over her chest, painfully aware that she had no bra on beneath the thin pajama top. The state of her nipples may as well have been an advertisement of her desire for him.

"Miranda, do you mind?"

The woman looked back and forth between them for a moment and then barely suppressed a knowing smile. "I think I'll go tackle those sheets now."

The insinuation that they would have any use for the bed made Brooke's cheeks burn. Ethan, however, didn't waste a minute. Before Miranda was even fully out of sight, he grabbed her by the wrist and marched her up the stairs.

She quietly went along, her apprehension building as they entered the studio. Finally she asked, "What's this about, Ethan?"

He reached into his breast pocket and took out a piece of paper. "This." He handed it to her.

When she unfolded it, she saw a printed screenshot of a computer desktop. In the middle was a pop-up warning highlighting a discovery of suspicious activity. As soon as she realized what she held, it was as if the heavens opened up and rained joy down on her.

"It came up this morning," he said. "I know you wanted me to email it to you, but I wanted to be here when you traced it."

She looked at him in surprise. "I was sure you'd decided not to use it."

"I almost didn't."

But she could swear that his eyes said something different. They were dark as if a storm was brewing behind them. He was experiencing the same turmoil as she, but he was determined not to show it.

A bubble of insane laughter welled up at the thought that Ethan Wolf, no longer hampered by rules against office romance, would not touch her. Brooke turned away from him and focused on the task at hand: busting the hack.

Putting on her game face, she sat down at her desk and brought up her computer's home screen. She felt Ethan hovering. Excitement over finally getting the proof she needed to bring Monroe's hack to justice quickened her breath. She looked down at the highlighted area on the warning message Ethan had given her and began typing in the series of numbers. Halfway through it, her fingers paused in mid-air.

"What's wrong?" Ethan asked.

Brooke's heart was flip-flopping inside her chest. "When did you say this came up?" she asked.

"Look at the time." He pointed to the bottom right of the screen-shot. "Eight forty-five this morning. Shannon whispered in my ear, I took the screenshot, printed it out, and came right over."

But it couldn't be! "This doesn't make sense," Brooke cried in a state of panic.

"What doesn't make sense?" He knelt down to get a better look at the screen.

She turned to him with wide eyes. "This internal IP address doesn't belong to a computer inside Monroe Graphics. It belongs to *mine*." As she said it, her hands jerked away from the keyboard as if it was hot.

"But you haven't finished entering it in yet."

"I know it's mine, Ethan. What I don't get is how this could happen when I wasn't even up here at 8:45, I was downstairs taking a shower."

With an increasing sense of dread, Brooke finished her thoughts in silence. She wasn't up here...but Miranda could have been. Was it just coincidence that this warning waited to pop up the first time she'd let anyone walk through her front door?

Her computer system, with its rootkit programs to keep it stealthy, had been left on—an open invitation for any spy.

"Hey," Ethan touched her shoulder. "Talk to me. You look like you've seen a ghost."

When his voice brought her back to reality, Brooke found it suddenly hard to breathe. A friend had betrayed her, alright, but it wasn't Roger. "It was Miranda," she said out loud.

Sensing a presence behind her, Brooke turned around to find the woman of her thoughts in the doorway. Ethan rose up to his full height. They both watched as Miranda's chest rose and fell in dramatic breaths. "What are you two talking about?" she asked, her voice higher than usual.

Brooke got up from her chair. The stink of guilt was growing stronger with each step she took toward the woman. Unable to hold back, she slapped Miranda hard across her beautiful cheek. "How long have you been selling me out?" she ground out. "Coming here under the pretense of being my friend?"

Miranda's hair fell aside to reveal a face haggard with anxiety. "Brooke...what are you talking about—"

"Don't even think of lying to me! I can see it in your eyes!"

Very slowly, Miranda's face changed. Though still visibly shaken, she gathered her emotions behind a mask of hope. "I did it for you, Brooke. Everyone had just lost their jobs, and we all wanted to see you get that VP position." Her attention turned toward Ethan. "You can't blame me for helping a friend."

"But you weren't helping me," Brooke spat out through her misery. "You were helping yourself. And don't use my competition with Ethan as an excuse; this goes way back before Ken Stevens even entered the picture."

"That's not true!"

"What do you mean by that?" Ethan asked.

"The day Ken fired me," Brooke explained without taking her eyes off Miranda, "I called my father to tell him what had happened. He told me the reason the business had failed was because we'd been slowly losing our biggest accounts to a more competitive market. When he looked into it, he and Roger had come up with a pattern of high-end bids that had been beaten out by mere dollars and cents. The evidence pointed to a leak. I thought it was awfully strange that the leak had survived the takeover."

Ethan stepped into her peripheral vision. "So, naturally, you suspected Roger."

"Is that what you counted on, Miranda?" Brooke added, her eyes narrowing to dangerous slits. "To throw me and Roger under the bus in case someone caught on to what you were doing?"

The woman backed up a step, shaking her head in emphatic denial. "No, I didn't want to hurt anyone."

"Of course, it was easy for you to steal from us when you worked there. It wasn't until your access was cut off that you helped yourself to my computer system, my *home*, my *friendship*, all in order to accomplish the same thing. My father trusted you," Brooke ranted in all-out rage. "But you took advantage of that kindness. You used it against him, and against me!"

"Oh, stop it!" The hurt was gone from Miranda's face, replaced by a look of righteous indignation. "So I sold some information. Don't blame me for taking advantage of an opportunity. This is fucking Florida, Brooke. The cost of living here bleeds the average working person dry, not that you would know anything about *that*. You have the luxury of hibernating in a fancy townhouse that your parents bought for you. Tell me one time you've ever had to scrape for a penny."

Angry disbelief clouded Brooke's vision. "You lost almost thirty *hard-working* people their jobs all to earn an extra buck for yourself," she spat out. "Tell *them* your sob story."

Miranda tightened her lips as she fought some internal battle, but she must have realized there was no point in arguing. With a sad slant to her mouth, she turned toward the stairs and paused to say, "Despite what you think, I've always valued our friendship, Brooke. I hope you can forgive me someday."

When Brooke remained rooted to the spot, Ethan passed by her and followed Miranda downstairs. Words were exchanged, and the front door opened and closed.

Brooke hugged her arms and turned away before Ethan reappeared. She didn't want to see him, especially now.

"How are you holding up?" he asked her.

Having taken yet another monumental hit, she feared that she could very well be on the verge of a nervous breakdown. "Not so good," she whispered. "I'd like you to leave, please."

Instead of doing what she asked, he came closer until she felt the warmth of his body against her back. "It isn't your fault, you know," he said.

A choked sob escaped from her throat. It absolutely was her fault. She'd left her computer running and unsupervised while another person had been in her house. Furthermore, she'd accused Roger. He had been the most logical culprit. Oh, how wrong she'd been, and the guilt she felt for essentially betraying *him* was nearly too much to bear.

"Brooke...," Ethan struggled for words. "You're allowed to trust your friends."

But she didn't want a pep talk right now. The heavy weight in her chest simply wouldn't allow it. She turned to him with as much poise as she could muster. "Thank you for bringing this to me. You should get back to work now."

Ethan's eyes filled with doubt. "I don't think you should be alone right now."

Her frazzled nerves instantly revolted against the patronizing tone in his voice. "It's my house. I get to do what I want, and once again you're standing in my way."

He shoved his hands into his pockets. "Is that how you see it?"

"I don't want to fight," she retorted in panic. "I just want you to leave."

"I'm not leaving."

How dare he bring that lord-and-master bullshit into her home! "Why not, Ethan? You don't want to miss yet another opportunity to throw my naïveté in my face?"

He released a frustrated breath. "I was wrong to do that. Right now, I just want to help you."

"Ha!" she scoffed. "How original. Tell you what, I may or may not email you in a week and let you know if I've decided to accept it or not."

"Brooke—"

"Just get out!" She felt a flood of tears coming and needed him to be gone before it started. When he reached for her instead, she pushed hard against his chest, but he caught her in his arms as she made a dash for the door. They fell down on their knees together, and he held her tightly against him as she completely broke apart.

Her loud sobs filled the room. The humiliation of Ethan witnessing her misery was just too much, but she didn't have the strength to break away. Unable to hold it in any longer, she let go of several weeks' pent-up frustration, sadness, and betrayal. As her tears soaked through his shirt, he held her in a tight grip while stroking her hair with quiet reverence. They stayed that way for a while, on the floor of her studio, surrounded by her hobbies, her achievements…, and now her failures.

When exhaustion took over and her sobs had died down, he rose to his feet with her in his arms. Brooke wondered how she could be so tired. Oh, yeah, she'd practically been awake for five whole days. Eyes swollen and scratchy, nose stuffed up and raw, she curled up against his chest and let him walk her downstairs and to the bedroom. On the verge of sleep, she heard a faraway curse and then felt herself being lowered to the couch instead. Then he draped a blanket over her shoulders. His voice came from somewhere in her dreams, telling someone that he wasn't going back to work for a while.

And then everything faded to black.

When consciousness returned, Brooke was in her own bed, her face burrowed in soft pillows. They smelled lovely, fresh…as though they'd been pulled straight from the dryer. She inhaled and rolled over slightly to find somebody lying next to her. She blinked, lost focus and blinked some more. "Ethan?" she groaned.

The body moved and sat up a little. "Brooke, dear, it's Mom."

Her mother's voice shocked her into a near heart attack. Brooke grabbed her eyeglasses. Once they were on, she looked at her mother with a mix of happiness and disappointment. Just how long had she been out?

"Mom?" she said in confusion. "Aren't you in Texas?"

Brenna Monroe's lean features bore, as usual, the mark of eternal patience. Her casual lemon-yellow slacks and patterned blouse were new and her light red hair was shorter than usual. Other than that, she looked like the same striking woman who'd occupied the corner office before Brooke had. She smiled and pulled Brooke's hair away from her face. "Apparently not. How are you feeling?"

"I—I'm okay. What are you doing here?"

And where was Ethan?

"Your father and I were worried," Brenna explained with a hint of tension. "You wouldn't answer your phone or return our emails, so we decided to come down."

Still in a state of confusion, Brooke sat up and rubbed the sleep from her eyes. The intense glow lighting the curtains from the sliding glass doors boasted an early afternoon hour. "You shouldn't have done that. I'm fine."

Her mother got up and opened the curtains bathing the already bright room in painful sunshine. "Not according to the young man we found here when we arrived."

"Is he still here?"

"No. But, before he left, he filled us in on what happened."

Shit. Swinging her feet to the floor, Brooke adjusted to this bit of news quietly. "I should have been the one to tell you."

The mattress dipped as Brenna sat beside her. She put a hand on Brooke's knee. "It's okay to let other people handle things once in a while. He seems to genuinely care for you."

Brooke squeezed her mother's hand, glad for the company. "If there was anything between us, it's over," she stated miserably.

"Are you sure?"

She straightened and gave her mother a smile. "You cut your hair. I like it."

Brenna pulled at her shaped, chin-length ends. "Not too short?"

"Nope. How's your heart? Are you taking care of yourself?"

With an airy laugh, the woman got up and helped Brooke to her feet. "Your father's taking better care of me than I ever did." She retrieved a pair of slippers and plopped them into position. "Now that we're both retired, the man's driving me insane."

"Where is Dad, by the way?" Brooke asked as she slid her feet into the slippers.

"He went out shortly after your friend left. They talked for a while."

A groan escaped. "About what?"

"I don't know, I came in here and fell asleep beside you." Brenna threw a sweater at her and headed out through the door toward the kitchen. "Come on, lazy bones, let's get a snack."

Feeling somewhat better, Brooke decided to face the rest of the day in complete denial. The fact that her parents were there now to act as blissful distractions had a lot to do with it. Brenna went about the kitchen as if she owned it, pampering her daughter just like Brooke knew she would. She felt like she was fifteen again, and she allowed herself to believe it for as long as she could.

Thoughts of Miranda, Ethan, and Monroe Graphics didn't enter her head, despite the stark reminders that remained. She did, however, have distant recollections of strong arms wrapped around her...a welcome safety as his heartbeat thrummed against her back while she drifted in and out of sleep.

Wait a minute...had that been real?

As Brooke added honey to the mug of hot tea her mother had prepared, she sat at her kitchen island in thoughtful silence. Brenna was looking through the fridge. "After our snack we'll go grocery shopping." The door closed and she approached with an apple and some cheese. "There's more space in your fridge than a Kmart parking lot."

Brooke watched as she took out a knife and a wooden block and began to chop. "Sorry. I haven't exactly been out."

Her mother looked up from her task. "So tell me more about Ethan. He's adorable."

Thoroughly depressed, Brooke reached for a slice of apple. "There's nothing to tell."

"Would you rather I speculate on my own?"

She chewed slowly, her focus blurred. "He's the new vice president of Monroe Graphics. Needless to say, we didn't get along very well."

"That's not the vibe I got earlier."

What her mother didn't understand was how thoroughly Brooke had screwed up. "That vibe you got was pity, mother. He hates me."

"Oh, I don't know about—"

"Mom, please." Brooke held up a hand in a pleading effort to make it stop. "We were at each other's throats from day one, and when we finally started trusting each other, I lied to him. I'm no better than Miranda in that respect, and he'll never trust me again. So can we talk about something else?"

"No, we can't." Brenna put down the knife. "You're miserable, darling, and I think it goes deeper than what happened with Miranda."

It was always an open-book type of scenario with her mother. Brooke's eyes began to tear up. "So, Ethan told you about her?"

She nodded with sadness. "Your father, especially, was pretty devastated."

Of course he was. Those two had laughed together as much as she and Brooke had. "Do you think he'll want to go after her?"

"Ethan sure wanted him to. He even offered to testify if it came down to that."

Then again, he hadn't been close to Miranda. Perhaps they needed an outsider to keep things real. "I think of all the times she came over," Brooke said with sadness. "She was always so eager to help me with my problems or to just chill. I have to wonder how much of it was real and how much wasn't. I'm so paranoid now that I don't even know what to think of Amy. Will she be devastated too, or did she know about Miranda all along?"

Brenna sipped tea, her face full of sympathy. "It's a tough call when you've been deceived by the people you love."

Brooke swallowed back another wave of emotion. "Ethan told me I was too naïve to be senior manager, let alone vice president. Boy, was he right."

"Trusting your friends doesn't make you naïve, darling. It makes you human. He knows that."

She sighed. "I hated him, Mom. I'm the one who started this fight between us because he was such a pompous jerk at the beginning. I guess a snake in the open is better than one in the grass, right?"

Brenna set the mug down and looked at her squarely. "You are so in love with that man you can't stand it."

Yes, of course she was, but hearing it out loud only made her feel worse. "Look, Mom...I was thinking of getting out of here for a few weeks. Maybe go back to Texas with you and Dad."

"Didn't you just take a vacation?"

She watched her mother clean up. "If you haven't heard, I'm kind of on another one."

The front door opened and closed. Brooke turned on her stool to see her father stroll into the kitchen wearing the classic navy-blue slacks and buttoned-down shirt he liked to travel in. The colorful band of his Panama hat reflected the artsy side of him and also hid the thinning hair beneath it. When he saw her, he took it off, his face familiar and loving. Despite all that had happened, he was the blast of fresh air she needed at that moment. Brooke got up and let him enfold her in a warm bear hug.

"I'm so sorry, Dad," she said against his chest, breathing in the comforting scent of his aftershave. "I shouldn't have been so mad at you."

He pressed a kiss to the top of her head. "I shouldn't have kept the truth from you. Maybe a lot of this could have been avoided."

"You're right about that." She broke away and peered up at him. The man wore such a look of sorrow that it broke her heart. "Guess we both learned a lot, huh?"

He gave her a tired half-smile. "You're a sponge, sweetheart. You've always had immeasurable talent and once this all settles, you'll be alright. I promise."

"She wants to come back to Texas with us for a while," Brenna broke in.

Brooke gave them an encouraging nod. "Yes, for a visit. And, since I'll be far away from here, I can find a job and stay in Texas permanently."

Her father held her at arm's length. "What in hell for?"

Her smile faded. "Why in hell not?"

"This is your home, Brooke. You love it here. Don't run away from it because of what happened. You're stronger than that."

"You didn't think so before," she argued with a scowl.

"I was wrong," he retorted with stern reprimand. "Let's keep it that way."

"I wholeheartedly agree." Brenna came up to her and ran a loving hand down the length of her hair. "The first thing you need to do is get out of this townhouse for a few hours. You must have an awful case of cabin fever."

Stanley took a piece of cheese from the plate. "Right. You can help us settle in at the house and then we'll go to the yacht club for dinner. Maybe take the boat out for a sunset spin. The gulf air will get your wheels turning again."

Remembering her vow not to wear shoes that day, Brooke's shoulders slumped with dread. "But I don't want—"

"Hey." Brenna gave her a gentle shake. "You'll do as you're told, young lady." Then she linked arms and steered her toward the bedroom. "Maybe we'll see dolphins. Remember how you loved to watch the dolphins?"

With a sigh of surrender, Brooke gave a reluctant nod and let herself be guided. She did love seeing the dolphins keeping pace with their trawler as it navigated the choppy waves. As a child, when they'd go on weekend trips to Key West, she even used them to decide what she wanted to eat. If a dolphin appeared, she'd have a ham sandwich for lunch. If not, it would be tuna. When it came time to raid the cooler, she'd know exactly which sandwich to take.

Even if it wasn't always the one she wanted.

ON THURSDAY AFTERNOON, THE SUN DOMINATED a cloudless blue sky. The temperature was cool enough to eat outside in Naples's Fifth Avenue South shopping district. Royal palms lined the sidewalks, adding their lofty tropical sprays to the already colorful historic and modern architecture around her. Brooke loved to eat there and watch the tourists and locals lingering at the windows, their arms hooked through bags filled with lavish purchases.

Wearing a light sundress and sandals, her hair down and moving with the occasional breeze, Brooke reveled in her newly acquired positive attitude. She took her attention away from her laptop long enough to accept a refill of iced tea and the check. When the waiter left, a shadow fell over her table.

"You're getting pretty good at avoiding the rain."

While Ethan's voice moved over her like a warm caress, Brooke ignored the skip of her heartbeat and kept her eyes trained on the computer screen. "Though it seems like a cloud just rolled in," she replied with the barest hint of a smile. When he didn't respond, she looked up through her prescription sunglasses and found him in full GQ mode, from the fitted lines of his three-piece suit to his sexy smolder. His sleek shades gave him movie star appeal, something that was clearly getting noticed by several young women on the sidewalk.

But he was here for her...and she didn't have to imagine what was beneath that suit. She cocked her head. "How did you find me?"

"When you wouldn't answer your cell, I called your father. He said you'd be here."

Brooke sipped from her straw. "He gave you his number?"

Ethan flipped his car keys. "Not everyone thinks I'm a turd."

The reminder made her smile. She leaned back, her voice soft. "When I called you that, you *were* a turd. But you're not anymore."

"Gee, thanks. May I?"

She watched him with a wry frown as he pulled out a chair without waiting for her answer. "Help yourself."

"You look different from the last time I saw you," he said. "Hell, you look different period." The waiter came by and Ethan declined his offer for anything to drink.

"I feel better," Brooke replied with a nod of appreciation.

His next words came out husky and full of meaning: "You look beautiful."

Sensing his intense gaze from beneath the sunglasses, her face instantly warmed. "Thanks for everything you did last Friday." She gave an embarrassed smile. "Tolerating my little breakdown and handling my parents."

He nodded once. "I'm glad I was there."

Though she wholeheartedly agreed, she refused to say it, at least not until she accurately deciphered his reason for seeking her out.

Ethan watched the busy scene around them from his chair. "Your father also said that you went for a boat ride and came back with a new career goal in mind. He made some comment about dolphins that I didn't quite get."

She smiled while flipping through a list of job prospects on her computer screen. "When I was younger, I sort of let them make decisions for me." She found one that seemed promising and wrote it down on her notepad. "Of course, my problems were a little more mundane back then, but I figured I might as well give it a try. See what happens."

Ethan leaned over and took a peek at her list. "How does that work exactly?"

"I told myself if I saw dolphins I'd stay here and find a new career. If I *didn't* see dolphins, I'd move to Texas with my parents and stay with my old career."

He snorted in disbelief. "You based a decision like that on dolphins?"

"Why not?"

The annoyance in his tone was palpable. "I don't know, I thought maybe you'd put a little more heart into it." She only shrugged and took another sip from her straw. Ethan scowled and pointed to the notepad. "Since those are local phone numbers, I guess that means you saw dolphins?"

Her pen scribbled across the page. "Nope, not a single one." When she looked up, it was to find him fighting a smile.

"But you decided to stay anyway," he concluded, relaxing back into the smug Ethan that she'd come to know so well.

"This is my home," she said simply. "And despite having no formal degree, I figured I can try my luck with something in software."

"That's the only reason you wanted to stay?"

It was posed as a dare—a dare to tell the truth and admit her feelings for him. Brooke stared right back, unwilling to break first. "Are you ever going to get around to why you're here?"

He tapped his fingers on the table for a moment and then said, "Ken wants to see you."

Her face fell a little. "What for?"

"No idea."

But Brooke had a feeling she knew. Her shrimp salad began to rumble in her stomach. "Did you tell him about Miranda?"

"You know I did."

She released a long, drawn-out breath. "I guess it's best to get it over with."

When they both stood up, Ethan asked, "What exactly do you think is going to happen?"

"Probably something that will require the presence of lawyers and henchmen," she answered with a grimace.

"I don't know. What if he wants you to come back?"

Brooke stopped halfway while closing her laptop. "Is that what he said?"

Ethan shrugged. "At this point, I'm speculating as much as you."

She continued to pack up. "Then it's doubtful. As VP, you would be privy to something like that."

"Would you take your old job back?" he asked. "Even if it meant honoring the deal we made?"

A laugh escaped from her lips. "You mean as your secretary? You'd like that, wouldn't you?"

His grin said it all. Rolling her eyes, Brooke put her laptop into the case. Then she noticed that Ethan was slipping money into the bill sleeve. She made a grab for it. "I can pay for my—"

"Just speeding things along, Monroe." He put a hand under her elbow and directed her toward his parked car. "You can ride with me. I'll bring you back here afterward."

For the first time since that awful day, Brooke sat in her father's old office feeling awkward in her sundress. The masculine combination of dark walls and wood surrounded her like a long-lost home, yet it was a place she never expected to see again. The fact that another man occupied it and had even fired her was an open wound that she never expected to heal, which is why she sat before Ken Stevens in a state of extreme confusion. "I don't understand. This *isn't* about Miranda?"

Ken propped a hip on the edge of his desk. "Your father and I are dealing with Miranda together," he said, "but that's an entirely separate issue. Brooke, I'd like you to come back."

She ignored the skip of her heartbeat and recalled Ethan's proposed scenario. What sort of plans would he have for his personal secretary? "Not to sound ungrateful," she cleared her throat, "but...doing what, exactly?"

Ken's mustache twitched. "You want that corner office, don't you?"

It was the last answer she expected. With a mixture of joy and discomfort, she rubbed her palms on the arms of her chair. "Look...I know I was leading that competition when you fired me, but it would be wrong to take Ethan's job. He's way more entitled to it than I am."

Amusement lit up Ken's eyes. "Did I say you would be taking Ethan's job?"

Her face burned with mortification. "No."

"And your answer proves what I already know about you. Aside from the spying, you have a great work ethic," he leaned forward for emphasis, "and you *care*. You are someone I need on my team."

With each compliment, Brooke became more and more wary. "That's quite an about-face from last week."

He shrugged. "I'm a reasonable man. In light of the discoveries we've made since then, is it hard to understand why I want you back?"

"Kind of. After all, I did spy."

Ken crossed his arms and put a finger to his lips in contemplation. "Your father and I discussed your actions, and I've come to see why you did what you did. Though you were entirely in the wrong, your heart was in the right place."

For the first time, Brooke truly understood why her father had chosen to sell to this particular man. A renewed sense of wellbeing flooded her heart. "So, I assume you want me to come back under the same terms as before? As Ethan's secretary?"

Ken's face morphed into a comically solemn mask. "Is that what you want?"

Brooke laughed. "With all due respect, not really."

"Good." The man got up, circled around his desk, and retrieved a thick folder. "Because I'm not a big fan of wasted talent, something your father and I also discussed." He slid the folder across the desk. When Brooke reached for it, he sat down and assumed the position of a man ready to negotiate. "Ms. Monroe, how would you feel about earning a degree?"

STILL REELING FROM KEN'S PROPOSITION, BROOKE tucked the file he'd given her beneath her arm and reentered the main work area. Several people stared, no doubt wondering what she was doing there. Most of the faces were ones she never would have missed—people who never really knew her. There were only a few she wanted to see: Letreece who'd greeted her with a warm smile when she'd arrived, and Roger, to whom she owed an apology. Did he even know about Ken's plans for her? Did he know she was here?

But first things first. Though Roger was an important factor in her life, he was little more than an afterthought compared to the man she knew was waiting for her. Their short drive to Monroe Graphics had been laden with flirtatious remarks, ones that left her with little doubt of Ethan's intentions. But just how deep could his feelings for her possibly be, especially when he'd turned her in without so much as a blink?

When she passed by Shannon's office, her familiar voice called, "Brooke!"

Closing her eyes, Brooke backed up the few steps to her door and waited patiently for the rant to commence. When none was forthcoming, she looked up and found Shannon behind her desk, regarding her with a curious gaze. Brooke shrugged her tacit permission to fire away.

Instead, Shannon pursed her lips and then smiled. "Nice going with that anti-malware stuff."

So, Ethan must have pulled some serious strings in order to get the woman to go along with her plan. "I'm surprised he told you it was from me."

She waved away the notion. "Of course he didn't, not until afterward."

It was an honest answer that put Brooke more at ease. "I guess I should apologize for targeting you in the first place."

"Hell no," Shannon retorted with a look of horror. "Then I'd have to apologize for targeting you, which would make things way too awkward."

They both smiled a little and Brooke nodded once. "Okay, then. Glad we cleared that up."

When she went to leave, Shannon delayed her escape with another question. "So are you back now?"

How to answer that… "Yes and no," Brooke replied.

"What does that mean exactly?"

"It's something that Ken should probably explain."

The man had been hatching plans that were best kept under wraps until more real estate had been acquired—a detail that no longer stood in Ken's way. With that in mind, Brooke left Shannon's office and headed for the one she used to call her own. The door was open. She found Ethan standing at the window, staring down at the scenery with his hands in his pockets. Several personal photographs were on the shelves behind the desk. The first was one she'd seen before, of him and his family in suspended animation, celebrating in front of a car covered in sponsor logos. Beside that one was a photo of the white BMW racing past a blurred crowd of spectators. Then there was a cute portrait of Adrianna. Another was of a couple that she assumed were Ethan's parents, flanking a small boy and his homemade derby car.

And, of course, there was the bowl of candy corn. Indeed, Ethan had made himself quite at home, though now he jingled the change in his pockets as if he were restless.

Brooke studied his broad shoulders, recalling a time when she'd hated him on sight. She'd hated his confidence, his drive, and his ability to charm his way through anything. But all those things were what had ultimately saved her. If not for Ethan, she'd still be paying for a very personal and stupid mistake.

How on earth had they come to this point? If not for Shannon's interference, would they have ever found their way to each other? Would doubt have turned to trust? Disdain to respect? Would their hatred have ever crossed over to love?

Brooke shook the thought from her head. Yes, she was very much in love with Ethan, a fact that she couldn't deny if she tried. Whether or not he felt the same…knowing him, it was a detail she'd need to extract with the use of clever tactics. "This office looks good on you," she said from the doorway.

When he turned, his stiff features softened with hope. "Are you back?"

Her smile confirmed it somewhat, just as his question confirmed that he had no idea what she was back for. Brooke remained tight-lipped as he crossed over to her with a focused look in his eyes. He pulled her inside, shut the door, and boxed her in between two strong arms. She swallowed, wondering if his heavy-lidded stare meant what she hoped it did.

"Good." He brushed a wisp of hair from her face. "Because I'm addicted to you, Miss Monroe, and I've been going through some pretty heavy withdrawal."

It still wasn't the declaration she hoped for, yet it did manage to stir her blood. "Are you expecting me to jump into that darkroom anytime you need a fix?"

"Can't," he answered, stepping closer. "The darkroom has been discovered."

Her surroundings faded away until all that was left was his body pressing against her sundress. Struggling to stay in the moment, Brooke gave herself a mental shake. "Let me guess. Someone got caught with his or her pants down."

"Mm-hmm." His lips brushed across her temple. "Ken had the revolving door removed."

"That's too bad."

He pushed back a little and gave her a look of intense purpose. "We still have to face him about us, though. It may take some work, but if we come up with some sort of written agreement, maybe...."

His voice trailed off when she shook her head. "We won't need to do that."

"Why not?"

"Because, Ethan...we won't be breaking that rule. Now or ever."

Brooke watched as his determination wavered a bit. The fact he just expected her to fall back in line meant that the man needed a final wakeup call...and that she'd enjoy giving it to him.

He paused for a brief second. "I understand why you don't want to take another chance on us. That said, this is me trying to change your mind."

He leaned in and captured her mouth in a slow, sensual kiss designed to burn the polish right off her toenails. As Brooke's insides turned to molten jelly, she wrapped her arms around his neck. With a soft sigh, she arched into his body as he softly touched the curves of her breasts.

Then he broke away, brushing a trail of light kisses along the side of her jaw, his thumb moving over her nipple in light, teasing strokes. "Would it really be so bad working under me?" he whispered against her cheek.

So, that's what he thought, huh? Brooke's eyes opened as she lounged against the door, fully enjoying the moment. "That depends," she murmured. "What exactly do you expect from a personal secretary?"

"Oh, I don't know, maybe bring me coffee in the morning. Schedule my appointments. Satisfy my sexual needs."

Brooke put her hands on his chest and gave him a push. "Then I hope you find one who's willing." Gaining her freedom, she strode toward the potted Ficus and pretended to inspect every perfect leaf.

"You didn't accept Ken's offer?" he said tightly from across the room.

She gave a nonchalant laugh. "Do you really think I could work under you? Whether it's outside your door or on top of your desk, I just have too much pride to give you that kind of control over me."

"Damn it, Brooke, I'm not the reason you should—"

"I accepted Ken's offer." She turned slightly and gave him her brightest smile.

His shoulders slumped in relief, but his glare was murderous. "Don't scare me like that."

"But he didn't offer me my old job back, which means that the terms of our original agreement are still null and void."

Instead of the disappointment she expected to see, his eyes filled with an optimistic light. "Please tell me you're replacing Bill Knight."

She blinked at him in surprise. "Is that what you hoped for?"

"It would be a smart move on Ken's part. At the least, Bill's ego could stand a good beating."

When Ethan sat on a corner of the desk, she moved toward him again. "He never even mentioned the creative department."

"What exactly will you be doing here then?" he asked, his mood considerably lighter.

"Ethan...I won't be working in this office anymore. He asked me to head up a new expansion."

His handsome features settled into a mixture of shock and delight. "He did what?"

Still dazed over Ken's proposition, Brooke explained as best she could. "I'll be supervising the new web design and security branch of Master Ink Innovations. It's something I tried to get my father to do before he sold the business." Her grin showed just how happy she was about it.

Ethan pulled her between his legs, his warm, appreciative gaze sweeping over her face. "Damn. I was looking forward to having a torrid affair with my new secretary."

She laughed. "You would have liked that, huh?"

They stayed that way for a while, enjoying the playful mood as he stared at their joined hands. "So, does Ken have an idea where this new branch will be located?" he asked. "Someplace close by, I'm guessing?"

Her gaze moved to his mouth. "Do you want me close by?" *Tell me you love me.*

"Of course. It would be easier for you to buy me lunch once in a while."

Annoyed, she broke from his grasp and sighed. "That might be difficult...unless I send you a gift card from Texas."

"Texas!" he shouted.

She nodded with a sympathetic smile. "I'll be leaving Wednesday."

"Wednesday!"

"So you see? We won't have to worry about that strict rule against office romance. Problem solved." Brooke twirled around and headed for the door. As she bent down to retrieve the purse she'd dropped earlier, Ethan caught up just in time to hold the door closed.

His breath brushed over her hair. "You don't really want to go to Texas, do you?"

"Why not? I can stay with my parents until I find my own house."

"You love your house here."

"I can make a fresh start and make new friends."

"You still have friends here," he countered, his own voice rising.

"Maybe I'll meet someone, fall in love, and start a family."

"You love me!" He twirled her back around. "And I'm here!"

With a mix of pity and sheer relief, Brooke watched him come to grips with what he had just said. "Come on, Ethan. Do you really think it could work between us?"

Without further hesitation, he pushed her aside and threw open the door. People scattered, clearing the way as Ethan stormed directly into Ken's office. With an impish smile, Brooke retreated back into the corner office. When Ethan later reemerged, she was sitting behind her old desk, her head thrown back in ecstasy as she enjoyed the many advantages of six-point massage.

The door clicked softly shut behind him. "Brooke?"

"Yes, Ethan?"

"I must have heard wrong." When her eyes fluttered open, he was rounding the desk with a promise of retribution in his look. "What you really said was that you'll be taking online courses from the University of Texas, and that you'll be running Ken's new division from the seventh floor of this very building."

Wary of his intentions, she gave him a sweet smile. "Yes, that's exactly what I said."

She yelped as he grabbed her arms and pulled her into a rough embrace. "That's what I thought," he growled. "Because you surely didn't just manipulate me into giving Ken a piece of my mind, right?"

Choking back her laughter, Brooke wrapped her arms around his waist and basked in her victory. "I hope you didn't make too much of a spectacle of yourself."

"I'm pretty sure I left him with a good idea of how I feel about you."

The warmth of his words dissolved her smile. Before she could ask him about those feelings, he leaned down and kissed her slowly. "You know what this means, don't you?"

Drowning under his spell, she whispered against his lips, "We both get a corner office with the same view?"

"Wrong," he whispered back.

She groaned. "Then please enlighten me." *Tell me you love me.*

"It means you are still, technically, working under me."

Squeezing her eyes shut, Brooke giggled against his chest. "You're hopeless."

"And I'm very much in love with you."

Her body went still. As time stopped, she looked up and met his gaze. "Really?" she breathed. "Are you sure?"

His hand touched her hair and he gently leaned her backward. The tenderness in his voice bespoke the truth in his words. "I don't need a weekend in the Keys to figure that one out."

Relief rushed through her with such force that she had to keep her knees from buckling. "Me neither," she whispered as tears blurred her vision. "I love you too, Ethan, though you're so very brave for admitting it first."

With a knowing smile, he murmured, "I couldn't let you go on all lovesick and moody now, could I?"

He had her there, and she confirmed it without a shred of denial this time. "Was I that obvious?"

His hold on her tightened, promising nothing but blue skies ahead. She kissed him with every ounce of love in her heart, not caring that several faces were pressed against the glass by the door. Let them watch. Let them wonder how two people on the same quest for annihilation had ended their fight in each other's arms, in crazy love, and on top of the world.

"But I still want my weekend in the Keys," she murmured against his mouth.

Ethan smiled. "I think we can arrange that."